Since 2004, internationally bestselling author **Sherrilyn Kenyon** has placed over sixty novels on the *New York Times* bestseller list; in the past three years alone, she has claimed the No.1 spot seventeen times. This extraordinary bestseller continues to top every genre she writes within.

Proclaimed the pre-eminent voice in paranormal fiction by critics, Kenyon has helped pioneer – and define – the current paranormal trend that has captivated the world and continues to blaze new trails that blur traditional genre lines.

With more than 25 million copies of her books in print in over 100 countries, her current series include: The Dark-Hunters, League, Lords of Avalon, Chronicles of Nick, and Belador Code.

Visit Sherrilyn Kenyon online:

www.sherrilynkenyon.co.uk
www.facebook.com/AuthorSherrilynKenyon
@KenyonSherrilyn

Praise for Sherrilyn Kenyon:

'A publishing phenomenon ... [Sherrilyn Kenyon] is the reigning queen of the wildly successful paranormal scene'
Publishers Weekly

'Kenyon's writing is brisk, ironic and relentlessly imaginative. These are not your mother's vampire novels'
Boston Globe

'Whether writing as Sherrilyn Kenyon or Kinley MacGregor, this author delivers great romantic fantasy!'
New York Times bestselling author Elizabeth Lowell

Dragonsworn

SHERRILYN KENYON

piatkus

PIATKUS

First published in the US in 2017 by St Martin's Press, New York
First published in Great Britain in 2017 by Piatkus

1 3 5 7 9 10 8 6 4 2

Copyright © 2017 by Sherrilyn Kenyon

The moral right of the author has been asserted.

*All characters and events in this publication, other than those
clearly in the public domain, are fictitious and any resemblance
to real persons, living or dead, is purely coincidental.*

A CIP catalogue record for this book
is available from the British Library.

ISBN {HB} 978-0-349-41327-3
ISBN {TPB} 978-0-349-41328-0

Printed and bound by CPI Group (UK) Ltd, Croydon, CR0 4YY

Papers used by Piatkus are from well-managed forests
and other responsible sources.

Piatkus
An imprint of
Little, Brown Book Group
Carmelite House
50 Victoria Embankment
London EC4Y 0DZ

An Hachette UK Company
www.hachette.co.uk

www.littlebrown.co.uk

For Tish, who will read this and know instantly why. Thank you so much for being my friend and a well-needed voice of reason. To Sheri, Kim Burdette, and Kim Turner for all the decades you've been my touchstones. To LaShon and Leisha for too many reasons to name. To Laura, Kerrie, Paco, Parker, Jacs, Alethea, Leanna, and Carl for coming to my aid when I needed you! I love you guys so much and am forever in your debt! And as always for my boys, who are ever my heartstones. I love you all!

I loved you at your most wicked.

—*Rev. Oscar C. Allred*

Acknowledgments

To Adam Ezra for allowing me to use the words from his song "Home Again Soon" off the *View from the Root* album. If you ever get a chance, make sure to check out his music. It's been my pleasure and honor to know him for years and to have featured his music in the Nick and Dark-Hunter videos, and at book signings. He is a great musician and a wonderful man!

DRAGONSWORN

PROLOGUE

In the year of Our Lord 417
May the fifth
Glastonbury Tor

Betrayal.

Cold and brutal, it always took the shape and form of the closest friend and ally. And stung so deep to the soul that it left you bleeding and weak, wondering if you'd ever find your way to trust again.

Left you adrift in misery and heartache. Unable to breathe for the pain of it.

Worse than that, the treacherous bastard always came when least expected. And at the worst fucking time.

Given the brutal circumstances of his birth, Falcyn Drago had never considered himself immune from its fetid claws. Far from it. Indeed, he'd been nursed on its most foul and bitter taste. He'd learned to anticipate it from everyone around him, at all times. And sadly, no one had ever disappointed him by being above it.

Never once.

Rather, they seemed to glory in stabbing him through his wounded heart as ruthlessly and viciously as possible.

And none more so than his own brother, who now stood before him in all of Max's sanctimonious and smug glory. Something that would have been galling had his brother been in his real and true dragon's body, but like this, in the guise of a man, the betrayal burned twice as deep.

And hurt all the more.

"Damn you, Maxis! Was it not enough you left Hadyn alone to die amongst the humans? Now you take my son, too!"

Maxis's hazel green eyes flared to gold, then to red as his anger ignited. "That's not fair! I did everything I could to save our brother. How dare you throw that in my face! I'd have given my life for his!"

"Bullshit! I should have strangled you the moment you crawled from your egg!"

Grabbing him by the throat, Max shoved him back against the wall of the stone room where Falcyn had thought to meet his son, but now instead found himself barred forever from the realm his child called home.

Because of Max! The flesh of his flesh.

His worst nightmare.

Max's eyes showed the depths of his own despair. "I wish you had, brother. I wish you had."

His brother's agony scorched Falcyn, but not as much as his own misery that ate him whole and left him bereft of anything save utter despair. Damn him for caring about Max's feelings when it was obvious that his brother didn't give one shit for his. Tears blinded him. "Maddor was all I had in this world. How could you!"

A tic started in Max's jaw as he stepped away. "I had no choice. Dammit, Falcyn! Be reasonable. The Adoni plan to use you as a tool. Nothing more. They bred a hybrid child with you, without your knowledge or consent, and you're fine with this?"

"Igraine was to be my wife!"

"Igraine is a faithless whore. An Adoni sorceress who has killed two husbands before you . . . think you that she'd spare you her treachery?"

"As you have?"

Max drew back as if he'd hit him, but he must have re-thought that stupidity. Because they both knew that Max would never survive a real fight with Falcyn. "If she truly loved you, brother, my spell on your child wouldn't have mattered to her, would it?"

Nay, it wouldn't. The truth was an even more bitter pill to swallow.

And for that, he hated Max most of all. Because now he

knew for an indisputable fact that he was every bit as unlovable as his *dearest* mother had proclaimed him to be upon his arrival into this hateful existence.

Max drew a ragged breath. "We were cursed from our births, and well you know it. The gods spurned us and our mothers abandoned us. The only hope your son has is that if he is more man than drake, he won't come under their fire . . . or notice. Or control."

"That wasn't for *you* to decide!"

"And you should have *never* allowed yourself to be used by the Adoni. You know the laws of magick the same as I. For this . . . some debt will be collected."

Falcyn winced at another truth he didn't want to face. "I was to protect him from it. Now . . ." He gestured at the veil that separated this world from the one where Igraine had taken their child to raise him out of his reach and care. There was nothing he could do for his son. So long as Maddor lived in his mother's fey realm, Falcyn couldn't get to him. Not even his powers were that great. "Never, *ever* speak to me again, Maxis. I'm done with you."

Returning to his dragon's body, he spread his wings, intending to fly.

"Careful of your ultimatums, brother. Like magick, they come with a terrible bite."

Falcyn shot a burst of flame toward him. "And so do I, Max! So do I!"

1

"Remi! You can't kill Daimons at the front door!" Dev Peltier shot across the main bar floor of Sanctuary at a dead run, with his wolfwere brother-in-law Fang Kattalakis hot on his heels.

"Sure I can," his identical brother snarled in his earpiece. "Watch me!"

Dreading the scene of his shapeshifting look-alike ripping the heart out of a demon on the busy streets of New Orleans underneath a closed-circuit police camera, Dev considered teleporting to stop the coming disaster, but that would only worsen this fiasco.

And guarantee them both some special quality time in a high-security government lab someplace where they'd never be seen or heard from again.

He and Fang barely reached the open front door in time to grab the tall, muscled mountain that sometimes passed as a human being before Remi ate the petite blonde standing nonchalantly under the outside streetlight.

And that bastard fought them with everything he had as they pulled him back from his would-be victim. A victim who didn't appear the least bit concerned that she'd narrowly escaped certain death at the hands of a savage bear-human-beast.

Remi even bit Dev in the shoulder as he struggled against them.

"Dammit!" Dev snarled. "You better have had your rabies shot, boy!"

Growling in that unique way that only a shapeshifting bear could, Remi continued to try and throw them off so that he could reach the woman, who still hadn't moved.

In fact, the Daimon yawned. Then checked her watch and manicure as if the entire event left her bored out of her mind. "Can I go in now? You two have him leashed, right?"

Fang's jaw dropped at her nonchalant tone. "You know, Medea, given what happened the last time a bunch of you showed up here, you've got a lot of nerve."

"'Course I do. It's what makes me the bad guy. And I'm told my half brother's upstairs, playing poker with your little brother. So if you don't mind . . ." She headed inside as if she didn't have a bar full of shapeshifters who'd love to make her their late-night snack.

Remi continued to curse them both. "They killed Maman and Papa! How could you let her waltz into our bar like that?"

Dev kept his brother in place with his forearm across Remi's throat. "Because if you harm one hair on her head, we'll lose our sanctuary license again. Think of your nieces and nephews and the danger you'd be putting them in!"

The last time they'd lost their license, Sanctuary had been razed and they'd lost their parents and several good friends.

Remi's gaze fell to Fang, and Dev knew *that* had finally reached through his brother's temporary insanity and need for blood vengeance. Their sister—Fang's wife—had just given birth to a son and daughter. And Dev's own wife was pregnant after having given up her immortality so that they could start a family of their own. Last thing any of them wanted was to risk enemies crashing the gate and burning Sanctuary to the ground.

Again.

Above all, they had to maintain their limani standing so that no shapeshifter or demon could war here. They'd all lost too much during the last battle that had shattered their family. Now, they had even more to lose.

Finally, the fire went out in Remi's eyes as he stopped struggling against them.

"We good?"

Remi nodded.

Releasing him, Dev stepped back to eye Fang. "So what idiot put hothead on the door tonight?"

Fang cast him a disgruntled glare. "I be said idiot. Thank

you very much. Thought he was you. Could one of your bastards cut your hair so that I can tell you apart?"

Dev rolled his eyes. Then pointed to the double bow-and-arrow tattoo on his biceps. "I do have one mark that distinguishes me from the other idiots I'm blood related to, you know?"

Fang scoffed while Remi started for the door.

"Hey, hey!" Dev caught his arm. "What'cha thinking, punkin?"

"That Maman should have eaten you when you were whelped. Or at least before you were weaned."

Dev snorted. "You can't go in there and start a fight with her. Need I remind you there's a shit-ton of human tourists in that bar and Max is a bit preoccupied tonight with his dragonswan. That boy ain't been up for air in days, so we can't count on him to help us out with mind-wiping the humans in the event they see something they shouldn't."

Remi's nose twitched in that way that said he was hell-bent for blood. "Can't his brother mind-wipe them, then?"

Good question. Falcyn might have the same powers as Max. Then again, he might not. Even if he did, there was no guarantee he'd use them, as helping others wasn't exactly the surly dragon's priority. "No idea. You want to ask Falcyn?" That shapeshifting bastard was the only creature alive with a worse attitude than Remi.

Unless you counted the former Dark-Hunter Zarek. Though to be honest, Dev would run Falcyn up against Z any day. Thrice on Sundays.

Proof to the point? Remi backed down immediately at the

thought of speaking to Falcyn, and that was something his brother *never* did.

"I'm going to go watch her," Remi grumbled before he headed inside.

Dev growled low in the back of his throat as he met Fang's irritated smirk. "I know. Dev, go watch your brother."

"And find me someone else to guard the door."

"Where's your ear p . . ." Dev's voice trailed off as he remembered that one of Aimee's favorite things was to nibble Fang's ears in the back room when no one else was around. Disgusted with the thought of his baby sister touching anything male in a sexual way, he grimaced. "Never mind. I'll grab Cherif. You can't miss him. He's the one who looks like me, but isn't."

"That could also be Quinn."

"Don't remind me." It was hell to be one of four identical quads. Only Aimee and the Dark-Hunter Acheron had ever been able to tell them apart.

And Dev's wife, Sam. She'd never once confused him with his brothers, which was one of many reasons he loved her.

"Double time, Bear!" Fang snapped. "Don't need your brother starting some shit while we've got humans around to witness it!"

Letting out a bear growl in his throat, Dev went to find Remi before the bear really did eat the Daimon, and start another war they didn't need to fight.

Medea screwed her face up at all the humans in the dark, noisy bar as they swayed to the music of the house band of shapeshifters

9

they'd ironically named The Howlers. Gah, how she hated them all. Though to be honest, it would be quite a feast for her should she choose to indulge, not that she needed their blood to feed—unlike the others of her kind.

For her, it was just fun payback. . . .

More tempted than she ought to be, she forced herself to ignore all the throats that would be so easy to rip open and searched for her half brother's familiar face. Though she and Urian were technically enemies who fought on opposite sides of this war, he was still one of the few people she considered her friend.

Right now, she had dire news he needed to hear.

"Hey, baby! You looking for me?"

Medea curled her lip at the cheesy come-on line. Worse? The filthy human stank of cheap alcohol and some cologne he must have bought off a clearance drugstore aisle. "Out of my way."

"Ah, now, why you want to do me like that, baby? Be nice and stay for a bit." He put a rough grip on her arm to hold her by his side.

Laughing, she bit her lip seductively. "Sugar, you have no idea what I really want to do with you. . . ."

His eyebrows shot north. "Oh yeah?"

"Ummm-hmmm." She stepped into his arms as she dreamed of gutting him on the floor.

An instant later, he was snatched back and shaken like a dog would do to its favorite toy. "Take a hike."

The human started to attack, until he caught sight of the

man who'd grabbed him. That took every bit of bluster out of him, and he quickly dashed away.

Not that Medea blamed him. This Were-Hunter was huge, even by their inhuman standards. Tall. Well muscled. His caramel skin would make any woman's mouth water. And to her instant horror, she wasn't immune to his charms.

In fact, she was strangely breathless as her gaze went to a pair of silvery blue eyes that practically glowed. Between that and his black hair, she'd almost think him a Dream-Hunter. Indeed, his powers were strong enough to be godlike.

The air around her was rife with them. It crackled in a way that was reminiscent of Acheron Parthenopaeus—an Atlantean god who pretended to be a Dark-Hunter for reasons only he knew. More than that, she couldn't even tell what breed this particular Were-Hunter belonged to. Bear, wolf, bird, lion, leopard, panther, tiger, dragon, jaguar, cheetah, or jackal. He was *that* powerful.

"What are you?"

Falcyn felt an odd half smile curve his lips. A rare, rare thing for him. But then it'd been a long time since he'd seen a morsel as tasty as this one. Her white-blond hair was an unusual shade, but natural. And it contrasted sharply with her black eyes.

And she wasn't just a Daimon. There was something a lot stronger inside her. Something he could taste and smell. The scent of it was like honey to his tongue.

"Hungry," he whispered.

She actually rolled her eyes and stepped around him.

A sound rumbled out of him that was even more rare than

his smile. So rare, in fact, that it took him a few seconds to realize it was a laugh.

No one had ever been so dismissive of him. Mostly because he ate those idiots and picked his teeth with their bones. And before he even realized what he was doing, he was after her.

She paused in the crowd to turn around and glare at him. "Oh, I see. You're a dog. Well, Fido, I'm sure there are some nice little humans over at the bar who'd like to take you home and pet you. I'm not one of them. So go on, boy." She clicked her tongue like a human would do their pet or a stray they were trying to get rid of. "Go on! Shoo!"

As she started to leave, Falcyn licked his lips. "So you're the queen bitch of the Daimons. They told me you were something else. But how many of them know you have demon blood inside you?"

She quirked a brow at his question, then gave him an insidious smile that made his cock jerk. "Before or after I kill them?" Her gaze narrowed as she swept a gimlet stare over him that said she was sizing him up for battle. "And you're wrong about my title. The queen would be my mother."

"Then what would that make you?"

"Daddy's most precious little girl."

He belly-laughed. Something that made every Were-Hunter near them step back and gape.

That finally took some of the bluster out of her, as she caught sight of their uncharacteristic reservation.

And fear. Especially since they never feared anything.

Except him. Yeah, he was *that* dangerous.

"Who *are* you?" she asked with a note of reservation in her voice.

"Wrong question."

"How so?"

"It's not so much who am I . . . as *what* am I."

Medea felt a tremor of fear finally roll down her spine. "You're not one of *them*, are you?" The Were-Hunters had been created aeons ago by the king of Arcadia in a desperate attempt to save the lives of his sons from a curse placed upon their mother's race by the Greek god Apollo—Medea's own grandfather. Seeking to elongate the lives of his sons, the king had bargained with a Sumerian god to magically splice their DNA with animals.

It'd worked, and the Sumerian god and Arcadian king had created two races of shapeshifters. Those who held human hearts, called Arcadians—human in their base forms, they could take animal form—and the Katagaria, who had animal hearts and were able to shift into humans.

The "man" in front of her shook his head slowly to indicate that he fell into neither group. As he said, he was something else entirely.

Yet he bore the scent of a Katagari warrior. An animal at heart and in base form. She knew the raw, preternatural musk that permeated their breed. It was unlike anything else in the world. And though tinged with something else, it was unmistakable.

This wasn't a man she was dealing with, but a creature of immense power.

"Like you, princess, I'm something much, much older than those half-Greek by-blows. . . . Deadlier. And unpredictable."

"I know you're not a god."

He approached her slowly, and while it wasn't in her to ever retreat, she found herself stepping back to keep from being overwhelmed by the sheer size of him. By the magnitude of his arcane powers that seemed to grow stronger the longer she was here.

"Perhaps, love," he breathed in her ear with that deep, resonant baritone. "But there are things in this world that even the gods fear."

And he was definitely one of them. She knew it with every single molecule of her being.

"Falcyn!"

Medea blinked at the sharp tone of her brother's voice.

The creature in front of her didn't react to it at all. Other than to give her an odd half smile. He tsked at both her and Urian. "Do you really think to make me heel at your command, lapdog?"

Tall and muscular, and unperturbed by that insult, Urian narrowed his eyes while he rapidly closed the distance between them. His white-blond hair fell loose around his shoulders, accentuating his sharp features as he kept his attention keenly focused on Falcyn, watching his every twitch. Which also told her how lethal and quick this being was.

A fearless, powerful beast himself, Urian was only wary around those who were worthy. He dismissed the rest.

Stepping between them, Urian gave her a bit of breathing room. "I would caution you to remember you're in a limani."

Falcyn snorted. "As if I give two shits for Savitar's laws." He raked a bitter stare over Urian. "Or *you*, for that matter. And even less for your boss. So don't even think of dragging Acheron's name into this as protection from my wrath. I dare him to say a single word to me . . . on *any* matter."

Urian scowled at his words and bravado, given the fact that Acheron was the final Fate of all. To defy him while knowing his real place in the universe was a special level of stupid and bravery that most lacked. "Is there nothing you fear?"

Falcyn's gaze went past Urian's shoulder to something in the crowd.

"Aye, but sadly she's not here."

Medea jumped at the deep voice that spoke near her ear. Startled, she turned to see another strange man in the crowded bar. One who stood out as much as Falcyn, but for other reasons. His hair was as pale as her own, if not more so, and his eyes a peculiar lavender shade. Yet for all his paleness, his skin wasn't white as she'd assumed someone's with albinism would be. Rather, it was a rich caramel like Falcyn's.

More than that, his ears held a bit of a point to them. For a moment, given the beauty of his features, she thought he might be fey . . . Adoni or such. But the way he moved, and given the scent of him, she dismissed the thought.

No, he was more animal than Adoni.

Languid and quick. A rare dichotomy that only a natural-born shapeshifter could accomplish. And like Falcyn, the air around him was rife with preternatural powers that danced for his command. This beast was every bit as powerful. Yet in a different way.

Nor were his powers as dark or sinister. This wasn't a creature who took pleasure in harm. Indeed, he seemed good-natured.

Falcyn tsked at him. "Now, Blaise, why would you go and bring Xyn into this? Especially given what a sore topic that is?"

Blaise let loose a charming grin. "Felt the need to rankle my big brother. Besides, everyone else fears you so. You need me to even you out." It wasn't until he stepped forward with his hand raised to feel his way through them that Medea realized Blaise was blind. "And if you're through scaring the natives, I've got something I need to speak to you about."

Falcyn sneered. "Rather spend time scaring the natives than listening to your petulant whine."

"Ah, now, you're going to hurt my feelings."

"You don't have any feelings."

"Not true. I had a lot of them, until you, Kerrigan, and Illarion shriveled them into oblivion. But I think I managed to salvage one or two. Please, try not to kill those last two off. I might need them one day."

Falcyn made a rude noise of dismissal. "Those are called hunger pangs."

Laughing, Blaise shook his head. "Hungry for a kind word, you mean."

"Well, you won't be getting it here." Falcyn gestured toward the stairs as if his brother could see his movements. "So off with you."

Blaise sighed heavily. " 'Fraid not. Must intrude. Can't wait."

Falcyn made another sound so deep in his throat that it vibrated through Medea's body.

Urian pulled her back. "Well, then. We'll leave you to your argument. Come, big sis. Let's get out of here before Godzilla and Mothra go at it and we're caught in the cross fire."

"Before who and what?"

Urian groaned under his breath. "One day we've got to do an all-day movie marathon to catch you up on my references." And with that, he pulled her toward the stairs.

But Medea couldn't resist one quick glance back at the stranger whose presence still haunted her. Worse? He continued to watch after her with that penetrating stare like she was a hare he was planning to devour as lunch.

"What are they?" she asked Urian as he led her upstairs to the less crowded area of the bar.

"Blaise is a mandrake. Falcyn . . . hell if I know. He's one of the dragon breeds, but not a Were-Hunter."

"If they're brothers, he'd be a mandrake, too. Right?"

Urian hesitated. "I don't think they're really related. The dragons have an even more peculiar idea of what constitutes family than we do."

She was so perplexed by that. "But if he's a dragon and he's not a mandrake or Were-Hunter, how can he be human?" Those were the only two kinds of pureblood dragons who could take human form.

At least that she knew of, and given the fact she'd walked this earth for more than eleven thousand years, she knew quite a bit about shapeshifters and the preternatural world that had birthed her.

And them.

Especially since her father was one. But his dragon form

came from the fact that he was a demigod, not a true shape-shifter. Unlike them, he couldn't hold his form for long, or live in it.

Urian paused to look from her to the two dragons in the crowd below. "*That,* Medea, is the question we've all asked and no one will answer. All we know is that he's a bloodthirsty beast who's best avoided."

2

"So what is your trauma?"

Blaise snorted derisively at Falcyn's growled question. "Lack of parental support. Failure to bond. Kerrigan knocking me into one too many walls for lipping off whenever he was in a foul mood, which was pretty much always. Fear of fluffy bunnies, but that's not why I'm here."

"Fluffy bunnies?" Falcyn wasn't sure he wanted to know the answer to that question, but it was so out of place for this audacious, lunatic mandrake that he just felt compelled to hear his explanation, even against all common sense.

"Ever seen the movie *Bambi*? Those little bastards are some strange brew. And don't get me started on Monty Python's *Holy Grail* and *that* hare-y nightmare." Blaise visibly shook. "It's to the point I don't even want to see that stuffed pink thing Nim carries."

At the mention of the harmless slug demon, Falcyn rolled his eyes so hard back in his skull, it actually burned. "You're so effing weird."

"Oh yeah, 'cause you're hogging all the normality. Have you ever bothered to look into that abyss, my friend? I promise the pot is calling the kettle twin."

"Have you a point to this mission, other than to piss me off and insult me? In which case, mission accomplished, but your life is drawing perilously close to its end as a result."

"Wow, that's some serious hostility you got going there, buddy. Need to chillax."

Falcyn arched a brow at the uncharacteristic word. *Chillax?* "Who have you been around that you've picked up this all new vocabulary?"

Blaise grinned. "Morgen's new toy. He's addicted to all sorts of peculiar things. . . . And not just porn. Which is why I'm here."

"What? For porn? Sorry. Not a pimp. Don't need a pimp. Don't want a pimp."

"Wasn't planning to act as such. Nor did I know you were into guys."

Falcyn grimaced. "Talking to you always gives me a brain

tumor. Explain to me how it is that no one's murdered you to date?"

"Not from lack of trying on their part, I assure you. Let me revisit the whole Kerrigan slamming me into walls. But I'm just that fast with my reflexes. And lucky for me, you're an old dragon. Decrepit."

"You really want to test that theory?"

"Not without backup. So to the point of my visit . . ."

More agitated than he wanted to be, Falcyn crossed his arms over his chest as he waited for Blaise to finish that sentence. "Have you lost your thought, your mind . . . or just your nerve?"

Cocking his head, Blaise narrowed his gaze as if he were listening intently to something. "They're here."

"They?"

"Morgen's dogs. That's what I was trying to tell you. She was given a hole, and while *she* can't come through it, her Circle now can."

"So? Why should I care? That's your battle, brother. Not mine."

And before Blaise could let out another word, the door behind him opened.

Falcyn's gut drew tight at the sight and arrival of Narishka duFey Morgen's right-hand bitch.

And the creature Falcyn hated most.

So much for this being Blaise's battle alone. Falcyn's blood flowed thick through his veins as he started for the tiny blond Adoni who'd robbed him of everything he'd ever hoped to love.

Holding her hand up, she caught him with her powers and tsked. "You know better, dragon. What were you thinking?"

"How much I want to feast on your entrails, fey-bitch!"

And still she didn't flinch. Rather, she shook her head at him. "Now, now, is that any way to speak to the stepmother of your child?"

Those words only fired his anger more as they awoke a pain so profound inside him that not even all these centuries could quell it. "You mean the murderess of my son, don't you?"

Blaise gaped. The birth of his son was something Falcyn had never mentioned to another living creature.

Other than Max.

And neither of them spoke of Maddor, as the mere mention of it made him most violent against his brother.

Narishka only knew because she'd helped her sister conceive and birth his son. And to what purpose? To become a slave for Morgen le Fey—thanks to Max and his interference. Because of his brother's actions, the mandrakes were nowhere near as powerful a race as they should have been. Hence why they all lived in servitude to the fey whores of Avalon and Camelot.

Maddor, as their progenitor, had been the first to suffer— shouldering the bulk of Morgen's blind rage because of Max's actions. And there had been nothing Falcyn could do to stop her or help his son.

Nothing.

Not even on the day they'd finally killed Maddor because of Max's curse. For that alone, Falcyn still wanted their hearts in his fists. Not a day went by that he didn't burn in anger over the loss of his child.

And that was why Falcyn had loved and protected Blaise for all these centuries.

Because Blaise wasn't really his brother.

He was his grandson. One he'd been forbidden to meet until long after Blaise had grown into his own. Which was why Falcyn had kept the knowledge of his birth from Blaise. Nothing save more pain could come from Blaise learning the truth.

He hadn't been abandoned by his father. He'd been torn from them and left to die by the Adoni, who were even more cruel.

And it stung him enough for them both. There was no need in burdening Blaise with a reality he couldn't change. Come hell itself, Falcyn would die before he allowed anyone to ever again harm Blaise.

"Bitch, please!" Falcyn used his powers to break her hold and slam her back against the wall hard enough to put a dent in the sheetrock.

Finally, panic and fear sparked in her eyes as she realized the true extent of his powers and her own weakness in comparison. She fought against his invisible grip. "Kill me and your son dies, too."

"My son died a long time ago."

Narishka shook her head. "Maddor still lives."

Those three unexpected words saved her life. "What do you mean?"

Grimacing, she glared at Blaise. "Tell him! Maddor still rules over the mandrakes at Camelot."

Falcyn felt the blood drain from his cheeks. No . . . she was lying.

She had to be.

"You play with me, Adoni whore, and so help me—"

"I would never!" Choking, she spat at Blaise. "Tell him, damn you!"

Blaise licked his lips slowly. His complexion paled as much as Falcyn's. "Is Maddor really your son?"

Falcyn couldn't bear to answer that question. Not while silent tears choked him. "Does he live?" His voice cracked on those words.

Blaise nodded. "Yeah, he lives. He's a cold-blooded son of a bitch, though."

Like father, like son.

With a bitter laugh, Falcyn closed the distance between him and Narishka. "She was a whore, actually. Treacherous from her first breath to her last."

Narishka lifted her chin with a courage that would be admirable if not for the sheer stupidity of her defiance, given his hatred and blatant disregard for her life. "I told you not to kill my sister."

Hissing, he moved to end her so that she could join Igraine in hell.

"Wait!" she screamed.

"For what?" The question was out before he could stop it. He didn't even know why he bothered, since he had no desire to spare her life or to even hear another syllable from her lips that were more used to spilling lies than truth.

"You have something we need."

So what? Was she effing kidding? He couldn't care less about them or their needs.

He quirked a brow at that. "I own nothing."

"Didn't say you owned it. You *protect* it."

He scowled even more, as there was nothing left in this life he protected.

Nothing other than Blaise and Illarion. And he'd *never* allow her to have either of them.

"Pardon?"

A dark, insidious light played in the depths of her eyes. "Let us negotiate, shall we?"

Urian scowled at Medea as they talked inside the small private room in Sanctuary that was reserved for whenever preternatural clientele became rowdy and needed a time-out away from human witnesses who might not react well to the reality of what they shared their world with. Barely more than a closet, their quarters were cramped, but it allowed them to not be overheard by any of the humans outside.

Or the Were-Hunters, who as a rule had *very* sensitive hearing.

And given the fact that his sister had just told him about a mysterious plague that was about to destroy her people, he was glad no one could overhear them.

"Why are you telling me this? I'm no longer a Daimon."

Medea crossed her arms over her chest. "Yeah, but for all you know, this plague could infect you, too. Whatever it is that Apollo unleashed on us is taking an awful toll. I know you hate our father, but—"

"Stryker's *not* my father!" he reminded her coldly.

"Biologically, true. However, he did raise you as his own. His wife birthed you."

"After I was ripped from the stomach of my real mother by that bitch you serve . . . and shoved into her womb without anyone's knowledge or consent!" And Medea reminding him of how the gods had screwed him over wasn't warming him to her cause.

At all.

Honestly, he'd had enough of being their bastard stepchild they kicked whenever they became bored.

"*That* bitch is also the mother of your current boss and the beloved protector of your real father and mother, don't forget!"

Urian hissed at her less-than-subtle reminder about Apollymi's position in his world. "You have some nerve to come here and ask me to help Stryker or Apollymi, given what they've both taken from me."

"I know that. Which tells you how desperate I am." She swallowed hard. "They're not the only ones who are sick, Uri. Davyn has it, too. He'll die if you don't help us."

She saw the uncertainty that tormented him as she mentioned the one Daimon he still considered his family. While Urian might be angry at her parents and Apollymi, he would never turn his back on Davyn. Not after all the centuries they'd been more brothers than friends.

Not after all the intel Davyn had risked his life to bring to Urian.

The one truth about her brother—he was loyal above everything else.

Even his own pride and ego.

And they both loved Davyn and appreciated him for the rare Daimon he was.

"Please, Urian. I lost my husband and only child because my grandfather—*the grandfather of* your *birth twin*—was a bastard. Watched them both be slaughtered in front of my own eyes by the human vermin you protect. For no reason, other than they feared us when we'd done nothing to cause their suspicions. We were innocent and harmless, minding our own business when they attacked us. So don't think for one minute you own some kind of market share on pain. Because trust me, brother, you're a novice. You've no idea what I went through in my mortal life or this one. I'm sorry for what Stryker did to your Phoebe. I am, but I've lost too many to sit back and watch the rest die and not do something to at least try to help them. That's not who I am."

Urian froze as if her words finally reached through his pain to open his eyes to a truth about his sister that he'd never seen before. "That's why you tortured Jared, isn't it?"

Medea winced at his mention of the Sephiroth who'd been held captive by her mother and aunt. To this day, she was ashamed of some of what she'd done to him while he'd lived in their custody.

But not completely. In her mind, he more than deserved everything they had put him through. "He turned on his own. Led them to slaughter for the very gods who betrayed us while his soldiers put their faith and lives in his hands. And for what? His own gain. Nothing more. He knew exactly how treacherous the gods all were and it didn't matter to him. Only his bargain did. He let his soldiers die under his command. So aye, I took my anger out on him when it became more than I could cope with. How could I not? How could anyone betray people who trusted him the way he did? Sit back and let his enemies tear apart his friends and family. Brutally. I'd go down fighting to the bitter end for a stranger. And I'm supposed to be the villain. The hypocrisy of what Jared did to his army sickens me every time I think of him. He sold them all out to save his own ass so that he would survive that war. There's nothing I hate more in this world than a coward."

"Except humans."

A single tear slid down her cheek as she saw the face of her baby in her mind's eye. He'd been so precious and beautiful with his curly blond hair and bright eyes. Dimpled cheeks and a laugh that had come from the angels themselves. So innocent and sweet. Medea had never truly lived until the day she'd held that bit of heaven in her arms.

And her heart had followed him into his grave.

"Praxis was five years old, Uri. Five. And he died in agony at their merciless hands, screaming for me to help him while they . . ." She choked on the words that she still couldn't utter. Not even all these centuries later. The horror was still too fresh and raw in her heart.

No amount of time had rectified what they'd brutally taken from her.

Nay, not taken.

Shattered. She might have physically survived, but inside she was as dead as her husband and son. Only a husk of the woman she'd once been.

And never again the doe-eyed innocent who once thought this world a beautiful place.

So instead, she glared up at her brother. "Tell me, Urian, how am I even sane, given what they violently stole from me? No amount of time can dull a pain that sharp!"

He pulled her against him. "I'm so sorry, Dee."

Her tears dissolved into rage, as they always did. Because she couldn't handle the full weight of her sorrow. It was a worthless, horrid emotion that made her weak and vulnerable. Anger motivated her. Rage kept her in motion past that most wretched pain.

That was the only reason she was still standing. It was what had seen her through the horrors of her life and what allowed her to function. It fed her like a mother's milk and kept her strong. It was what she embraced with both fists.

Her breathing ragged, she pushed him away from her. "I don't need your pity. It's worthless. You can keep it, especially if you're not going to help me."

Urian caught her arm as she started to leave. "Wait!" He wanted to deny her this request. In truth, he wanted Stryker to go down in flames and to laugh as he watched it happen. After all, the bastard had cut Urian's throat in cold blood and murdered his precious Phoebe—the only woman in the world he'd ever love.

But Medea was right. He couldn't allow the rest of what had once been his family and friends to die and do nothing. Unlike Jared, he couldn't stand by and see his friends slaughtered unjustly.

Not if he could help it.

"There is one thing that might be able to save them."

"What?"

He hesitated. Not because he didn't want to help them, but because he didn't know what Stryker might do with the cure. In his hands, it could prove most lethal.

No good deed goes unpunished.

Somehow this was going to come back on him. He knew it. Such things always did, and they left him bleeding and cursing. Yet even so, he couldn't allow Medea to be hurt any worse than she already had. She was right. She'd been through enough, and at the end of the day, they were family. Maybe not in the conventional sense, but he felt a kinship with her. And he had grown up thinking himself one of Stryker's sons. Thinking of Stryker's daughter as his own sister.

Every time he looked at Medea, he saw Dyana's beloved face. Remembered their time as children and the day they'd renamed her Tannis because they could no longer bear to call their only sister the name of their aunt who'd allowed her own brother—the god Apollo—to curse them to die over something none of them had participated in.

They'd all been innocent victims of a fetid power game between the ancient gods. All of them had paid a high cost to continue living, just to spite those who would see them fall for no reason whatsoever.

For better or worse, Medea was every bit as much his sister as Tannis had been. And because he loved her, he refused to add to her pain.

"I don't know if it'll work or not."

Medea chafed at his hedging. "Oh for goodness' sake, just say it, already!"

"A dragonstone."

Pulling back, she scowled at him. "A what?"

Urian hedged as he sought a way to explain it. But it wasn't as easy as it should be. "For lack of a better term, it's an enchanted rock the dragons have. Supposedly, it can cure anything. Even death. It even brought Max back after he was killed saving his wife and children. So I would assume it could cure this, too."

"Where do you get one?"

That was the easy part.

And the hardest thing imaginable. "As luck would have it, there's one here."

Joy returned to her dark eyes. "Where?"

He visibly cringed at the last place either of them wanted to venture. Because asking for help there was all kinds of rampant stupid. "That would be the stickler, as it belongs to Falcyn."

"That surly beast I met earlier?"

He nodded. "To my knowledge, that's the last one in existence. The rest were all destroyed or have gone missing."

Medea groaned out loud as her stomach shrank at the very thought of having to negotiate with Falcyn over something so rare. It flipping figured. She might as well stick her head in the mouth of a hungry lion and ask him not to bite.

Or her mother to shed blood when she was in one of her moods.

"Great. So how do I go about getting this thing?"

"Word of advice? Ask nicely."

Falcyn stared at Narishka. "You want my dragonstone?" He laughed in her face. "Fuck off and die in agony, you worthless bitch."

"Does your son mean so little to you, then?"

"About as much as you value your life." He smirked pointedly.

Blaise stepped between them, aggravating Falcyn, as it prevented him from killing her. "Why do you need his stone?"

Narishka raked a cold glare over him. "This doesn't concern you, maggot. Stay out of it."

Falcyn crossed his arms over his chest as he cleared his throat. "Can I kill her now?" he asked Blaise in a bland tone that belied his fury.

"I'm about to give her to you, but aren't you curious why she's here?"

"Not enough to spare her life."

Blaise laughed. "Wow. Remind me to never really piss you off."

"I would, but you don't listen." As he moved to make good on his threat, the door opened to admit Urian and Medea into the room.

Falcyn drew up short at the sight of them. And at this point, he was rushing through the last of his patience for anyone. Even a woman with an ass that fine. "Here to help or to hinder? Declare yourself."

Urian's eyes widened before he answered. "Whichever choice ends with me on your good side."

"Grab the bitch."

But before anyone could move, a bright light pulsed inside the room, blinding everyone except Blaise, who couldn't see anyway.

Falcyn cursed as pain radiated through his skull, leaving

behind a flashing strobe that made him queasy as he tried to see past the swirling white dots that peppered his vision.

"Urian?"

"Blind as a bat!" he snapped in response to Falcyn's call. "Dee?"

"Can't see shit." Medea held her hand up to shield her light-sensitive eyes.

"It's demons in the room." Blaise moved to cover them. "Gallu."

Ah, that's just great.

"Who invited the assholes to our party?" Falcyn snarled.

They were one of the few breeds that could infect a victim and turn them into mindless slaves.

Or killing machines. Neither of which appealed to Falcyn. While he didn't mind senseless violence for the sake of it, he wanted the ultimate decision for who and what he killed to be his alone, and not the behest of some evil overlord. No one would ever hold dominion over him.

No one.

Something grabbed Falcyn.

He moved to punch the fool.

"Don't you dare," Blaise growled in his ear. "Or I'm leaving you to them."

In another quick blur, Falcyn felt himself falling. He reached out and started to transform, then stopped himself, since the transformation could kill Blaise, or him, or both, depending on what it was Blaise was up to. Because this suddenly felt like inter-dimensional travel. And transforming during the middle of *that* was never a good idea.

"Blaise? What are you doing?"

"Hang on! Everyone stay calm!"

Yeah, right. Calm wasn't his natural state of being.

Pissed off?

Check.

"Then why do you sound panicked and why am I still blind?"

No sooner had Falcyn finished that sentence than he slammed hard against a mossy cushion. And something soft and curvaceous landed on top of him with a loud "huff." Worse than that, it elbowed him right in the stomach.

And would have kneed his groin had he not twisted and moved with lightning speed.

"Hey, hey, love! You only touch the no-zone if you intend to make it happy."

Grimacing, Medea gave him a look that said he was some unwelcome goo that had attached itself to the bottom of her bare foot on her way out of the bathroom. "There's not enough beer in the universe for me to touch your no-zone, dragonfly. Don't flatter yourself."

"Says the Daimon crawling all over it."

"Jumping off it, you mean, before I catch something I'm sure antibiotics won't cure."

He scoffed at her insult. "Not what it feels like from where I'm laying, and you're still on top of—umph!" He growled as she elbowed the air out of his lungs.

With a fierce scowl, he rubbed the abused area and pushed himself to his feet so that he could look around at something other than her shapely ass. He'd expected to find himself either in the bar or Peltier House—the residence the bears owned that was attached to their bar.

This was neither.

Irritated, he faced the cause of this particular disaster. "Blaise, what did you do?"

They were out in a meadow. A dark, dismal, creepy-ass meadow, the likes of which human kids used to scare each other. Or B-movie directors favored for the backdrops of their cheesy sets.

Yeah, he could definitely see some axe-wielding lunatic coming at them from the brush. 'Course, the mood he was in, *that* lunatic might be him before much longer.

Blaise turned around slowly in a way that said he was using his dragon-sight to feel the aether. "Well, this wasn't what I had planned."

"What?" Urian's voice dripped with sarcasm. "You weren't wanting a trip to Halloween Town? I'm so disappointed, Blaise. Was hoping to get my Jack Skellington underwear signed."

Falcyn snorted at the sudden image he had of Urian in his head, posturing in Jack Skellington briefs like some Calvin Klein model. Actually, he could see the freak in that. Which was the most disturbing part about all of this. 'Cause really, he'd much rather be wasting that brain capacity on picturing Medea naked than imagining Urian in his twisted Disney underwear fetish.

Pushing the images out of his mind before he went as blind as Blaise, Falcyn scratched at his whiskered cheek. "So how'd we get here?"

"Not sure. I was aiming for the parlor of Peltier House."

Blaise screwed his face up. "Epic fail. Not even sure where we are."

Urian let out a long, tired breath as he surveyed the twisted landscape. "I think I know. But you're not going to like it. I sure as hell don't."

Medea pursed her lips. "Try us."

"Myrkheim."

Falcyn grimaced at how right Urian was, as an ulcer started in his stomach.

Blaise made an expression of exaggerated happiness. "Oh goodie! The borderlands where heathens go to rot! Just where I wanted to build my vacation home! Where's a lease? Sign my scaly ass up!"

Medea rolled her eyes. "What's Myrkheim?"

Falcyn laughed bitterly at her innocent question. Which made sense, all things considered. "Guess the Daimons don't spend a lot of time here, as it's not really part of *your* mythology. It's a nether realm. A holding ground, if you will, between the land of light and dark where the fey can practice their magick."

"Who's feyfolk?"

Legitimate question, he supposed, as there was a lot of fey in the world to go around, and he hadn't specified the pantheon. Falcyn sighed. "At one time, everyone's. But nowadays, it's mostly reserved for Morgen's rejects. And some other IBS-suffering bastards."

"Yeah, okay . . . So what's the—" Before she could finish her sentence, a bolt of light shot between them, narrowly missing her.

In fact, it only missed her because Falcyn deflected it. "Stray magick. You have to keep your head up for it. If it hits you, there's no telling what it might do. Could vaporize you. Turn you into a toad. Or just ruin your chances for children."

Medea's eyes widened as she watched it explode and morph a tree not far from them into a chicken that screeched, then dove under the ground to burrow like a frightened rabbit. "That happen a lot?"

Falcyn nodded. " 'Round here? Good bit."

"Great. Anything else I should watch out for?"

"Yeah," he said bitterly. "Everything."

Blinking, she met Urian's gaze. "Joke?"

"Falcyn has no measurable sense of humor. At least none that we've identified to date."

Blaise braided his long white hair and secured it with a leather tie he'd unwound from his wrist. "Well, Max said that Falcyn wasn't always the pain in the ass we know him as. But I can only speak about the last few hundred years. And he hasn't changed as long as I've known him."

"Not helping, Blaise," Urian said drily.

He spread his arms wide to indicate their surroundings. "In case you haven't noticed, I'm not real good at that. Tend to fuck up all things whenever I try to help."

"And Merlin chose you for a Grail knight. What the hell was she thinking?"

Blaise hissed. "We don't talk about that out loud, Falcyn! Sheez! What? You trying to get me killed?"

Falcyn shot a blast of fire at the sky. "Still trying to figure out how we got here . . . and why. 'Cause let's face it, we didn't get sent here for anything good."

"Was hoping you wouldn't notice that." Blaise cleared his throat. "Way to harsh my zen, dude."

Falcyn rolled his eyes at Blaise. "You need to stop hanging out with Savitar. I hate that bastard."

"You hate everyone," Blaise reminded him.

"That surfboard-wielding bastard I hate most of all."

Blaise arched an inquisitive brow. "More than Max?"

Falcyn growled. "Are we going to argue inconsequentials or look for a way home? 'Cause I just tried my powers and they didn't do shit for getting us out of here."

Cringing, Blaise rubbed nervously at his neck. "Mine either, and I was hoping to keep you distracted so that you wouldn't beat my ass over this situation."

Falcyn glanced to Urian. "What about you, Princess Pea? You got anything?"

"Besides a throbbing migraine? No. My teleportation isn't cooperating either."

They all looked at Medea.

"Really? If mine was working do you think I'd be here, listening to the lot of you? Promise, I'd have vanished long ago."

Blaise sighed. "I think I saw this movie once. It didn't go well for the people, as they turned on each other and it involved chainsaws . . . and a whole lot of blood."

"But was there silence? That's the real question."

Urian snorted at Falcyn's irritable comment.

Worse?

There *was* sudden silence. It echoed around them with that eerie kind of stillness that set every nerve ending on edge. The kind that radiated with malevolence because it was a portent.

The men drew together to stand with their backs to each other so that they could face and fight whatever threat was coming for them.

Medea wasn't so quick to trust. While they were allies, they weren't hers. And trust didn't come easy to her—it hadn't in a long, long time.

Actually, she wasn't sure if it'd ever been part of her vocabulary. So she stood as she'd done the whole of her life.

Alone.

K-bars drawn. It was, after all, what she knew best. And she waited for the imminent storm that would do its damnedest to tear her to shreds. Just as it always did.

Falcyn froze as he caught sight of Medea and her warrior's stance. She was a thing of exquisite beauty and he wasn't describing her physical appearance. Rather it was that raw determination in her dark eyes. The steel in her spine as she stood ready to take on whatever threat was coming for her with shrewd confidence.

Damn.

That kind of grit reached out and touched him on a level unexpected. Bonded them. Because only someone who'd been through the hell he'd known could look like that.

And before he reconsidered his actions, he moved to stand with her.

She scowled at him. "What are you doing?"

"Covering your flank."

"I've got jeans for that."

He bit back a wry grin. "Yeah, you do. And a fine ass they cup. I'm here to make sure you keep it attached where it is and unbloodied."

An unidentifiable shadow passed behind her eyes, but whatever it was softened her features and hit him like a blow. More than that, it caused his cock to jerk at the worst possible time. And he didn't know why, when he needed his blood in his brain so that he could think through how best to defeat whatever was planning to take them out.

Suddenly, a bright light flashed near them. One that momentarily blinded him with its intensity.

He pulled back to confront the mist that solidified into a tall, lanky male with brown hair and red eyes.

Raking a sneer over the demon dressed in black-on-black designer snobbery, Falcyn glanced to Urian, who seemed to recognize the Fabio wannabe. "So, Slim, who is *this* designer asshole?"

3

The demon quirked a grin at Falcyn's question. "That's Mr. Asshole to you, Dragon."

"Sure, punkin. Whatever floats your shit."

Medea poked Falcyn on the shoulder before she rose up on her toes to whisper in his ear. "You might not want to antagonize him."

"Says the woman who knows me not at all. Trust me. I've pissed down the throats of monsters that make this posh boy look even lamer than what he is. On my scared-o-meter, he doesn't even move the needle."

The demon smiled grudgingly. "Which is why you've held your dragonstone longer than any other dragon in history. Now be a good boy, hand it over."

Falcyn snorted derisively as he raked a less-than-impressed stare over him. "Uh . . . hell to the no."

A slow smile spread over the demon's chiseled features, but didn't quite reach his red eyes. "Give us the stone and I'll tell you how to save your sister."

Falcyn went still at those words. "My sister's dead. And if you pull a Narishka on me, I swear, demon, I'll eat your heart for lunch and burp it for dessert."

"I don't know what Narishka did, but your sister was turned to stone. So while she's not technically living, she's not exactly dead, either."

Falcyn felt the blood drain from his cheeks as those words sank in and he realized that for the second time today, he'd been lied to. Not that he should be surprised. His biggest shock came from the fact that they'd all managed to keep the secrets. "Blaise? Did you know about this?"

"No. I was told she went down fighting against Morgen with Anir." Anir was King Arthur's son, who'd been turned into a gargoyle due to another curse the fey bitch had put on him and his knights.

Medea placed her hand on Falcyn's forearm in a comforting gesture before she leaned against his back. "Kessar is a treacherous bastard. Don't trust him. He wouldn't know the truth if it bit his furry little ass off."

Kessar.

Now that was a name Falcyn knew well. "So posh boy's the

gallu leader the Sumerian gods turned against. Bet that ruined your day, huh?"

"You should know, son of Lilith."

Blaise sucked his breath in sharply between his teeth. "Never, ever ... *ever* bring his mother into things. That's just a good way to get your ass kicked, as he tends to madly lash out whenever you mention she-who-should-never-be-named."

"You should listen to my brother, demon. At least I know my mother's name. Which is more than you do." He swept a grimace over Kessar. "And if you know that much about me, then you know who and what fathered me. So if I were you, I'd run before I decide to pull the wings off you for fun and pin you to a wall somewhere to throw darts at whenever I'm drunk."

Unperturbed, Kessar examined his claws. "Fine. I take it you've no interest in learning where they sent your sister?"

A slow, insidious smile spread over Falcyn's face. "Oh, I'll find her. As soon as I eat your brains and absorb the information."

Faster than Medea could blink, Falcyn was on Kessar, tearing at his flesh. With an unholy growl, he snatched the demon's head back and would have ripped out his throat had Kessar not vanished.

Blood dripped from Falcyn's hands and chin as he sneered up at the dismal sky. "What? Was it something I said? Come back here, you pussy bastard! What kind of demon runs like a bitch over a small bite?"

Urian crossed his arms over his chest as he met Medea's shocked stare. "And now you know why I had my reservations about seeking out our not-so-friendly dragon for conversation. You just can't take him out in public. Or private either."

Medea would have made a comment had Falcyn not decided to lick the blood from his fingers. "They have these things called napkins, you know? Been around for thousands of years now. You should try one."

Wiping the blood from his lips with his knuckle, he grinned at her. "A squeamish Daimon? Seriously? Besides, I like the taste of my enemy's blood. It soothes me. Blood of my friends is even better, but they tend to get a little testy whenever I partake of my favorite delicacy."

Blaise sighed. "Really, we tried home-training. He failed miserably. But he's awesome when you need someone killed and you don't have a place to hide a body. He eats all traces of it. Better than a pet Charonte demon."

With one last lick to his middle finger, Falcyn turned back to Blaise. "Can you transform?"

"Haven't tried. Why?"

"I can't."

Blaise looked sick to his stomach at that realization. After a second, he shook his head. "Why can't we turn?"

"That would be the disturbing question of the moment, wouldn't it?"

Urian laughed nervously. "How do we get back?"

"There's always a portal of some kind." Falcyn turned a slow, small circle as he surveyed the land around them. "We just have to figure out where it is and what it looks like. You know . . . fun shit that, always."

"Yeah. Lots of fun." Urian's voice dripped with sarcasm. "And avoid stray magick and demons."

"And everything else," Medea added.

"Exactly what she said," Falcyn muttered under his breath.

"So glad I got up this morning." Blaise sighed heavily. "Hell, I even bathed."

Falcyn passed a smug sneer at him. "So glad I'm stuck here with all of you. Bitching and moaning. I suddenly feel like I'm teaching kindergarten."

Medea shook her head at Falcyn's droll tone. "I know why *I* need your dragonstone. What's the deal with the others, anyway? Why are they so hot to lay hands to it?"

"Aside from the fact that they're assholes?" Falcyn headed for the woods. It seemed as likely a spot as any to find an enchanted portal. "Narishka wants it to bring Mordred back to life."

"Mordred le Fey?"

He inclined his head at her. "Yeah. Apparently, they think they've found his tomb, and Mom wants a reunion with her precious little boy." He smirked. "Personally, I'd like to reunite them in hell. Who's with me?" His gaze went first to Urian, then Blaise. "Really?" he asked drily. "No takers?"

Medea shrugged. "I might be tempted if I knew who you were talking about."

"Queen Bitch, Morgen le Fey. Can't miss her. Tall, gorgeous, meaner than shit. Blond and lethal."

"Sounds like me . . . except for the height."

He laughed. "That's what all the stories about you say. Are they true?"

"Depends on your side of things. My mother says I'm not mean enough."

"Ouch." Falcyn sucked his breath in sharply. "Take it Mommie Dearest has some issues?"

Medea snorted. "Her issues carry Samsonite."

Urian came up between them. "Enough getting along, you two. It's starting to creep me out. The last thing any of us needs is a meeting of the two evils."

She rolled her eyes. "Already had that. My parents. Besides, Falcyn doesn't strike me as evil."

Falcyn cocked his head at that, instantly intrigued. No one put him in any other category. Ever. In fact, most ran from him as if he were *his* father—the fount of all evil itself. And the majority of beings had no idea what spawned him. They only assumed it, given the nature and position of his father. "Really?"

"Hmmm." She swept a probing stare over his body. "While you are definitely cantankerous, you don't take pleasure in hurting others."

"And how do you know that?"

Medea smiled. "Been around real evil long enough to know the difference. Trust me, sugar, you ain't got it by a long, long shot."

Falcyn slowed as she quickened her steps to catch up to Blaise. What the hell was *that*?

A compliment?

He wasn't quite sure, since he didn't normally get them from anyone.

Kicks in the ass and teeth?

Those he took routinely.

But strokes to the ego? Foreign, alien beasts he had no concept of. Weird. And it left him with a strange feeling in his stomach.

Maybe those were the aforementioned hunger pangs.

Yet it felt like a hunger for something other than food, for once. And made him harder than he'd ever been in his life.

Urian reached over and brushed his thumb against Falcyn's jaw. "You're gaping, brother. Might want to close that before you catch some flies."

He slapped at Urian's hand. "Don't be an ass."

"Can't help it. Spent too many centuries as the right hand of evil, myself. Left a black mark on my soul."

As they neared the edge of the woods, Falcyn had the eerie sensation of being watched. Thankfully that curbed his attention where Medea was concerned, and distracted his gaze from straying to her constantly.

Damn, she was a lot more distracting than she should be. If his body didn't stop, he was going to start cutting pieces of it off.

Falcyn rubbed at the hairs on the back of his neck that had risen. "Blaise?"

"Yeah . . . I feel it."

Medea's dark eyes met his and did the strangest things to his stomach. Which made him even harder, damn it all. "What is it?"

"Not sure." Falcyn walked backward so that he could scan the meadow as he tried not to think about why he wanted to stay close to her to protect her from whatever threat he sensed. That was an innate dragon trait. One he didn't want to scrutinize, because the ramifications terrified him.

He saw nothing around them.

Not that it meant anything, given the powers some of their preternatural brethren possessed. And he really missed being in his dragon's body right now. A dragon's sight was very different from that of a human's. Much sharper and clearer. And while a trace of that followed him into a human body, it still wasn't as good as it'd be in his other form. Which was why Blaise wasn't blind as a dragon.

Only as a man.

Then Falcyn heard it.

A mere wisp of breath. So low as to be virtually inaudible. To a normal creature. But he wasn't normal. Too many centuries of fighting for survival had left him paranoid and highly attuned to everything around him.

Like Medea's soft lily scent.

Especially that subtle shift in the air that said he was being stalked by something invisible. Something approaching fast on his right . . .

With lightning reflexes honed by battle, he reached out and grabbed their pursuer.

"I mean you no harm!" The sound of a woman's voice shocked him.

Falcyn tightened his grip on what felt like a throat. "Show yourself."

She materialized in his fist and, as he'd assumed, his hand was wrapped about her neck. Large lavender eyes swallowed a face that appeared more girl than woman, and yet the fullness of her leather-wrapped body said that she was well into her twenties. Physically, anyway.

Probably older given the amount of power and confidence he sensed from her. That level of expertise came from a creature who was centuries old.

"What are you?"

She rubbed at his wrist to remind him that his death-grip was cutting off her ability to speak. Another action that said she was older than a frightened teen.

Falcyn relaxed his hold, but not enough to allow her to escape. He wasn't a fool and he hadn't lived to his own advanced age by playing one.

"I'm Brogan."

"Didn't ask your name. Don't really care. I asked *what* you are."

"Cursed. Exiled and damned. Please, let me go and I can help you."

She was hedging and he didn't like it. Creatures who played games usually had something to hide. "Why?"

"Why should you let me go? So that I can breathe."

Falcyn ground his teeth. "No, why should we trust you to help us?"

"Because I want out of here more than anything, but I lack the powers to break the seal or bargain for freedom. If you take me with you, I'll show you where a portal is."

Still suspicious, he released her. "And again, I ask what you are."

"A kerling Deathseer."

Falcyn conjured up a ball of fire and held it so that she knew her own death was imminent. "Deathseer or seeker?"

A seer saw death. A seeker caused it.

Holding her hands up, she stepped back from him. "*Seer,*" she said quickly, letting him know that she got the less-than-veiled threat in his actions. "Though ofttimes the Black Crom uses me to find his victims."

"And why is that?"

"I was sold to him for such."

Falcyn moved to kill her, but Blaise caught his arm.

"Don't hurt her."

Aghast, he stared at him. "Are you out of your mandrake mind?"

Blaise snorted. "All the time. But not about this." He held his hand out to the petite brunette. "Come, Brogan. I won't let him harm you."

Allowing the fire in his hand die out, he scowled at Blaise. "Can you see her at all?"

Blaise shook his head. "I can only hear her voice. Why?"

Because she was exquisitely beautiful. Her long dark brown hair that had escaped her tight braids made perfect spirals around her elvish features and pointed ears. Enchanting features the fey often used to lure others to their doom. And that included her tight brown leather pants and corset that were covered by a flimsy green robe, and the fey stone necklace and diadem she wore.

But if Blaise couldn't see it, then it wasn't a trap for him. "Why are you attracted to her?"

"Didn't say I was. I only hear the truth in her voice. She's not lying to us. So I think we should help her."

"And no good deed goes unpunished. You help her and you're likely to pay for it. In the worst way imaginable and at the worst possible time."

Blaise sighed heavily at Falcyn's mistrust that had come from a lifetime of betrayal. "What I love most about you, Fal. Your never-ending optimism. It bowls me over."

Perhaps, but sadly he expected only the worst from those

around him, and *very* seldom had they risen above his low expectations.

Tucking down her gossamer wings so that they couldn't be seen, Brogan retrieved her knapsack.

As she started past Falcyn, he stopped her. "You harm him . . . or cause him to be harmed in any way—even a hangnail—and I will make sure you die in screaming agony."

Her eyes widened at his threat. "I see no death for him. You've no cause to threaten me on his behalf."

As she moved to walk beside Blaise, Medea dropped back to Falcyn's side. "What's a kerling?"

"A conjuring witch."

"That why you asked if she sought death?"

He nodded. "Kerlings can be a handful."

"Known many?"

"No, but I've killed my fair share."

Brogan gasped and glanced over her shoulder at Falcyn.

With a fake smile, he waved at her.

She let out a squeak and sidled closer to Blaise, who cast a fierce grimace in his direction. "What did you do?"

"I smiled."

"Ah, that explains it, then. It's such an unnatural act for you that you look like some questing beast whenever you try."

Falcyn screwed his face up as Blaise allowed the kerling to lead them.

Medea frowned up at him. "So what's the deal?"

"With?"

She jerked her chin toward Blaise. "You only heel for him. Why is that?"

"I don't heel for him. I protect my brothers."

"So you say, but that's not what it looks like from where I'm standing."

"Then you need to get a pair of glasses, a better vantage point, and look again."

"Don't get testy with me, dragonfly. I merely find it fascinating that you'd tuck your claws in for your brother. It just seems out of character for you. And weird."

"Weird?"

"Yeah. I never tuck mine in for Urian. Rather I use him as a sharpening strop."

"That's the truth. She lets blood every time she gets near me."

Falcyn bristled under her probing stare. "We're dragons, not Daimons."

Medea went cold at his words. "What's that supposed to mean?"

"We're cold-blooded. The only warmth we have is our family, so we tend to shelter them more closely than others do. Why? What did you think I meant?"

"She thought you were taking a dig that we feed off each other's blood."

Falcyn snorted. "Oh . . . there is that. Honestly, hadn't thought about it. Or I might have pointed it out."

Brogan glanced at them before she leaned in closer to Blaise. "They always carry on like this?"

"Not really. They just met."

"Yet they argue like a married couple . . . hmmm."

Falcyn summoned another fireball for the witch.

Medea caught his arm before he could launch it. "Barbecue her, Simi, and we're stuck here with no way back."

"Not stuck. Just detained."

"Yeah, well, I need to get home. Can't afford to be detained any longer than necessary. So tuck the fire and temper, princess, and be nice."

"I'm never nice," he said sullenly.

He didn't even like the sound of that four-lettered word. Hmmm, maybe there was some Simi in him, after all.

Suddenly, Brogan stopped.

Falcyn scowled at her as she cocked her head. "There a problem?"

Her eyes turned a peculiar color that defied all description. It was a strange fey hue that said she was tapping arcane powers to read their environment.

With the faintest whisper in her voice, she spoke. "Death is upon us."

4

Before Falcyn had a chance to ask Brogan what she meant, the ground around them began to boil. Literally. Chunks of soil bubbled and churned as if it were a living, breathing creature about to rise up under their feet.

Medea cursed as she danced around it to avoid being tripped. Likewise, he jumped over a segment of the ground that burst beneath him. It shot chunks of earth, grass, and mud everywhere.

"What the hell is this? I'm too old for hopscotch."

Brogan gasped as she jumped over another erupted rut. "Svartle Orms. Whenever the smiths break for the day, the orms are let loose from the forges and they stampede to freedom."

The head of one ugly, foul beast came up from the ground. It opened its mouth, showing off rows of serrated fangs.

"They're also starving," Brogan added. "And will eat anything they catch the scent to."

"Not on your menu, buddy." Falcyn let loose his fireballs into the beast's throat.

Howling, it lunged for him.

Medea fell in at his side, adding god-bolts to his fire to help fry the bastard. Urian and Blaise covered Brogan.

"What should we do?" Blaise asked her.

Brogan lifted her arms and began to whistle gently. The crooning went through Falcyn, making his sensitive ears ache. Blaise made a sound of sharp disapproval.

Still, she continued. Until it began to drive the orms back. "Run!" she said. "Head for the boulder caves! They won't enter there."

As they started for them, a cold wind came whipping through the trees.

"Ignore it and keep going! Don't look up. Eyes ahead!"

Don't look up? Was she kidding? Now it became an imperative need to do so. But conventional wisdom said it would be all kinds of stupid to defy Brogan's order.

All kinds of—

Crap!

Falcyn glanced up before he could stop himself.

And the moment he did, fire rained down from the sky.

Not just fire. Rocks. Lava. And some kind of stinging larvae.

Brogan made a sound of supreme disgust. "What part of *don't look up* did you not understand, dragon!"

"The part that it's a dragon's nature to do what we're told not to!"

Blaise cursed and swatted at the bugs. "What are these things?"

"Bloodvlox. Don't let them break your skin or they can infect you and take you over. If they land near your ears, they can crawl inside and ingest your brains! And keep them away from your eyes, too."

Medea hissed and slapped at one that was trying to burrow under her skin. "How do we get rid of them?"

"Fleabane, but I don't have any on me and can't conjure any until we get away from the orms." Brogan swatted at them. "I'll boost your powers so that you can teleport to the caves over there. It should be enough to get you to safety. But you'll have to do it fast, before they catch on and you lose the ability again."

Growling at the thought of blindly trusting her, Falcyn glanced around and decided there was no other out. "All right. On three, we teleport to just in front of the caves." And if she was lying or betrayed them, he'd eat her whole. "Ready?"

"Ready!" they said in unison.

Falcyn counted down.

On one they went, but just as he started to follow, an orm grabbed his leg. He turned on the creature and caught it with his claw, wishing he could give it what it really deserved.

His dragon's venom.

He stomped and kicked until he broke free, then he tele- ported, making sure he didn't take any stray beast with him, since that could cause its DNA to merge with his—something he definitely didn't want to happen. He was damaged enough. His luck, he'd sprout another arm or head.

Or another piece of anatomy he didn't want to think about duplicating, because one was enough to get him into all manner of trouble. It definitely didn't need a twin.

Especially not around Medea.

By the time he made the cave and retook a solid form, the howling had picked up volume and the fleas were stinging even more as they swarmed him the moment he was solid again. Blaise whipped at them with his shirt while Medea jerked Fal- cyn inside by the arm.

Urian used his powers to seal them in the cave.

Teamwork . . .

He shuddered. It gave him the willies. He'd never really bought into that. Dragons were solitary creatures, and while he'd fought with his brothers a handful of times, it wasn't enough that it left him comfortable with such things. And definitely not when sur- rounded by this many strangers.

"Can the orms find us in here?" Falcyn asked while Blaise pulled his shirt back on.

Brogan shook her head. "But there are others who can. The forges are all in places similar to this . . . as are their homes. It's why the orms avoid them when they're free."

"Awesome," Urian breathed. "Are the portals here, too?"

"Not close by. That would be too easy."

Of course it would.

Urian growled. "You think if I called for Acheron he might hear me and come to the rescue?"

"You can try." Falcyn waited.

After a few seconds, Urian growled again. "It was worth a shot."

"Anyone know a dark elf?" Falcyn glanced to Blaise, who made it his habit to party with them.

"None that I want to call. Thank you very much. Want to knock up Narishka?"

Falcyn glared at him. "I knocked up her sister. It's what got us into this, remember?"

"Ha, ha, ha, American slang. You suck so much," Blaise whimpered.

"Yeah, well, not real big on your slang either, Yobo."

Blaise shook his head irritably. "Bloody Yank."

Falcyn lit the cave with his fireballs. "Too bad we don't have Cadegan here. A dark hole like this is right up his alley."

"Illarion's, too," Urian reminded him.

Falcyn nodded. He was right about that. They'd both lived in drab caves for centuries.

Medea gave him an arch stare. "I would have thought you were at home here, too."

He grimaced at the ex-Daimon. "Stop with the stereotypes. Not all dragons hibernate in closed quarters. I lived on an island, on top of ruins. In the open and quite happy not to be penned in. My brother Max lives in a bar."

"Aye to that," Blaise chimed in. "My home was a castle in Camelot. Usually under the Pendragon's feet, but we won't talk about that, as it's just a dismal memory. Retrospect, don't know why I brought it up."

Brogan cocked her head. "Most of the dragons here are cave-dwellers. They fire our forges. The rest hide so as not to be enslaved."

"How many reside here?"

She scowled at Blaise's question. "A few dozen that I know of. Not counting the orms. They were bred once the dragon numbers began to thin."

"Makes sense." Falcyn passed a sad look at Blaise. "We don't do well in captivity."

"Is that why you're blind?" Brogan asked.

"No. My father blinded me, hoping I'd die in the wild when I was a babe. . . . At least that's what I was told."

Brogan paled. "Pardon? Why would he do such a terrible thing to his own child?"

"My mother had me to be a tool to control my father, but when he rejected me because of my albinism, my mother abandoned me to him and he took me out into the woods and left me there to die. I was to be an offering to the gods. Luckily, they rejected me, too."

With every word he spoke, fury rode hard on Falcyn, and he crossed the room to Blaise's side. His features turning dark and deadly, Falcyn fisted his hand in Blaise's hair and jerked him close. "You were *never* rejected by me. Never!"

Raw sadness hovered in his sightless eyes. "I know."

With a gruff growl, Falcyn released him and stepped back.

Medea felt a strange lump in her throat as she saw the moisture Falcyn blinked away from his eyes and the way Blaise licked his lips and cleared his throat as if biting back his own round of tears. That was love in its purest, gruffest masculine form.

Now she knew why Falcyn protected him so zealously.

And that thought brought a wave of strong emotion surging through her that she couldn't quite identify. But it was definitely tender and overwhelming.

There was a lot more to this dragon than just the beast he let the world see.

And Brogan saw it, too.

Clearing her own throat, Brogan motioned toward the backside of the cave. "There should be a tunnel that leads toward the underground channels where we might be able to find a path to the porch."

"The porch?" Medea didn't understand the word, but the way the woman said it she felt as if she should.

"Aye. It's the plateau where the elders meet to watch the other realms. There's a portal there."

"Why do they do that?"

Brogan scoffed at her question. "In case you haven't noticed, my lady, there's not a lot to do here, other than survive and make weaponry for the gods and fey beings. So the elder wyrdlings look out, pick a happy mortal, and ruin their lives. For fun and wagering."

Medea gaped. "You're serious?"

Her features grim, Brogan nodded. "They call it the yewing. The mortal is randomly selected and his or her fate is up to whatever lot they draw from their skytel bag while they're watching them. They think it entertaining."

"I knew it!" Blaise growled. "I knew my life was nothing but a sick joke to the fey. And all of you said I crazy." When no one commented he drew up sullenly. "Well, you did. And I *was* right."

Falcyn snorted. "Anyway, let's find this porch and see if we can locate the portal back home. Or at least to Avalon or Camelot. From there, we can return. For that matter, I'd take Vanaheim or Asgard."

"You could travel from there?" Medea asked in an impressed tone.

"I have friends in low places."

"Those aren't low places," Brogan admonished.

"That depends on your point of view." Falcyn winked at her. "From where I stand, they're in the gutter."

"Who *are* your parents?" Medea asked, even more curious about him now.

Blaise shook his head at her. "Don't go there. It's a dark place of pain we don't want to visit, as it will send him to a level of pissed off he won't return from for quite some time. We just say that he was spawned from the fount of evil and leave it at that."

"So you two didn't have the same mother?" Brogan asked.

Blaise shook his head. "They were only the same lethal species."

"Can we change the subject?" The bark in Falcyn's tone added veracity to Blaise's words.

Medea held her hands up in surrender. Obviously, he had about as much love for his parents as Urian did for Stryker. And speaking of . . . she really needed to get home and help her family. "Can we not teleport to the portal?"

Brogan shook her head. "I wouldn't advise it. Those powers tend to attract unwanted attention in this realm. The less magick used that they're unfamiliar with, the safer you'll be."

Awesome. Just flipping awesome.

Suddenly, another streak rushed past Medea's face.

"Case in point," Brogan said quietly. "There's enough trouble with things such as *that* attacking us. Last thing we need is to be adding to it."

"What causes that to happen?" Medea watched it ricochet off and explode behind Urian.

Brogan touched the wall. When she did so, it began to glimmer with a faint green glow that allowed them to see deep into the darkness. Oddly enough, it appeared more like a shimmering night sky than an underground cavern. Truly, it was magical and breathtaking. Like something from a dream.

"Well, it depends. Some of those lights are sparks left over from the creation of magical items in the forges. They dance about until they extinguish on their own. Others are certain spells that never weaken. Some actually grow stronger. When they can't be contained in their own worlds or environments, they're naturally drawn here."

Medea frowned at that. "Why?"

"It's what this was set up for." Brogan gestured to the walls around them. "Myrkheim. It's a magnet realm for that magick to protect the other worlds."

Her scowl deepened. "You use that word as if it makes sense to my Apollite ears."

Smiling, Brogan glanced to Blaise. "By your coloring, my lady, I assumed you to be a Ljósálfr like Blaise."

Blaise choked on the word. "Actually my mother was Adoni. So you'd be wrong with your assumption, Lady Brogan. The bitch what birthed me was definitely a member of the dökkálfar. The black fey," he explained for Medea. "The ljósálfar are those who follow the light and practice magick that only benefits others. Adoni are selfish and practice the dark arts. Hence their dökkálfar moniker, or the dark fey, as they're more commonly called." He glanced over his shoulder toward Medea. "'Myrkheim' means 'dark ward,' which is why it was given to this world."

Ah, now she understood the distinctions. Medea narrowed her gaze on Brogan. "Which side are you on?"

"I'm what's called a myrkálfr. Shadow fey. I draw my powers from both the light and dark as needed."

"In other words, she hasn't declared a side." Falcyn narrowed his gaze on her. "No one trusts them as a result. And they're weaker in their powers because they haven't committed to one cause or the other."

"That's one theory." Brogan lifted her chin. "But I like to keep my options open. You never know when you're going to need light or dark powers. The world's a tenuous place."

"And I prefer not to judge others." Blaise offered her his arm.

Medea didn't comment. "I always thought the light and dark fey thing had to do with their coloring."

Brogan tucked her hand into the crook of Blaise's elbow. Medea didn't miss the way Brogan's features softened ever so slightly toward him as he placed his hand over hers. "A lot of people mistakenly do, but it has nothing to do with our features or coloring. Most of the Adoni are very fair, and almost all of them are dark in their powers. The designations are more religious in nature and thereby are choices we take voluntarily."

And by the way Falcyn's eyes narrowed on that intimate touch, Medea had a feeling he didn't miss their burgeoning affection either. More than that, he didn't appear to approve of the way Blaise was doting on his new friend.

At all.

"You okay?" she asked him.

Falcyn turned that glower to her with an unnerving ferocity. She half expected him to breathe fire out his nostrils. If she didn't know better, she might think him jealous.

"Down, boy. I didn't do it."

He arched a brow at her. "What?"

"What, what. Whatever it is that caused that look of hate in your eyes. I didn't do it. So breathe in, relax, and blink."

Baffled, Falcyn glanced to Urian. "She always this flippant?"

"Yeah. You have no measurable sense of humor. She has no measurable sense of fear. Bad combo if you ask me. But semi-amusing for the rest of us."

"Brogan . . ."

Slowing, Falcyn paused at the musical whisper that echoed off the walls around them.

Brogan froze.

"What is that?" Blaise breathed.

"A haunt. Ignore it. It's merely another joy that comes with living here."

"Brogan . . ." it repeated.

Medea shivered as a chill went down her spine. It was like someone walking over her grave. The singing voice was so creepy in its tone, and at the same time, strangely beckoning. "What are these things?"

"Cousins to púcas, they live in the darkness and lure the unwary to their deaths. I told you that I'm a Deathseer, so they call to me whenever I'm near. To claim one of my ilk is a bonus for them."

"Medea! Come to me and see what I have for you! You want to visit the past! Come. Come see what I have! You'll like it, I promise!"

"Ignore it." Brogan raised her voice louder to cover their tones. "It's only trying to get you to walk off the edge and plummet to your death."

"Falcyn . . . don't you want to see Hadyn again?"

He patted his ear. "Is there a way to get rid of it?"

"They fear hellhounds . . . light."

Urian grimaced as he cringed from a piercing cry. "But apparently not dragons or Daimons."

"Or Deathseers," Blaise added.

"Anyone have Aeron's number?" Falcyn asked, thinking of the Celtic war god who traveled with a Cŵn Annwn. They'd get a twofer with him and Kaziel—actually a threefer since Aeron had once been cursed to be a púca.

More whispers began to echo and sing with the first voice, adding to the volume and making the lure harder to ignore.

Their combined voices became deafening to Falcyn's sensitive ears. Blaise stumbled and went down.

Urian cursed at the sound.

Her features pale, Brogan turned to Medea. "What should we do?"

"Is there a way to kill a haunt?"

"Not that I know."

The men were now on their knees with their hands over their ears, in utter agony.

"Me-dee-ah!" They continued to try and call for her, too.

But that singsongy tone gave her an idea.

Closing her eyes, she took a deep breath and started singing her favorite Adam Ezra Group song at the top of her lungs to drown them out. "She puts a light to the candles 'round the room like a shrine. . . ."

Oddly enough, it seemed to be working. At least Falcyn had a bit of a reprieve.

Hesitating as their eyes met and she saw his deep gratitude, Medea began to sing louder. "She says, 'If it don't come in vinyl then it ain't music divine . . . she calls me her lost and found!"

Falcyn blinked as he heard Medea's angelic voice over the pain of the haunts' cruelty. Like a heavenly choir, it overrode their agony and drove it from him. More than that, she wrapped her arms around his head as if to protect him from them while she continued to sing in the most incredible voice he'd ever heard from anyone.

It was as if she were part siren or miren. And it captured him fully, pulling him away from the haunt's lure.

She held his head against her thigh. "Her voice finds hope and diamonds and fables all around and I'm taken over now, by the soul of a taste of a sound . . . when I'm lost in the darkness . . . when I'm cut at the knees . . . she says 'you can give your soul to the city . . . you just bring your heart home to me' . . . she says 'I know 'bout your problems . . . take a rest for a while,' and every sign on the highway says I'll be home again soon."

Closing his eyes, he savored the sensation of her hand in his hair while she sang and held him against her body. No one had *ever* held him with such affection.

Like he mattered.

Like I'm human.

As if he were hers to hold and keep . . .

Words failed him utterly as inexplicable emotions assailed him. An unknown wave of tenderness rose up and swallowed him whole. No words could describe this . . . inner warmth. It tasted like honey on his tongue and left him even more helpless than the haunt's crooning.

And still she sang while she gently swayed. Never once in his life had he ever wanted to belong to anyone. He'd always prided himself on standing alone. On being the sinister, solitary beast.

I am drakomai.

Yet in this moment, he surrendered himself to her completely.

Then, in a single heartbeat, the haunts were gone. And so was any resistance to her that he might have ever had . . .

Urian was the first to recover himself. "Damn, big sister. Had no idea you could sing like that."

Clearing her throat, she appeared embarrassed as she stepped away from Falcyn. "I don't do it often."

He caught her hand before she could leave him entirely.

Falcyn wanted to say something to her. To tell her what that had meant to him. How much she'd touched him in a way no one had before.

But words failed him completely. He didn't want to cheapen it with something so trivial as empty words people spoke to each other without meaning.

All he could do was stare up into those dark eyes, hard and aching, unsure and lost. In that moment, he realized exactly how inhuman he was.

How human he wanted to be.

For her. That realization terrified him to a level he'd never dreamed of.

She's a Daimon.

No, not a Daimon. An Apollite. Technically, she'd never converted over into the parasitic beast that had to prey on human souls in order to live. Her mother had saved her from that nightmare fate.

Thus the true tragedy of her life. The humans had attacked her and her family when they hadn't been Daimons. Neither Medea nor her husband or child had ever harmed a human being. According to Urian, they'd been dedicated members of the Cult of Pollux—Apollites who took oaths whereby they swore to harm no human and to die as Apollo intended, peacefully on their twenty-seventh birthdays.

Innocent victims to man's inhumanity and fear.

At the time of her death, Medea hadn't known how to fight or protect herself. Had never tasted human blood or violence of that nature. She'd been wholly unprepared for what they'd done to her. What they'd done to her child.

It wasn't fair. But then nothing in life ever was. He of all beings knew that.

Life preyed on the weak. It preyed on the strong. But at least the strong could fight back. They could weather the hell that rained down on them. The weak were seldom so fortunate.

In one heartbeat everything had changed for Medea. Her innocence had died a most brutal death. And she'd been baptized in the blood of her family.

Life made victims of everyone. Without mercy. Or compassion. It spared none.

Rising to his feet, he enveloped her in his arms, wanting to shelter her there. To keep her safe from any harm, as she'd done him. That was what his kind did. It was how they showed affection.

Not with words.

With action.

"Um . . . Falcyn?"

Blaise laughed at Medea's tone. "What's my brother doing?"

"Holding me in an awkwardly tight manner. It's very strange."

"But is he sitting on you?"

"No . . ." Medea stretched the word out. "Why? Should I be worried?"

"Well, it means he's not trying to hatch you. Yet. That's always a bonus."

"Stop," Falcyn growled. "Both of you." He tightened his arms around her an instant before he let go. "I was only saying thank you for helping me."

Medea smiled in spite of herself. "You're welcome." Biting

her lip, she watched as he ambled back toward her brother. Whom he summarily took a playful swipe at.

Damn, he was exceptionally handsome.

And she despised the fact that she noticed. Hated how edible his ass was in those tight black jeans.

Normally, she didn't really pay attention to such things, except in passing. Yet the longer she was around Falcyn, the more she was seeing how gorgeous he was and the harder it was getting to dismiss it.

Worse? She liked the way he'd held her. It'd been way too long since anyone touched her like he did.

Like she mattered.

She'd forgotten what it felt like to be part of a couple—to have a man stare at her as if he hung on her every word. But Falcyn made her remember things she'd done her damnedest to forget.

More than that, he made her crave it again.

Don't! She didn't want to be hurt. Not like that. Not after what she'd gone through with Evander. It'd almost killed her to lose him, and she never wanted to hurt that way again.

And yet . . .

This was different.

He was different.

And it wasn't just because Falcyn was a dragon. Though that was a large part of it, there was a lot more.

Something in her reached out for him against her will. She didn't understand it.

And she hated that weakness with every part of herself. *You're stronger than this.*

She didn't need anyone. Ever. Not for anything. On her own two feet. That was how she lived. It was what she knew best. What she liked. Nothing could hurt her unless she allowed it and she refused to be vulnerable.

No connections. She had her brother and Davyn. Two warriors who were virtually incapable of falling. They were the only ones she was attached to.

And her parents, who would fall to no one.

Not even the gods.

That was all she'd allow herself. *I will stand below no more pyres to watch my loved ones burn.* She refused to be Urian. To live in absolute grief. A shadow of her former self. A shade lost in the anguish of heartbreak. She'd been there for too many centuries and it'd taken her too long to get over the death of her baby and husband.

Medea couldn't go back.

She *wouldn't* go back.

Not even for Falcyn.

Heartache was for fools. Love was for the weak. She had no use for either. *I'm stronger alone, always.*

No matter what, she had to make herself believe that and remember that. To live it.

And as they walked, Brogan drifted back to Medea's side and cocked her head in a very birdlike manner. "They called you a Daimon?"

"Sort of."

"I don't know your species. Are you like the fey?"

"My people were created by the Greek god Apollo and then cursed by him."

"Why?"

Why indeed. That had been the question that had galled her the whole of her exceptionally long life.

Medea sighed as she was driven against her will to remember the tragedy of her mother's mortal fate. Head over heels in love as a girl, she'd married Apollo's son without hesitation. And then, pregnant with her, her mother had been forced to divorce Medea's father or see herself raped and murdered by the vengeful god.

Leaving her father had emotionally destroyed her mother. Had killed something deep inside her that hadn't come alive again until the day they'd reunited.

Centuries after Stryker had married and raised another family with another wife—Urian's surrogate mother.

And thus had begun the curse of her people, as Stryker had made a bargain with an Atlantean goddess to save his family from his father's curse.

"Apollo had a Greek mistress that caused his Apollite lover-queen to become jealous, as she felt betrayed by him because her own son had died. Or so she thought . . . The queen didn't know that her son had lived because Apollo had spared him. That Stryker had been taken from her womb so that he could be safely raised by his father in Greece, with a surrogate mother. So when Apollo fathered another son with his Greek whore, she sent out her soldiers to murder Apollo's mistress and child. Only the Apollite queen didn't have the backbone to stand by her decree. Rather, she told them to make it appear as if an animal had ravaged them—as if a god couldn't figure out the truth.

Tells you exactly what kind of moron my grandmother was, and I shudder over the fact that I share genes with that brainiac."

Medea growled and rolled her eyes over the nature of people's jealous idiocy. "Anyway, in anger over their murders, Apollo cursed not only Stryker's real queenly mother and her soldiers who'd actually done the deed, but every single member of the race he'd created—my people, including my father and mother because he totally forgot that they shared her blood—to die at the age of his mistress. We were given the fangs of an animal and forced to seek our only sustenance from each other's blood, as no other food could nourish us ever again. We are banned from the sunlight Apollo's known for so that he will never have to endure the sight of one of us again. And if that wasn't enough punishment, on our twenty-seventh birthday we wither away and decay into dust in the most painful way you can imagine."

"That's horrible!" she breathed.

"It is, indeed." More so because she was Apollo's own grandchild—his very flesh and blood—and the rotten bastard had spared none of them his wrath. Not her. Not Urian or any of his brothers or other sister.

Nor Stryker, Apollo's own son.

All of them had been damned by the god's anger for something they'd had no part in or any ability to stop. They hadn't even lived in Atlantis at the time the queen had done it.

How Medea hated Apollo for his vindictive cruelty.

For that matter, they all did. For a god of prophecy, he'd proved very short-sighted, indeed.

"I'm so sorry, Medea."

She shrugged. "I got over it. Besides, I was six when he cursed us. I barely remember life before that day."

"You don't eat food?"

She shook her head.

Brogan fell silent for a moment. "But if you were to die at twenty-seven and you're not a Daimon now, how is it that you're still alive?"

"A bargain my mother made for my life."

Sadness turned Brogan's eyes a vivid purple. "Tell me of a mother who so loves her child. Is she beautiful? Wondrous?"

Medea nodded. "Beyond words." She pulled the locket from her neck and held it out to Brogan so that she could see the picture she had of her mother. "Her name is Zephyra."

"Like the wind?"

"Yes. Her eyes are black now, but when I was a girl, they were a most vivid, breathtaking green."

Brogan fingered the photo with a sad smile tugging at the edges of her lips. "You admire her."

"She's the strongest woman I've ever known. And I love her for it."

Closing the locket, she handed it back to Medea. "She looks like you."

"Thank you. But I think she's a lot more beautiful." Medea returned it to her neck. "What of your mother?"

A tear fell down her cheek. "My mother sold me to the Black Crom when I was ten and three. If she ever loved me, she never once showed it."

"I'm sorry."

Wiping at her cheek, she drew a ragged breath. "It's not so bad. She sold my siblings to much worse. At least I had Sight. Had I been born without anything, my fate would have been . . ." She winced as if she couldn't bring herself to say more about it.

"What exactly is the Black Crom?" Medea asked, trying to distract her from the horror that lingered in the back of those lavender eyes.

"A headless Death Rider who seeks the souls of the damned or the cursed."

Medea jumped at Falcyn's voice in her ear.

"A kerling can sing to them to offer up a sacrifice before battle. Or summon them for a particular victim."

"Can," Brogan said, lifting her chin defiantly. There was something about her, fiery and brave. "But I don't. I hate the Crom. He springs from Annwn to claim the souls of his victims with a whip made from the bony spines of cowards. He rides a pale horse with luminescent eyes that can incinerate the guilty and innocent alike should they happen upon him and stare into them. None are safe in his path. To the very pit with him and his insanity. I've no use for the likes of that beast. You've no idea what it's like to live in its shadow. Subject to its pitiless whims."

Though she'd just met her, Medea felt horrible for the woman. "Can you be freed?"

She shook her head. "Not even death can free me, as I am bound to him for all eternity. What's done is done. I only want to be released from this realm so that I'm no longer used by the dökkálfar for *their* schemes where he's concerned."

"Used how?" There was no missing the suspicion in Falcyn's tone.

"They can bargain with the Crom for my services, and when they do so, I have no choice except to give them whatever it is they've contracted for. I've no say whatsoever in the matter."

Medea grimaced at the nightmare she described. "Will that change once you leave here?"

"It will weaken their hold over me. Aye."

Suddenly, Brogan stopped moving.

Medea became instantly nervous at a look she was starting to recognize. "Is something wrong?"

"We're approaching the porch," she whispered.

"Is that bad?"

She didn't answer the question except to say, "The Crom is here."

5

"So that's a Crom. . . ." Medea felt her jaw go slack as she caught sight of the massive glowing horseman. At first, he appeared headless. Until she realized that his head was formed by mist at the end of the spiny whip he wielded as he rode. The white horse was giant in size . . . almost as large as a Mack truck. An awful stench of sulfur permeated the cavern, choking her and sticking in her throat as if it had been created from thorns.

Even more disconcerting, the baying horse

made the sound of twenty echoing beasts. And its hooves were thunderous—like an approaching train. The sounds reverberated through her, rattling her very bones.

"I won't do it!" Brogan shouted. "I refuse you!"

The horse reared as the Crom cracked its whip in the air. Fire shot out from the whip's tip as more thunder echoed.

Unfazed and with fists clenched at her sides, Brogan stood stubbornly between them and the Crom. "Beat me all you like. I will not give you that power. Not again! Not over my new-found friends!"

"What's going on?" Medea asked.

Brogan kept her gaze locked stubbornly on her master. "He wants the ability to speak. But if I give it to him, then he can call out your name and claim your soul to take it with him to hell. And I will not allow it."

With a long, bony finger, he pointed at Brogan.

She shook her head at him. "Then take me, if you must. I'm all you'll be getting today! I won't let you have them! You hear me? No more!"

He charged at her.

In an act of absolute bravery, she stood her ground without flinching.

Blaise caught her an instant before the Crom would have mowed her down. Lifting her in his arms, the mandrake whirled her past the razor, blood-encrusted hooves that were mired with the remnants of the Crom's past victims.

Falcyn and Urian went charging in to cover them.

Rolling her eyes at their brave stupidity since none of them were armed, Medea joined their cause. She manifested her sword and twirled it around her body. Falcyn unleashed his fireballs while she watched the fey creature turn around for another pass.

It started for them.

Until it saw her sword.

With one last shrieking cry, it vanished in a puff of pungent green smoke.

What the hell was that?

"Okay . . . that was effing weird. Where did he go?" She glanced around, half expecting him to manifest behind them. "What just happened?"

Brogan inclined her head to Medea's sword. " 'Tis the gold of your blade and hilt. It's his weakness. With that, you could have maimed him."

Medea gaped at her. "You couldn't have told me that before he charged?"

"Wasn't allowed to say it until you found it on your own. I'm forbidden to."

"Well that just sucks!"

Brogan smiled. "For me more than you, my lady. Believe me." She had a point.

And Blaise had yet to set her back on her feet. In fact, he seemed reluctant to let her go.

"My lord?" Brogan blushed profusely.

Blaise hesitated. "Not sure I should let you down. You seem to keep finding trouble whenever I do."

Medea looked away as a strange tenderness went through her at how adorable the two of them were. Especially when Brogan wrapped her arms around his neck and snuggled against his chest as if content to stay right where she was.

But Falcyn wasn't so kind. "Blaise! Set her down! Now!"

Medea popped him on the arm as Brogan appeared stricken by his sharp tone. "What is your problem?"

Falcyn gestured at Brogan. "He doesn't know where she's been."

Was he serious? "Oh my God, Falcyn! He's not some two-year-old child and she's not a piece of candy he found on the floor that he stuck in his mouth!"

"Well, that's how he's acting. He looks at her like he could eat her up."

"And you're acting like a baby. Get over it. He's a grown dragon. He's allowed to be nice to any woman he wants to. *Without* your permission or approval, you know?"

Falcyn's nose actually twitched and flared. "Doesn't mean I have to like it," he groused like that two-year-old she'd just mentioned.

Blaise rolled his eyes and shook his head. "He always acts like an old woman. I'm used to it. He's the same way with Il-larion. Max is just as bad, if not worse. At least they no longer try to burp me after my feedings. Or check my nappy."

Brogan laughed as Blaise finally set her back on her feet, but he kept her tucked by his side.

And yet there was a profound pain deep inside Falcyn's eyes that Medea didn't miss. What was that dark shadow that haunted him so?

Before she could ask about it, Brogan drew their attention to the stones that, when they stepped back, Medea realized formed a half-broken demonic face suspended on pedestals over a deep, fiery abyss.

"Well, that's different." And the dais was impossible to reach. . . .

Medea arched a brow. "I take it that's the portal we're looking for?"

Brogan nodded. Her mood now was subdued and quiet. Gone was any hint of the playful sprite she'd been a few seconds ago.

Medea cast a dry stare to Falcyn. "This is when having a flying dragon would come in handy." Falcyn snorted. "So would rope . . . and a gag."

Before she could stop herself, Medea swept a hot, seductive glance over his long, lush body. "A rope and a gag come in handy for *lots* of things, princess," she said suggestively.

"Ew! Hey, brother over here, and I do not approve of this entire line of conversation with my sister! Back to a G rating, folks."

Laughing, albeit a bit nervously, Brogan started toward the platform.

She'd only taken a step before a light flashed and smoke exploded in front of them—this realm seemed to like that a lot. Apparently, the entire place seemed to be rigged for a heavy metal concert tour.

The peculiar portal in front of them churned into action, spinning and turning like a rusted nickelodeon. Light shot out from the demon's mouth and eyes, with a blinding intensity. Symbols twisted around it in a frenetic ballet that was painful to watch.

And out of that madness came more smoke and mist. As if an angry beast snorted at them with a furious hatred. Spiraling up and dancing to a jerky beat, the mist solidified into the shape of a tall hooded beast.

No, not a beast.

A man.

At first, Medea thought the emerging figure was a wizard of some kind. Or shaman. Indeed, his flowing feathered robes and chains, along with the braided black hair and the huge elaborate raven skull headdress, would have lent themselves to that assumption. Especially since bells chimed as he moved and he held a bloodred torch staff in his left hand. One that belched more fire and smoke as it shot arcing balls of light upward around his head.

Yet there was something more to him than that. Something powerful and ancient.

Timeless.

As he turned to face them, she saw that he'd painted a thick black band over his golden eyes that made their unusual color more vibrant. He stepped down from the dais with the grace of a man half his age. And when he neared them, he flexed his dark gray gloved hand that held the staff, digging the wooden claws that were affixed to his fingertips into its leather-wrapped shaft. His gaze bored into them with the wisdom of the ages, and with the sharpness of daggers. As if he were cleaving secrets from their very souls.

"Kerling," he growled in the gruffest of tones. "What is this?"

Brogan curtsied to him. "They were brought here against their wills, copián. They don't belong in this realm. I seek to send them on their way."

A deep, fierce scowl lined his brow. The red light of his torch flared again, and turned blue.

Confused, Medea leaned toward Falcyn. "What's a copián?"

"Hard to explain, exactly. Lack of a better term, they're time wardens and keepers of the portals."

That only confused her more. "Why don't we have one for the bolt-holes in Kalosis, then?"

"You do," the copián said. "Braith, Verlyn, Cam, and Rezar were the first of our kind. They set the perimeters for the worlds and designed the portal gates between them. It's how they trapped Apollymi in her realm—by her own blood and design. It's why her son is the only one who can free her from her realm where she was imprisoned by her own sister and brother for crimes they imagined, that she never committed."

Ah, finally she understood. Because Apollymi was the ancient goddess Braith. One of the very gods who'd first set the gates.

Medea gaped. Holy shit . . . literally. No wonder the ancient Atlantean goddess was so pissed off all the time.

Now it made sense. That was how Apollymi had been able to open the portal originally and bring Stryker through it. How she controlled it to allow the Daimons to come and go, while keeping everyone else out.

Apollymi was one of the creators of it.

Medea had always wondered about that. No wonder Apollymi spent hours in her garden at her mirror pool, watching the human realm. . . .

She was one of the first portal guardians.

Brogan gestured toward them. "As you can see, their presence disturbs the balance. This isn't their world and they shouldn't be here. We have to return them before they're discovered by the others and chaos ensues."

Two lights shot out of his torch. They streaked up like the stray magick blasts had done earlier, and circled around the old copián to land on each side of him. There they twisted up from the floor to create two tall, lean, linen-wrapped plague doctors. With wide-brimmed cavalier hats, they stared out from their long-beaked, black linen masks from shiny ebony eyes. Soulless eyes that appeared to be bleeding around the corners. Even the linen was stained with their blood.

It was an eerie, macabre sight that made the hair on the back of Medea's neck rise. And given the creepy Charonte and gallu demons and Daimons who called her realm home, that said a lot.

"What are those?"

"Zeitjägers," Falcyn whispered to her.

Another term she'd never heard before. "What do they do?"

"Guard time. But mostly they steal it."

Was he serious?

"How do you steal time?"

Falcyn laughed. "You ever been doing something . . . look up and it's hours later and you can't figure out where the time went 'cause it feels like you just sat down?"

Yeah, of course. Everyone knew that feeling.

She nodded.

"Zeitjägers," he said simply. "Insidious bastards. They took that time from you and bottled it for their own means."

"Why?"

"So that we can sell it." The copián glanced to his companions. "Time is the most precious commodity in the entire universe. The most sacred. And yet it is the most often squandered. From the moment of our births, we're only allotted so much of it. And for even an hour more, there are those who are willing to give up anything for it." An evil smile curled his lips. "Even their immortal souls."

A chill went up her spine at the way he said that.

The copián stepped down to approach Medea. "Surely a child of the Apollite race can understand that driving desperation better than most."

He was right about that. Nothing like being damned to only twenty-seven years for something you didn't do to make someone realize just how precious life was.

Even more so while watching everyone around you die long before their time.

For one more breath, her people were willing to take human lives and destroy their immortal souls. Her one saving grace was that her mother had sacrificed her own soul to save Medea from having to make that choice.

Because the sad truth was, Medea had been too much of a coward to do it. Unlike Urian and her father, she hadn't been able to destroy a single human soul for her own salvation. She'd been content to die as Apollo had decreed. Honestly, she'd thought that it wasn't her place to do that to another living being. That humanity was innocent and undeserving of such a horrendous fate.

It wasn't until the humans had robbed her of the ones she held most sacred that she'd lost her own soul in the process and learned not to care. It wasn't just her child they'd killed that day. It was her compassion and ability to feel empathy for anyone else. If they were incapable of respecting her loved ones, be damned if she'd respect theirs.

That was a two-way street.

So she'd become the monster they thought her to be. And had been on a centuries-long quest for survival ever since. Putting the good of her race above theirs. Humans could all rot as far as she was concerned.

Nothing else mattered. On that cold winter's day, they'd become parasites to her.

No. Worse than that.

They'd become *food*.

The copián cocked his head in such a way that she half expected his elaborate headdress to fall off. Yet it stayed perched perfectly atop his head, as if part of his body. "You've heard the expression 'living on borrowed time'?"

"Yeah."

He gave her a crooked smile. "We're the ones you borrow it from."

Oh yeah, that sent chills over her entire body.

He swept his sinister gaze over them. "My price is simple. An hour from each of you and I'll open the portal."

"An hour?" Falcyn sputtered. "How 'bout I just rip some heads off all y'all until you yield?"

The copián smirked. "You could do that, but you can't open the portal without me."

"Sure I could find someone."

"You really want to chance it?"

Falcyn's expression said he was willing to gamble.

The copián tsked at him. "So very violent from an immortal who can spare an hour with no problem whatsoever. Think of it like those humans who donate spare change for charity. An hour is but a penny, and you have a jar full of them just sitting in your home that you'll never use. Why not give one to someone who really needs it? Why be so selfish?"

"Because you're assuming they'll use it for good, when I know for a fact that most people who barter with you don't have kindness in their hearts."

"True, but sometimes that trash they take out on their way to the grave is a service in and of itself, is it not?" He cast a pointed stare toward Urian, whose gaze narrowed dangerously as the old bastard struck a tender nerve with the former Daimon who'd once made his meals off the worst sort of humanity so that he could elongate his life.

Blaise sucked his breath in sharply. "Word of advice when dealing with these two? I wouldn't go for the twofers on the insults. Even with the zeitjägers as backup. I mean, let's face it. They're not being peaceful at the moment because they don't know how to be violent . . . however, I'll be the first to say have at it if you can get us out of here. You can take two hours from me."

The copián scowled at Blaise. "Two?"

"Yeah. One for me and one for Brogan. I'll pay her fee."

She gasped at his offer. "Why would you do that?"

Blaise shrugged. "Being stuck here has been punishment enough for you. As noted, I won't miss two hours out of my life. I'd have just wasted them in a movie theater, anyway. And this way, I get to do something useful with them and be a hero to you. That's a loss I can live with." He winked at her. "Besides, I don't intend to leave here without you."

"Suck up, show-off," Falcyn muttered. Then louder, "Fine, take mine."

Medea hesitated as a bad feeling went through her. She couldn't explain it, but something in her gut didn't like this. And the look in Falcyn's eyes said he was every bit as suspicious.

If the others felt it, too, they gave no clue that anything was out of the norm.

"So how do you take this time from us?" Medea glanced back to the zeitjägers.

The copián laughed. "It's already gone. As I said, you don't even miss it. You didn't even know we did it."

Falcyn leaned down to whisper in her ear. "Told you. Insidious bastards."

No kidding. The only clue was the strange slurping sound the zeitjägers made. At least, she assumed it came from them.

Maybe not.

Yeah . . . *c-r-e-e-p-y.*

The copián walked toward the portal and lifted his staff. The moment he did, the portal came alive with swirling, vibrant colors. He moved his staff through it until the mist began to mimic his movements.

Red fire shot out from the torch and was absorbed by the mist.

"It's ready."

Urian grinned at Medea. "Ladies first."

She rolled her eyes at her brother. "Like you'd know if I didn't make it."

"You might be polite and scream . . . then again, it is *you*. Maybe Blaise should go first? I know he'd scream to warn us."

He turned an angry glare to Falcyn. "I thought you weren't going to tell anyone about my screaming fits?"

"I didn't. That was Max who outed you."

"Oh. . . . Remind me to kill him later." Blaise headed for the portal. "Fine, I'll go through first."

Brogan took his hand. "I'll go with you."

Touched by the gesture, Medea headed up the platform to the strange humming beast that seemed to have a life of its own. Yet as she reached the portal, Falcyn held her back.

He quirked a peculiar smile at her. "In case my usual luck holds and this all goes to hell."

Before she could tell what he intended, he lowered his head and captured her lips with the hottest kiss she'd ever been given. He held her as if she were the most precious thing in his world.

As if he loved her.

Stunned, she couldn't breathe. It actually took her a moment before she could even react enough to kiss him back. But when her brain began to work, she had to admit he was exceptional at this.

More than that, he set her on fire. It'd been far too long since anyone had kissed her in such a manner. Since any man had made her feel exceptional. While she hadn't been chaste, she hadn't been promiscuous either. Mostly because she'd avoided any emotional entanglement with another living being, other than her mother.

It didn't matter how much time passed. Thoughts of her son and husband forever haunted her. Nothing could chase away the memory of their smiles. The warmth that she'd once taken for granted.

Fear of losing another had kept her heart locked in ice.

Apollites and Daimons were hunted creatures who often lived exceptionally brief lives. Even their strongest were often annihilated by Dark-Hunters, sooner rather than later. And that only compounded her fears to the point that she'd been incapable of opening herself up for more heartache.

But Falcyn wasn't an Apollite.

He definitely wasn't a Daimon.

And when he pulled back, she was left dazed and breathless by the taste of him. A gorgeous smile hovered at the edge of his lips as he stared down at her.

Without a word, he led her into the portal and kept her steady. . . .

Falcyn cursed the moment he felt the energy pulling at his body.

And then it sucked them into the stinging vortex.

He'd always hated stepping through one of these gates. Blaise was a lot more used to it than he was, since he held one of the keys that enabled him to travel to and from the veil world where Merlin had pulled Avalon and Camelot to so that she could protect the other worlds and realms from Morgen's evil. After the death of King Arthur, it'd been the only way to secure the realm of man, and the other eight worlds from Morgen and her evil Circle. Otherwise, Morgen's fey court would have enslaved them all.

But as for Falcyn, he liked to stay planted in one dimension. This kind of hopping through nether portals crap was not his forte.

And as the colors swirled and he lost his bearings and feared his lunch would follow, Falcyn definitely understood why he'd always felt that way. This shit sucked! Give him wings and flight or teleportation any day.

Especially when he went slamming hard into a dark, damp ground a few minutes later.

Gah! That was going to leave a mark.

Groaning, he lay on his back as everything spun around like a Tilt-A-Whirl. And he hadn't even got a funnel cake or fried Twinkie out of it.

With a grimace, Falcyn rubbed at his eyes. "Blaise? You dead?"

"No." He didn't sound like he was in any better shape than Falcyn, though.

"Good. I want the pleasure of killing you myself, you bastard!"

Blaise snorted.

"Don't scoff, dragon," Urian said, his tone every bit as peeved. "Soon as I can move again, I intend to help with your murder and dismemberment."

Falcyn turned his head to the right, where Medea lay a few feet away from his side, unmoving on the grass. "Medea?"

She finally lifted a hand to brush her hair from her face. "Not dead, either."

That made him feel a bit better. "Brogan?"

"Just wishing I was." Shifting her legs, she made no move to rise. Rather she seemed content to lie on her back, staring up at the dismally gray sky. "Is it always this miserable to travel in such a manner?"

Blaise sighed. "Pretty much. Least I didn't slam into an invisible force field this time."

Rolling over, Falcyn pushed himself into a sitting position, then scowled as he caught sight of the dark, twisted trees around him. Trees that lined an equally screwed-up, bleak landscape the likes of which he hadn't thought to ever see again.

Oh, this can't be right.

Yet he knew he wasn't dreaming. And he definitely wasn't imagining this.

"Hey, Blaise . . . Why the hell are we in Camelot?"

"Whaaaaat?" He rose with a fierce scowl and looked up as if he could see the sky, which he couldn't. But it didn't stop him from trying.

Falcyn let out a tired, irritated sigh. "Correct me if I'm wrong."

His white-blond hair shimmering in the fey light, Blaise paled as he sniffed the air. "Well . . . you're kind of wrong."

"How so?"

"This isn't Camelot . . . exactly."

That only made his stomach tighten with dread. "What's *not exactly* Camelot?"

"Val Sans Retour."

Ah shit . . . He'd rather be in Camelot. With Morgen, tied to her throne. Naked and declawed.

Muzzled even.

Sitting up immediately, Medea scowled at them both. "The what?"

Falcyn let out another groan before he answered. "The Valley of No Return. So named because no one ever comes out of here *alive*. Like Blaise . . . because I really am going to kill him as soon as I find my strength."

"Not true!" Blaise stood and took a defensive position. "I came out alive a few years back when I was here."

Falcyn made a rude noise at the reminder of the mandrake's less-than-stellar adventure.

Medea rose and brushed herself off. "Did you?"

"Yeah. Me and Varian. Merewyn, too."

His anger rising, Falcyn went to the mandrake, dreading an answer to a question no one was asking. "But *why* are we here now, Blaise? How did we get here?"

Blaise quirked a sarcastic smirk that really tested Falcyn's patience and restraint. "Did you sleep through the part where we stepped into a magick portal and were sucked through a vortex?"

"Don't make me beat you with my shoe."

"Well, I'm just wondering. 'Cause you asked. I mean, you were there, were you not? You didn't miss that rather large, ghastly light we stepped into, did you?"

"Yeah, but I have a head injury, right now. Maybe a concussion. Thinking some kind of serious brain damage. Definitely trauma of some sort. And a migraine the size of *you*."

Urian broke off Falcyn's tirade by jerking on his sleeve to get his attention.

Even more irritated, Falcyn barely kept himself from slugging him. But there was something in the man's eyes that stayed his reaction.

Curious, he followed Urian's line of sight and turned his head to where Urian was staring at something over Falcyn's left shoulder.

The moment his gaze focused on Brogan and the man who'd materialized by her side, he scowled. "Who's that?"

"Don't know, but she seems to know him."

By the look on Blaise's face, he did, too.

And they weren't friends.

Falcyn narrowed his gaze on him. "Blaise?"

A tic started in his jaw. "I know that essence when I feel it. It's Brevalaer. Morgen's pet whore."

6

Brogan hissed at Blaise. "His name is Brandor! Not Brevalaer! And you will *not* disrespect him again in my presence by using such a fey insult for him! Do you understand me?"

Falcyn's jaw went slack at her unexpected outburst.

Okay, then . . .

Nice fit from our new companion.

In a complete huff, Brogan embraced the tall, dark Adoni male. Eyes wide, Medea met Blaise's equally shocked expression. While he couldn't see her current actions, he'd definitely heard her verbal explosion.

A tic started in the mandrake's jaw. "Are they kissing?"

Stunned by the amount of jealousy betrayed in that single question, Medea screwed her face up. "No, but she is hugging him like she hasn't seen him in a really, *really* long time."

Falcyn cocked his head. "Does kissing his cheek count?"

Medea popped him on the stomach as Blaise's expression turned into one of extreme pain. "That's mean! Don't torture the poor mandrake!"

With a fierce grimace, Falcyn and Urian stepped around her to approach Brogan and Brandor with those predator gaits she knew so well. "What's going on here?"

Medea stayed back to cover them.

Just in case. As she'd quickly learned that when hanging out with these two, literally *anything* was possible.

Brandor, who was the same height as Falcyn, put himself between Brogan and them. Even though his clothes were ragged and it was obvious he hadn't been living well, he kept one arm on Brogan as if to protect her while he braced his body to confront Falcyn. Medea would give him bonus points for that. Spoke well of him that he was concerned for Brogan's welfare.

Still, she reserved judgment.

Even assholes could have consciences from time to time.

Extremely tall and handsome, he had the same chiseled striking features that marked all Adoni. Of course a lot of that had to do with the fact that if any child was deemed "unfit" their mothers abandoned them to die. Or dumped them in the human world to fend for themselves with no knowledge of their other-worldly ties.

Yeah, the fey and demons had a lot in common.

She could almost feel bad for the guy even if he was gorgeous, with his long, wavy black hair and hazel eyes so green they all but glowed with an unholy fire.

By his predatorial stance, it was obvious he knew how to fight and wasn't afraid to bleed.

But as Medea shifted her gaze from him to Brogan and back again, she realized that their features were extremely similar. Not just because they were both fey and both had pointed ears . . .

"I had Brogan bring you here so that I could speak with you."

The look on Falcyn's face said that if he'd still possessed his dragon's fyre Brandor would have been incinerated on the spot. "Excuse me?"

Brandor tensed, watching them for any hint of a coming attack. "I know you don't trust me. You've no reason to, but Blaise can tell you that I've been privy to Morgen's most secured council for years."

"True, and why are you here and not buried in some part of her body, where you normally live?" Blaise all but growled those words.

Anger sparked in Brandor's eyes, but he restrained it admirably. "I was caught trying to smuggle a portal key to my sister. Morgen gave me no chance to explain before I was banished here in one of her more stellar rage-fits."

That news seemed to shock Blaise.

"Who's your sister?"

Medea laughed at Falcyn's question, unable to believe he could miss the obvious, given how observant he normally was in all other matters. "Brogan."

"Brogan?" Urian, Blaise, and Falcyn spoke in unison.

Brandor gaped at Medea. "How could you tell?"

She gestured at the two of them. "It's obvious. You look just alike. And while she hugged you, it wasn't what one would give to a boyfriend or lover. It was definitely familial. Are you twins?"

Brogan finally stepped away from him. She cast a sheepish glance toward Blaise. "Aye. I told you it could have been much worse. My brother's life makes a mockery of mine and my sisters' combined. To protect me from their fate, Bran gave up the bulk of his powers at puberty—transferred them to me so that I'd be stronger and have more value."

Sadness darkened Brandor's eyes. "I've been trying to help Ro for a long time. But Morgen can't abide Deathseers in her Circle or the fey court. And as Ro said, I have little power left. The moment I heard you'd been pulled into her realm, I knew this was the only shot we'd ever have of helping each other, and getting her free."

"So what news do you have to share?" Medea wanted to keep him on point and not let him wander to inconsequential details.

"Morgen has made a pact with the god Apollo. They're after the goddess Apollymi and intend to use her army of Charonte to kill Acheron and take over Myddangeard and Olympus."

That was all well and good, except for one thing.

Her people.

"And the Daimons protecting Apollymi?"

"Apollo has sent a plague to kill them and the gallu to punish them for their rebellion against him."

Well, that explained the foreign illness that was tearing through their ranks. No wonder they couldn't fight it off. Damn her grandfather for it! Was he never to grow a heart and leave them in peace?

"Why do they want my stone?" Falcyn asked.

"It's the only thing that can stop them. The gallu need a dragonstone to repair your brother's tablet. Apparently, Hadyn's treasure is a key of some sort they need to free their dimme sisters."

The expression on Falcyn's face said there was much more to it than that, but he didn't comment. "Yeah, well, they can rot." He shook his head. "I'm not about to help any of them."

Brandor gave him an arch stare. "Not even to save your own sister?"

That cold steel hatred returned to Falcyn's eyes, and it made Medea's blood run cold. "Don't go there."

Brandor glanced to Brogan. "I would never taunt anyone with such a cruelty. Family should never be used as a bartering tool. But it's what they will hold over you and use against you if you don't do what they want. It's why I told Ro to bring you here. I know where Sarraxyn is, and I will take you to her before they hurt her to get to you."

"For what price?"

He took his sister's hand. "You've already paid it. You freed my sister from her realm and brought her to me so that I can protect her from her master. I'll help you free yours from hers. It's the least I can do."

Blaise shook his head. "Bullshit. I don't believe you."

Brogan's cheeks brightened with color. "You can trust him, Blaise. He's a good man."

"I don't trust anyone who beds down with Morgen."

"Says the mandrake who served the Kerrigan?" Urian cocked a sarcastic brow.

Finally quelled, Blaise cleared his throat. "Okay . . . valid point taken."

Urian sighed as he cast his gaze around each of them. "Yeah, I don't think anyone in this group can judge another for their past deeds."

Medea didn't comment on that. Mostly because he was right. All of them had served evil at some point.

Of course, she and Brogan were the only two who continued to do so.

But still . . .

"This is all well and good, but let's not lose sight of the fact that Urian and I aren't here on a vacation. I need your dragonstone, Falcyn. There's still the matter of the plague that's spreading through my people. I can't watch my parents and best friend die. I've had enough of death and I don't want any more of it."

Brandor scowled at her. "You're the daughter of Stryker?"

His question brought her suspicion straight to the forefront and put her instantly on guard. "How do you know that?"

"Morgen and Apollo. As I said, I've been privy to Morgen's most intimate councils. The word *brevalaer* is fey for *nothing*. Which is exactly what she considers me. Therefore she never worried what I heard or saw, as she didn't think I could use it against her."

Falcyn narrowed his eyes on Brandor. "How much have you heard?"

"Everything."

Blaise nodded. "She kept him literally chained to her throne or bed most of the time. I can attest to that."

"Well, if you know so much, any idea why we can't turn into dragons right now?"

"No, but I can tell you this. If Narishka made a bargain and you turned her down, they'll put a hit out on you."

"What kind of hit?"

"Ever heard of a strykyn?"

Medea had no idea what that was, but the anger flaring up in those steely blues said that Falcyn had dealt with more than his fair share of them.

"I've killed a few." Oh yeah, his voice was scarcely more than a fierce growl.

"That's what they'll be sending . . . along with anything else they can bribe."

Medea waited for an explanation, but they didn't seem eager to elaborate. So she prompted them. "What's a strykyn?"

Falcyn gave her a cold stare. "Children of Stryx."

"The water witch?"

He nodded. "Yeah, and they're what your father was named after. Fierce birds of prey who once served Ares in his larger battles. They are the black war owls with red wings and gold beaks who live on the edge of Hades where they feast on the souls of the damned and eat the carcasses of cowards."

The ones that traveled in swarms and could bring down entire armies . . .

She gaped at the old legend her mother had used to frighten her into behaving when she'd been a girl. But instead of using their real name, her mother, being an Atlantean Apollite, had referred to them as Greek War Birds. "His prized birds he suckled on the blood of misbehaving infants and children?"

"Yeah. For battle or to fight, they shift into large, mountainous warriors with serious attitude problems. Bastards so irritable, they make me look friendly."

That she'd like to see.

Urian cursed. "Apollo must have seized them when he defeated Ares and the others on Olympus and took it over."

"Would be my guess and our luck." Falcyn cursed under his breath. "Damn it. We really got to kick their asses out of that place soon."

Great. Medea's head was starting to throb again. "How do we fight and defeat them?"

Brogan crossed her arms over her chest. "The fruit of the strawberry tree can paralyze them."

"Good to know." Medea glanced around the bleak landscape that sadly lacked strawberry trees. Too bad they weren't allergic to drab gray ick. . . .

"Any other tricks?"

Brandor considered it a moment. "They can be diverted with other meats. Even if it's raw. But if they catch you, there's no way to escape them."

"Beautiful."

Falcyn snorted derisively. "Cut their hearts out. Their heads off. Incinerate them. Best of all, they taste like duck and are quite filling, if not a little gamey."

Medea arched a brow at Falcyn's dry tone. "Pardon?"

"You asked how to kill them. It's what always worked for me. I am a dragon, you know."

With a sarcastic laugh, she sighed at him. "You really are violent to your core, aren't you?"

There was a light in his eyes that she didn't quite understand. "From the moment I made the mistake of crawling out of my egg, everyone around me has tried their damnedest to kill me, for one reason or another. Starting with my own mother. That kind of survival doesn't exactly lend itself to benevolence or trust. Just a whole lot of pissed off."

Those words choked her as they gave her an insight into him that was brutally honest.

As hard as things had been for her, no matter the hell life had unleashed, she'd always had the shelter of her own mother's love. She couldn't imagine being alone the way he had. Of being left to fend for herself.

And while the death of her family haunted her, there for a time, she'd been deliriously happy with them. It was a happiness Falcyn couldn't even begin to fathom.

That thought brought an unbelievable ache to her chest. How could he keep going when they'd taken everything from him?

In that moment, she saw him for what he really was.

A survivor in the purest sense of the word.

With a coldness she knew was only surface protection, he turned toward the others. "Blaise? Can you open the portal out of here?"

"The key I have only works in Avalon. My father keeps everything locked here because he doesn't want anyone to discover that he's still alive. But we should be able to find him in his palace, and get him to open it. Although . . . he pitched a glorious fit about opening a gate the last time I was here with Varian and we asked him. Might be easier to get a kidney from him than a key."

Brandor scowled. "Your father?"

"Emrys Penmerlin."

"Your father?" he repeated. "That bastard?"

"Hey now! No shit-talking the man who took me in and saved my life. I owe him everything."

And still Brandor sputtered as if he were an overinflated tire that had sprung a leak on a hot afternoon. Really, the sounds were quite impressive.

A part of her had the urge to tip his teakettle before he exploded.

But after a few seconds, Brandor pulled himself together. "Well, we have him to thank for the lovely traps in this place. So I'd caution all of you to be wary of where you step and to keep your senses alert. At all times."

Blaise let out a fake laugh. "He would not be wrong about that. My father was a little overzealous when it came to populating the landscape with terrifying creations." He rubbed awkwardly at his neck. "You definitely don't want to fall into the pits of despair."

Medea scowled. Did he really mean what he'd just said? "The who . . . what?"

Blaise flashed a nervous grin at her. "They have a gas in them that makes you unbelievably depressed and you lash out at everyone. Although . . . Merewyn was kind of entertaining when she stumbled into a pit—at least for a while. Still, it's best to avoid them."

"Goodie. What else?"

"Standing water," Brandor said irritably. "It explodes when you touch it."

"Oh yeah." Blaise smirked. "I forgot about that."

Brandor snorted. "Wish I could. Lucky me, I learned the lesson when a hare made the mistake of trying to drink it before me. Least I got some hasenpfeffer out of it."

Medea wrinkled her nose at his offbeat sense of humor. Although, she appreciated his ability to turn lemons to lemonade, or in this case, rabbit entrails to stew.

Without pausing, Brandor continued with the warnings. "Basically, Merlin controls everything here except for the sylphs, who hate his guts. They hate ours, too. So, again, avoid any water where the water sylphs might live—including deep puddles—and the trees where the tree sylphs are, as those are nasty men-hating bitches who will rip our limbs from us just for entertainment."

"And the rocks will attack, too." Blaise flashed another grin.

"Are you shitting me?" Urian was aghast.

"Nope. A lot of them are bantlings and goylestones."

"Who? What?" Medea asked again.

"Baby gargoyles. They're not real bright, but they are rocks and they will attack en masse. So *get your rocks on* takes on a whole new meaning."

Why wasn't she surprised? Damn. It was as challenging to live here as Kalosis—which was the Atlantean hell realm where you had to avoid all manner of scary things. Things that included hungry Charonte and her parents. "Lovely."

"And whatever you do, you have to avoid the SOD."

Medea looked down and shifted her feet as a wave of severe trepidation went through her. "The dirt? Seriously? Why? What's it do?"

"Not sod. *SOD*." He stressed the word as if there was a difference to her ears. "S-O-D. Shadows of Doubt. Cousins to the sharoc, they reach out from the shadows, grab you when you least expect it, and suck the life out of you. You won't feel them at first. Just a little twinge that you can't complete what you're doing. Next thing you know, you're paralyzed with doubts. Incapacitated and they have their fangs in you. Once they do . . . you're theirs. They own you and you're dead."

Medea passed a less-than-amused gape at Urian. "And they think Daimons warrant a dedicated execution squad? Seriously? At least we give the humans a quick, painless death. And a choice. We don't come at your back."

He shrugged. "What do you want me to say? They're shadows. No one's afraid of a shadow—that's Peter Pan kid shit. But everyone fears the dark. Besides, only cowards and thieves lurk in the shadows. It takes a true warrior to hunt in the darkness where your actual fears and threats thrive, and to kick the ass of real evil where it lives and breathes. That's a real man or woman. Not some sneaky piece-of-shit coward."

Falcyn snorted. "Hence the other so aptly named branch of Were-Hunters they use for my brethren."

Because *Were* was the Old English word for *man* and was a shared root word for *fear* and *war*. Meaning that the Were-Hunters were men-hunters or those who hunted what men feared most and weren't afraid to kick its ass wherever they found it.

And speaking of the great evil . . . "So where do we find this Merlin?"

"Dad!"

Falcyn cringed at Blaise's unexpected shout. Not that Medea blamed him. Her own ears weren't happy about that shrill decibel level, either.

And no one answered the bloodcurdling screech.

Blaise cocked his head to listen. "Weird."

"What is?"

"My father always answers me." Stepping back, he put his hands to his mouth to shout louder. "Father? Nimue?"

Again, nothing.

Not even an animal stirred. And now that she noticed it, that was very peculiar indeed.

Medea had that bad feeling again. Something about this wasn't right. She could feel it deep inside.

Without a word to them, Blaise headed for the trees. "Sylph?"

Curious, Medea headed after him, toward the forest. She'd never seen a real sylph spirit before. Only heard legends and stories about them.

But as the tree came awake with a reddish color and in a

twisted form, she had her doubts about all the great beauty they were supposed to possess.

Let's hear it for creative license.

She thought it was just her being judgy about them until Blaise jumped away with a curse.

"What is it?" Urian asked.

Transforming into a bleeding, demonic body, the sylph advanced on them with a round of cursing and hissing.

Blaise turned pale before he grabbed Brogan to pull her back from the tree. "She's a gallu! Run!"

7

Light and sound exploded all around. It was as if the entire forest had come alive to consume them. Or at least tear them down. Everything was blowing up like some kind of slick heavy metal light show.

Temporarily blinded and disoriented, Medea had no idea in which direction to head.

Someone grabbed her.

She spun to slug them, only to catch the crisp masculine scent she knew more intimately than she cared to admit. And it was one that was starting to give an innate comfort to her that she didn't even want to investigate. "Falcyn?"

"Yeah, hang on." He lifted her and pulled her with him toward her left.

Normally, she'd protest being manhandled like this. But she was so grateful to have someone who could see what was happening that she went along without complaint or assault. Especially since he was being remarkably gentle. In fact, he kept her cradled against him as he twisted and dodged past things she could only guess about.

And that terrified her. She hadn't trusted anyone like this— with her safety—in more centuries than she could count. Truth be told, she couldn't remember ever being *this* trusting. It just wasn't in her. Yet something about Falcyn made it a lot easier than she'd ever thought possible.

By the time they made the woods, she could finally see again. And it was only then that she realized how tightly she was holding on to him. The fact that she had her face buried in the crook of his neck and had surrendered herself completely.

That was even more terrifying than the attackers she couldn't see.

He was her anchor in this madness that kept her grounded and sane.

Better yet, he was her life preserver. And she both hated and adored that sensation.

What the hell is wrong with me?

How could she ever trust a stranger like this? A dragon, no less?

With her still in his arms, Falcyn turned around slowly to

survey their surroundings and to make sure they'd escaped the possessed gallu sylphs.

Although it was a bit painful and her sight was peppered with pinpoints of light, she scanned with him and saw nothing. They appeared safe for the moment.

To her instant regret, Falcyn set her down on her feet. She didn't know why, but a part of her wanted for him to hold on to her the way Blaise had done with Brogan. To be as reluctant to let her go.

Are you insane?

She had to be. Medea Theoxena needed no one. Not for anything. Emotions were for suckers and fools. Neither of which was her.

Ever.

I will never *be weak again.* Not for any reason.

Not for any person.

That had been the promise she'd made to herself the day she stood over the bodies of her husband and child. The day she'd torn through the human village like a vengeful harpy, laying waste to every being there.

To this day, she could hear their screams and see their faces as she made them pay for what they'd ruthlessly taken from her without regard or remorse. That was the only thing that had allowed her to live with the anguish of her loss. The knowledge that she'd returned to them the same pain they'd coldly served to her.

And still it wasn't enough. That thirst for vengeance continued to burn within her like the passions of Aphrodite. To that end, she understood why her grandfather had gone wild on the Apollite race over his own son and mistress. She would never fault him for that rage that demanded blood sacrifices to slake it.

But she could have never cursed her own children, even in the midst of that kind of unreasoning grief. Not for anything. That he could do such to her father and her was an unforgivable sin.

And Falcyn understood that loss himself. While they hadn't killed his son, he'd thought of him as murdered—which was the same range of emotions Medea had lived with. He'd gone through identical pain over the centuries.

No wonder he was barely this side of insane. He lived in the same dismal hell she called home.

That, too, weakened her for him. Bonded them together. It was rare to find anyone who could relate to her fury. To her need for blood atonement. Someone who didn't judge her for wanting vengeance, even all these centuries later.

Worse, those thoughts brought an unexpected wave of tenderness crashing through her. One that made her throat tight and eyes water.

Don't, Medea! She couldn't emotionally afford to go there. Rather, she needed to focus on something else.

Quick, before she lost herself entirely to this dragon by her side.

Blinking, she tried her best to clear her vision. "Where are the others?"

"Not sure." He glanced around as if looking for either friend or foe. There was a light behind his eyes that said he had something else going on in his thoughts. "They scattered, and like you, I was blinded enough that I couldn't see where they went. I'm trying to reach Blaise with my powers. Something has me blocked. I'd Bane-Cry for him, but given this place, I'm not sure I want to even attempt that. Who knows what might answer with him, or head toward his position. While I have no problem beating the hell out of anything that rears its head, I don't want to lead trouble to him."

She bit back a smile at the emotion in his voice. He always thought of Blaise first.

In every situation. Which made her suspicious . . .

"You love him a lot more than a brother, you know that? What's the deal with you two?"

Hands on hips, he turned to face her. "Don't know what you mean."

She tsked at the suddenly defensive dragon who confirmed her opinion and solidified it. No wonder he was so protective. . . .

There was only one logical reason for that.

"I had a moment where I thought he might be that son you mentioned, but since he knew your son in Camelot . . . my money says he's your grandkid, isn't he?"

Oh yeah, *there* was an expression that confirmed it on those handsome dragon features. Falcyn should never play poker. His opponents would clean house with his wallet.

His continued silence on this matter only added another layer of veracity.

Medea approached him slowly. "That's why I didn't ask

about it while they were around us. I knew it would piss you off. And I was right." No one could miss the fury that burned deep in those steely blues.

Tsking, she cocked her head. "So what really happened to separate him from his parents? 'Cause I know you didn't give him up without a fight."

Falcyn started to tell her to go to hell and take her ridiculous assumptions with her. It was what he'd always done in the past when someone asked something he didn't like. He couldn't stand being questioned.

And yet as he saw her honest sincerity and the tenderness of her expression and it touched a part of him that he hated, the truth ran past his lips before he could catch it and lock it down. "I don't know. I wasn't there when Blaise was born. Maybe his father did what Blaise said and left him to die. I've never met Maddor. Have no idea about his character or anything else. He could easily be as big a bastard as I am. Even though he's my son, he's a complete stranger to me."

"Why?" As soon as the question came out, she regretted it, because it wrung such a look of pain from him that *she* could feel it.

It was an expression of soul-deep anguish. The kind only a parent could feel at the loss of a child.

And she hated how well she related to it. How much she understood.

How much she despised herself for reopening his wounds when it was obvious that he wasn't really a bastard. In spite of his words, he cared about his unknown son as much as she'd cared about hers. And he ached over the loss every bit as much.

It was the loss of all those years together that never went away. The anguish of wondering what could have been. What kind of man her son would have grown into. What kind of relationship they would have had.

All those questions and all those doubts and the pain. It never dulled. Never stopped.

Damn life for it.

And Falcyn loved Blaise more than his own life. She'd seen that firsthand in everything he did for him. The way he doted and guarded.

Before she realized what she was doing, she pulled him against her and held him. "I'm sorry, Falcyn."

Falcyn swallowed hard, wanting to shove her and her pity away from him like a disease. He was drakomai. The first of the dragons. He didn't need kindness or compassion.

Damn sure didn't want it from a Daimon leader.

That was what his mind screamed out. But his body wouldn't cooperate or listen. In all these centuries, no one had ever held him when he was hurt.

Never once.

He was always abandoned during those darkest hours of his life. Left alone to ache and bleed until he'd learned to expect nothing else.

From anyone.

But instead of rejecting her for her unique kindness, he lifted his hand and buried it deep in her soft hair so that he could hold her close and savor the novelty of this moment. The novelty of being held and soothed by someone who smelled like gentle lily flowers.

Damn.

The warmth of her skin was unlike anything he'd ever felt or known. It shook him to the core of his being. And touched him more than he wanted it to.

He felt her smiling against his cheek. "Your skin really is cooler than most, isn't it?"

Again, such a comment would have normally moved him to righteous anger, but he didn't hear disdain or mockery in her tone. She was amused by the fact that he was a cold-blooded creature.

"My basal temp is significantly lower than yours, yes."

"It's nice. My skin's always hot. I can't stand it most of the time."

"Anytime you want to cool off, I volunteer to suck all the heat out of you."

Smiling even wider, she placed the most chaste kiss imaginable to his cheek before she stepped away, and yet it fired his blood more than any he'd ever had before.

How screwed up was that?

Even worse were the sudden fantasies in his mind of holding her in a much more intimate setting. Of making love to her for the rest of the day until they were both sweaty and spent.

Consequences be damned. And it left him harder than he'd ever been. Needier than he could stand. All he wanted right then was to be inside her.

Unaware of his hunger, Medea headed deeper into the forest to search for the others.

"My brother."

She paused at Falcyn's barely audible words. "Pardon?"

"You asked me why I wasn't around my son. My brother cursed him."

Medea froze instantly. Those words shook her on several levels. Not the least of which was the very personal one over what had resulted after her grandfather had cursed her entire race to die. While she didn't know Falcyn's brother, this knowledge made her instantly hate him. "What kind of curse?"

"That the mandrakes would never be able to sustain their dragon forms for long. They can fight in them, fly in them, but they can't live permentantly as dragons. Mandrakes are basically nothing more than men who have the ability to assume a dragon's power when they need it."

She scowled at his words. "Why would he do that?"

"For their own good and mine, he said."

She didn't miss the note in his voice as he spoke. "But you don't believe that?"

He let out a bitter, scoffing laugh. "My son's mother was so infuriated when she learned that Max had cursed them that she took Maddor to Landvætyria where I couldn't get to him. When Igraine and her sisters could find no way to work around Max's spell, the entire mandrake race they conceived was enslaved and tortured because of it—with my child being their primary whipping boy and the focal point of their hatred. So how can I? I was banned from ever seeing my child. From protecting him from their cruelty. He could stand beside me to this day and I wouldn't know him. I'm sure he hates me. Who could blame him for it?"

With a ragged breath, he shook his head. "I don't know. Maybe Max was right. The Adoni would have most likely still found a way to enslave them for their purposes, and sooner or later, we'd have been at war with them because of Morgen and her ambitions. Evil bitch that she is, she would have eventually pitted us against each other. That I don't doubt. It is how she is. War would have come regardless. Had Merlin not sequestered the mandrakes here behind the veil centuries ago, we most likely would have been forced to put them down for their sakes as well as ours. But the father in me doesn't care about any of that. I would have found a way to save my son."

"And your sister? Why is she trapped here?"

He winced. "She came here because of me and Maddor. While I was banned from visiting Landvætyria, she wasn't. Morgen and her aunts set about trying to breed more mandrakes with other dragons. They would lure them here, breed them, and then kill them. I didn't know the latter part until after Arthur's son, Anir, brought word to me that Xyn was dead. That she'd died while trying to free Anir, his army, and Maddor from Morgen."

"But she's a statue? Not dead?" That was what Brandor had said.

"I should have thought of that. It must have been what she was doing instead of killing them." He released an elongated sigh. "It was always Morgen's special cruelty for her enemies. Anir and every soldier under his command were turned by her magick into her personal Stone Legion."

Medea scowled at the unfamiliar term. "Stone Legion?"

"An army of gargoyles. The only reprieve Merlin could give them from Morgen's evil is that under the light of a full moon, they turn human until dawn. Otherwise, they're frozen statues during daylight and are her army whenever she needs it."

So she cursed them and then forced them to fight for her? Yeah, what a cruel bitch. Not even her mother was *that* bad, and her mother could be brutal.

"That's horrible!"

He nodded. "Compassion isn't one of Morgen's virtues."

"And Maddor's mother? Who was she?" She hoped it wasn't Morgen.

When he spoke, she learned she was right. But the truth was even worse.

"Morgen's mother."

Medea felt sick at that news. "Morgen le Fey is the half sister of your son?"

A tic began working in his jaw. "Indeed."

"Morgen knows this?"

"I'm sure she does. Not like Igraine or her sisters ever hid it."

And still Morgen had enslaved her own brother. . . .

Then again, why was she surprised?

If the legends were true, Morgen had done much worse than that to her family. Especially her brother Arthur. So why she'd expect her to have any compassion for Maddor, she didn't know.

This was why Medea had no regard for humanity. Why she viewed them as parasites. Their cruelty was truly spectacular and surpassed only by the gods themselves.

Wishing for a better world for all of them, Medea paused in the middle of the woods as she realized everything here looked the same. A person could easily get lost and never find a way out of the forest. Get turned around and walk in circles without ever knowing.

Yet Falcyn navigated the landscape as if he knew exactly where he was headed. "Where are we?"

He gave her a droll smirk. "A dark and enchanted forest."

She rolled her eyes at his sarcasm. "Uncalled for. Where are we headed?"

"Merlin's palace. Since it was the last place we discussed, I figure it's where we're most likely to find the others."

"And you know the way . . . how?"

"While my powers aren't up to par, I can still feel the heart, as it were, of this place. Can't you?"

"I thought it was indigestion."

He snorted. "Yeah, sure you did."

But he was right. She could feel those sharp, emanating powers. Had he not been with her, she would have avoided them. Not out of fear. Out of respect. One didn't walk into the den of a sorcerer without knowing what you were getting into.

With no better solution on how to get out of this place, she followed after him again. "So how did you get hooked up with Igraine, of all people?"

"Dragonvane."

That didn't make sense to her. "I thought that repelled you guys."

"Not *bane*. Vane. It's a special scent that mixes amber and musk with myrrh. Sadly, we find it as irresistible as a cat with catnip."

Ah, that explained it. "You were drugged."

"I promise you, I wouldn't have slept with her otherwise. While Igraine was highly attractive, I was well aware of how she'd brutally killed her second husband in order to seduce and then marry Arthur's father. Given her track record of murdering husbands and lovers, I would have never taken a dip into her pool, had I been in my right mind. No woman is *that* attractive." He let out a tired sigh. "Makes me wonder what spell she used on Uther Pendragon. I find it hard to believe he'd have succumbed any quicker than I did."

"At least you're in good company."

"Yeah, the Fucked-Over Club. Hooray. That makes it so much better."

She popped him on the arm.

Shocked, he gaped at her. "You have absolutely no fear of me, do you?"

"Should I?"

"Given *my* track record? Yeah, you should. I live to make meals off tender morsels like you."

Scoffing, she walked right up and smirked in his face. "Have you seen *my* track record, buddy? Between the two of us, you should probably be the one afraid."

"Now you're just trying to turn me on."

"And that does it for you, huh?"

With a wicked grin, he glanced down at the bulge in his jeans. "Apparently."

Medea blushed as she realized that he wasn't joking. He really was turned on.

Even worse? She wasn't offended by it.

Instead, it sent a wave of unexpected desire through her. And another of great curiosity. One that didn't really bear investigating. Or thinking about, as it led her thoughts into very dangerous territory.

"So how long has it been?" he asked.

"For what?"

A teasing grin curved his lips. "That long, huh? You can't even remember what I'm asking?"

More heat crept over her cheeks. "It's been a while. Hard to cozy up to men you know are only one minute away from death. Especially after you've already lost your heart and soul—the last of the good ones." She gave him a gimlet stare. "What about you?"

"I know exactly how long it's been since I last slept with someone. I wasn't asking me about me."

She snorted irritably at his continued sarcasm. "You're avoiding my question."

"I know. And I would like to continue avoiding it, as I just had a nasty altercation over this very topic."

"Meaning?"

He rubbed at his eye. "I was briefly and I do mean b-r-i-e-f-l-y involved with an Amazon dragonslayer."

She paused to gape at him. "I beg your pardon . . . are you insane?"

"Yeah, well, in my defense, it worked out well for both my brothers. They're quite happily married to dragonslayer dragonswans. In my case on the dating front, not so much. She definitely wanted to skin my hide more than climb it. But she's the only reason I hung around Sanctuary as long as I did."

"You were trying to work it out?"

"Not really. Even my masochism has its limits. I was getting ready to leave when you showed up."

Medea didn't know why, but she felt bad for him. And a

little jealous. But in the end, her curiosity got the best of her as she slowed her stride. "So what went wrong?"

"As long as I was in a human body, she was fine. Sadly, I can't stay in one. Sooner or later, I have to be what I am. And human's not it. The moment I shifted and Tis was reminded that I'm an animal, she lost her human mind."

Medea tried to imagine what he must look like as a dragon. It was hard to think of this insanely hot man with scales and claws. To think of him as a massive beast.

Of course, he was massively large in human form, too. Even his hands were gigantic.

Which made her even more curious. . . .

"So how is it you can shapeshift? I didn't think a full-blooded drakomai could do that."

"Most can't."

She arched a brow at him. "But . . ."

This time, he was the one who paused. He turned to look at her as if he wanted to see her expression. "I can shift for the same reason your father can."

You're an ass was the first thought she had, but it was quickly followed by the truth.

A truth that slapped her hard.

No . . .

Her stomach shrank. "You're a demigod."

"Technically, I'm a full god who was cursed at my birth."

Oh yeah, now an ulcer was starting to form. Either that, or she was getting ready to give birth to a diamond, because her stomach clenched hard enough to create one in the pit of her belly. "What?"

"You know," he said sarcastically. "Both my parents were gods. My mother made a play for the head of her pantheon, and when his wife found out, she reacted as any goddess would. Sadly, my mother's powers weren't what she thought them to be, and she learned the hard way how weak she was in comparison to Shyamala."

Medea furrowed her brow as she tried to follow his explanation. "Shyamala? I don't know a goddess with that name."

"Yeah, you do. You just know her by her more contemporary name. Azura."

Medea felt the blood drain from her cheeks as she made the most horrific connection ever.

If Azura was the goddess who cursed his mother for dabbling with her mate, there was only one male god who could have fathered him.

Holy fucking shit . . .

"You're a son of Noir."

The king god of *all* evil.

8

Falcyn let out a long, tired sigh. "No one can help who their parents are."

"Yeah, but Noir . . . I didn't know he had any children."

"We are few and far between, as Azura can't stand us and tends to put a hit on us from the moment we're conceived. Most of our mothers never survive to birth us."

Little wonder he was so paranoid. Angry.

And fierce.

No doubt he'd been looking over his shoulder his entire life.

"What happened to your mother?"

"As soon as Azura found out, my mother, Lilith, was cast from her pantheon, turned into a demon, and villainized. Of course, my mother didn't go quietly into the good night. Her wrath was such that she over-embraced her new role as lead bitch, and began plotting revenge on them all."

Medea had to bite back a sarcastic laugh at that. Azura and Noir were two of the most lethal and dangerous gods the universe had ever spat out. It said a lot about his mother that she'd ever think to take them on—it was something her own mother might have done in her youth.

Lilith was either extremely brave or radically stupid. Yet honestly, Medea couldn't imagine anyone being enough of either to ever try to take on one primal power.

Never mind two . . .

His mother's reputation in history was starting to make sense.

"How did she hope to defeat them?"

"She and her sisters began to breed a race of dragons to take down all the pantheons. If they were cursed to only birth monsters, they decided they were going to make the most of it and use us to battle them."

"No wonder your childhood was bleak."

Fire lit his eyes, turning them a vibrant orange. "You have *no* idea."

Was he serious?

"No idea what it means to be cursed? To bleed for the

actions of others over something I had no part in? Oh, yeah. I have no concept whatsoever of what *that's* like. At all."

Falcyn winced as he realized how stupid he must have sounded to make such a complaint to her. An Apollite. Of all the creatures, in all the worlds, she was the only one who understood him. Who knew exactly his pain. "Sorry. Forgot my audience."

She shrugged with a nonchalance he was sure she didn't really feel. "It's fine. I learned long ago that no one is immune from misery. And some of us, it stalks like its favorite bitch in heat."

He paused to cup her cheek. "I'm sorry for all you've lost. Innocents should never be forced to pay for the acts of others. Each drop of blood shed by them is an indictment against the entire world for its heartlessness."

She placed her hand over his as her eyes burned him with the depth of her pain and courage. His gut tightened as she met his gaze and he saw the truth inside her. Saw the horrors she didn't dare speak about because they hurt so much that to give voice to them only crippled you more. So the only way to survive was to bury the agony so deep that you could overlook it most days, and to pray to the gods that you never cracked open the door where they were kept.

And still her gaze burned him deep inside his soul. "You were the first dragon made, weren't you?"

He winced at a truth he never spoke of. Many suspected, but he'd never confirmed nor denied it. Not even Max knew for certain. A tiny, tiny handful of others knew, and they never breathed a word of it.

There was no reason to keep it a secret, really, other than he felt somehow responsible for all his siblings born to their demonic mothers.

As if he could have stopped it had he been a better killer for his mother and her sisters. A better dragon.

Xyn had shared in that. She'd been born only a year after him. Together, they had tried to placate their mothers' wraths.

And failed miserably.

The gods made vicious enemies, and the two of them had been bonded by their efforts to rectify the hatred. Bonded by their scars.

"Falcyn?"

"Yes. I was first."

Medea swallowed at those whispered words. Her poor dragon. She couldn't imagine the nightmare he'd been through. Her own was staggering enough. And here in this one moment, she felt closer to him than she'd ever felt to another.

"We are the guinea pigs," she said with a sigh. "And as such, we're always fried from the experimentation."

He laughed bitterly. "True."

With a ragged sigh, she glanced about the forest. "Where do you think the others are?"

"I don't know, and I don't like not knowing. I've never been without my powers in this manner. It's . . . irritating. And it's not something I'm used to."

She agreed. "We are such similar creatures, you and I."

"For a Daimon and a dragon, you mean."

"Both spawned by evil, to do evil. Like the Malachai."

Falcyn considered that as they walked. The Malachai was

one of the most evil demons out there. The king of them all, as it were. Luckily, there was only one of them left alive. The rest had been slaughtered long ago.

"Have you ever met the Malachai?"

Medea nodded. "The current Malachai served my father for a time. Killed my aunt. Have you met him?"

He passed a guarded stare toward her before he answered in an insidious tone. "I've met *all* of them."

Her jaw went slack at that knowledge. The current Malachai—Nick Gautier—was merely the latest in a line of thousands of them.

And each one lived for hundreds, sometimes thousands, of years.

For Falcyn to have met them all would make him older than her grandfather Apollo.

Make him older than she could truly conceive.

Crap on a shingle . . . literally.

"Exactly when were you born?"

He gave her an evil, cocky grin. "Let me put it this way, I fought in the Primus Bellum."

The first war of the gods . . .

Her jaw dropping, Medea froze as that knowledge staggered her most of all. And with it came another startling realization as she recalled something Urian had told her about Falcyn's dragonstone and why it was so special.

"Your stone isn't like the others, is it?"

He didn't answer.

And by that silence, he told her everything. If he were that old and the son of two gods—even one who was cursed—his stone would have to be older than the others, too. More powerful.

Urian's voice whispered through her mind. *"Can even bring the dead back to life."*

That power was reserved for very few, and out of the few able to do it . . .

"Holy shit," she breathed as all the pieces came together in a blinding realization. "You're the ancient war god Veles." That was why he could shapeshift when the others couldn't. He wasn't just a dragon.

As he'd said, he was a god.

"And that's not a dragonstone you carry, at all . . . It's the effing dragonsworn. The world egg!"

The birthstone of the original gods.

Staring up at him, she saw the truth that he didn't bother to deny. "I'm right, aren't I?"

Falcyn started to tell her she was insane. Since the dawn of time, he'd carried that secret. Told no one the truth about himself or his stone.

No one.

He had no reason whatsoever to trust her. And every reason to remain silent.

And yet when he looked at her, he lost himself to the darkness of those eyes. The softness of her lips. Before he could think better of it, he nodded.

Because he was the first, and because Noir was his father, he held more powers than any of his siblings. And it was because of his father and his mother's wrath that he'd been deemed and worshiped as the very first war god of the world.

"But how can it be?"

He shrugged at the simple, complicated truth of what he was. "When Chaos and Order spun together for the first time and joined to make life out of nothing, the egg came from the friction of their union. From that initial explosion, the north wind carried that first egg and set it down upon the earth to keep it from shattering. Out of the darkness sprang light that cracked it in two, and Shyamala emerged into existence first, followed by her other six siblings—though they often lie and mislead about who was born first and in what order. Never understood why, but apparently it's an issue between them. The order, however and regardless of what they claim, is simple. Braith. Cam. Rezar. Verlyn. Lilith. Kadar. Three born of order. Three of chaos. Three of light. Three of dark. When Lilith was born, they say she slipped or was possibly pushed, and was damaged in the fall, thus causing her powers to mix back together. She was neutral in the beginning. Willful. Insatiably curious, and in an effort to repair herself, she took the pieces of the egg and fused them back together with their conjoined DNA. But she never told the others what she'd done. It was her secret."

"Then how did you get it?"

"I was born from it, too, after Shyamala, or Azura as she's now known, forbid me to be born from my mother's womb. She made it so that my mother would never be capable of a live birth—that we'd be born dead. Contrary as always and determined that Azura wouldn't get the best of her, my mother cut me from her womb and decided that I and my siblings would be egg-born creatures who could be hidden from Azura's wrath. That way, even if Azura or one of the other gods killed the lilit mothers my mother had created from her own blood for the bitch to get in on her good graces, the cursed egg-born babies would survive without their mothers."

Medea frowned as she tried to understand Lilith's reasoning. "Why did your mother create the others, knowing the gods would try to kill them too?"

Raking his hand through his hair, he sighed. "The lilit were her decoys to distract Azura and the others from me and my sister. But my mother lost her sanity in the process and with it became the very demon they'd dubbed her. We were quickly forgotten as her children and became tools to be used in her war against them all."

"And your father?"

"Is a worthless bastard who makes yours appear loving in comparison. All he ever wanted me for was vengeance against the other gods. I never meant anything to him, other than to be used as a tool. If there's anything or anyone Noir values, I don't know it. I doubt if he even cares for Azura. I don't think he's capable of caring about anything."

"Well, from what I hear, world domination."

Falcyn snorted. "Yeah. That would be it. The gods know, it was never his children or sister-wife."

That made sense. Medea was silent for a while as they made their way through the forest. Her head reeled with this new information about Falcyn and his family. There was so much she'd have never guessed at, and it made her wonder something else.

"Why did you change your name from Veles to Falcyn?"

He shrugged. "I grew bored with pantheon politics. Was never much of a team player anyway."

"Yeah, I remember hearing those stories about Veles."

A playful light sparked in his eyes. "Probably all true. Especially the gory parts."

"And you're avoiding my question again. Why the name change?"

The light went out in his eyes and pain replaced the spark. "After the destruction of my last temple, I went to live in seclusion. It was my sister who renamed me Falcyn for the reaping-hook-shaped claws I have and because it was always my weapon of choice in battle whenever I fought as a human. Once she was gone, I kept the name to remind me of her as if it was all I had left of Xyn."

No wonder he'd avoided answering it. Now she felt terrible for having pressed the issue. "I like it, and it suits you better than Veles, I think."

A twisted half smile curved his handsome lips. "I'm going to take that as a compliment."

"Good, 'cause I meant it as one. . . . And tell me, Lord Falcyn, what does the dragon who has lived so long value?"

She realized too late that was the wrong question, as his eyes flared to a deep, dark red and he slowed his walk. More than that, he clenched his fists and lowered his head.

"Why would a Daimon leader want to know?"

"I was only making conversation. But I see now the depths of your mistrust. Not that I blame you. You've lived long enough to know better than to open yourself to a stranger. So I won't fault you for that suspicion. You are a wise dragon, indeed."

He pulled her to a stop. "Tell me what you value."

"Nothing, really. Just my mother and Davyn. Some days my father and brother."

"Only some days?"

She let out a bitter laugh. "Sad, right? I still barely know them. I want to love my father, but it's hard to forgive him for what my mother went through. For all the centuries I watched her cry for him."

"And what of Urian?"

"I love my brother because he's my brother. But by the time I came to know him, he served Acheron—our worst enemy, who hunts us and who trains Artemis's army to kill us. How can I trust someone who's in service to my enemy? I understand his hatred of Stryker. I won't fault him for despising someone who cut his throat and murdered his wife. But at the same time, I'm not dumb enough to trust Urian with anything more than a sister's love. I carry no expectations of him beyond that."

"Yet you sought him out in this matter?"

"Only because I trust in his love of Davyn. While I might not be able to put Urian at my back, his history with Davyn is such that I doubt he'd betray his one, true brother. They've bled far too often for one another in the past and have too much history with each other. I trust Davyn and Davyn trusts Urian."

Falcyn scoffed as they came to a jagged edge. He turned to help her up the small embankment. "That is some screwed-up logic, my lady. Sad that I understand it and can relate. As you said, we are similar creatures."

Medea didn't speak as he lifted her effortlessly to stand by his side. He was a massive beast. Stronger than any man she'd been with in a long time. And she'd always been a sucker for great strength.

Worse was how much she liked the scent of his skin. He was intoxicating.

Even now, she could still taste his lips from the kiss he'd given her. And when he met her gaze, she knew that those thoughts were bare to his sage dragon sense.

Before she even realized what she was doing, she leaned in to kiss him again.

Falcyn closed his eyes as he tasted her and the sweetest passion he'd ever known. Unlike Tisiphone, she didn't judge him for a birth he couldn't help. Or think him unnecessarily harsh for the feelings and grudges he had against a brutal world.

She understood. Especially since she now knew he was a war god. A secret he never let anyone else know.

And he'd never been held by a similar creature before. Because dragons shared a common gene pool and history, he'd avoided sleeping with one, as he viewed all their females as his sisters.

His hatred for his mother had kept him away from demons. So most of his lovers had come from humans and the fey. Never had he been with an Apollite or Daimon. Since they were Greek in origin and he despised the Greeks for what they'd done to his race and his brethren, he considered them disgusting creatures.

Yet there was no scorn inside him for this woman. Not even a tiny morsel of it.

She fisted her hands in his shirt, pressing him closer against her body. Breathless, he deepened their kiss, wanting her more than he'd ever wanted anything.

Terrified of where those feelings might lead him, he tore away from her lips.

"Push me away, Medea," Falcyn said raggedly. "Tell me how much I repulse you and that you don't want anything to do with a sullen, self-pitying bastard who has no use for this world or any other."

Medea frowned at his unexpected words. Who had said such to him?

"I don't find you repulsive, dragonfly. Far from it."

He cupped her face and stared at her. His eyes were dark and filled with a soul-deep torment she didn't quite understand.

"Say it, Medea," he insisted. "Because right now, all I want is to be inside you out here in the woods like the animal I am. And I know how very wrong it is to crave you when there's nothing for either one of us. I know you deserve better and that we don't have time for it. But honestly, I don't give a shit about that or anything else. All I can think about right now is you and how much I want you."

His words shocked her as much for his sincerity as for the ragged desperation she heard in his voice.

Worse, it made her body hot and shivery. Needful. Things she hadn't felt in so long that she'd almost forgotten what it was like to be this way with another. This wasn't just a biological itch. There was more to her feelings for him.

Something scary and demanding.

Something she didn't want to deny.

She'd felt it since the moment she'd walked into Sanctuary and first seen him in the crowd.

Strange, she'd always wondered what it would be like to lay with one of the other species—either a man or Were. In her wildest fantasies, she'd sometimes imagined how they would take a woman. If they'd be violent or tender. Or as gentle as her own husband, who'd won her heart when she'd been nothing more than an innocent girl so long ago in their ancient world.

But it was this fearsome dragon who called out to her now. A fierce, harsh beast who held tolerance for none. His anger was so evident, it was practically tangible.

Don't.

The word hovered in her mind like a breathless phantom. It would be all kinds of foolish to sleep with him. He was the son of two of the most powerful ancient bloodlines and she was the daughter of a cursed race and a god at war with his pantheon.

A race he hated. They had no future together at all. How could they?

She might even conceive his child. And then where would they be?

But instead of horrifying her as it'd always done in the past, the thought actually made her heart leap. The fear of having another child was no longer there. Because she knew that Falcyn would protect their baby with the same insanity that he used to keep Blaise safe.

That he used so that he could shield her.

How much more determination would Falcyn show for his own?

No . . .

This dragon wouldn't allow a mere human to harm their baby. Ever. He would give his life before he saw it skin its knee. He'd be the kind of father she'd dreamed of. Unlike her own, he would never leave. Never allow his child to be alone or be harmed.

And for the first time in centuries, she saw a future for herself where she wasn't alone. One that wasn't bitter.

Stop it, Medea!

It was too late. The floodgate was open and all those repressed dreams rushed over her. All she'd ever wanted was a baby to love. A life to share with someone else.

Her mother had always said her reckless heart would lead her astray.

Today it had led her straight to Falcyn Drakos. And even though she knew this was complete and utter insanity, she refused to back down.

"Make love to me, Falcyn."

9

Falcyn was completely stunned by her words. Medea was supposed to curse him and shove him away from her. Slap his face or cut out his heart.

She wasn't supposed to want him.

A decent man would pull away from her. But he wasn't decent. Nor was he a man. He was feral to the core of his dragon being and harder than hell. A dragon who took what he wanted, consequences be damned.

It was what had gotten him into trouble

with Igraine. Drugged and reeling, he'd acted out with her in the heat of passion, and then paid dearly for it.

In the blink of an eye, and as a result, he'd lost everything.

Because he didn't believe in rules or refinement. Those were for Max and his brothers and sisters. They were the ones who paid attention to Savitar's rules and dictates. Those who abided by the pacts and politics of the gods.

As a god himself, he'd always thought himself above such petty, irritating things that had been relegated to mortals and lesser creatures.

Just as he'd been above emotions and wants. He didn't need companionship. He was drakomai. They were solitary and happy to be such.

Until now.

In the one instant of her walking into his circle, Medea had changed everything in his bleak world. He craved her with a madness he didn't understand. Wanted her with him in a way he'd never wanted anything else.

Now he wished he knew what words could convey how much this moment meant.

How much *she* meant to him.

He'd lived his whole life without the warmth of a tender caress. How could he walk away now? He traced the curve of her swollen lips with his fingertip, before he parted her lips and kissed her deeply.

Falcyn closed his eyes and inhaled the sweetness of her breath as he let loose his tongue to dart against hers, to sweep up to the palate of her mouth until she moaned and writhed from it. The feel of her supple body pressed against his while he pulled her black shirt free of her pants.

"You really should push me away," he said, lifting his head to stare down into her gentle, dark eyes.

She quirked an adorable grin that exposed her fangs. "Never been one to do what I'm supposed to. Goes with my whole evil villain title."

"Yeah, and sicko me finds that one of your more endearing qualities."

"Are you mocking me?"

"Never, my love. I'd never mock you for fear of your kicking my ass."

Medea's heart fluttered as he offered her a real smile with those teasing words. It was unexpected and breathtaking.

His pale eyes glowed in the dim fey light as he gently picked her up and lowered her down to their knees. His heat surrounded her while his arms cushioned her from the cold, damp ground. The heat and strength of him surrounded her.

And against all sanity and reason, she wanted more of his hard body.

She actually purred as he returned to her lips to kiss her softly. She'd never been touched like this. Never thought a mere kiss could be such a wondrous experience.

And when his warm, callused hand closed around her breast, she jumped in nervous excitement. Pain and pleasure stabbed through her body as heat pooled itself between her thighs.

Never in her life had she burned like this. Craved another with such a vicious heat. She couldn't even begin to understand these foreign sensations. They were so confusing and consuming, and why she'd have them for him, she couldn't imagine.

Electrifying. Tormenting, and they left her wanting more of him.

Her enemy.

Falcyn left her lips to kiss a trail down her throat to the breast he cupped. Medea swallowed at the sight of his dark head at her breast, at the feel of his tongue teasing her taut nipple. His tongue was rough and hot, his lips soothing and tender.

She cupped his head to her, and let the waves of his soft hair tease her fingertips.

He was so beautiful there, tasting her, teasing her. The tense lines of his beautiful face showed the pleasure he received just from touching her. And it made her heart pound.

She sighed in contentment and let the incredible earthy sensations sweep her away until she was nothing but an extension of the dragon holding her.

Closing her eyes, she surrendered herself to him completely.

Falcyn had never tasted anything like her body. She was so warm. So inviting. More so because he knew she was sharing with him what she so rarely shared with anyone else. She wasn't a creature of trust any more than he was.

Why she would choose him right now, he couldn't even begin to imagine. He was so unworthy of what she offered. So unworthy of her, period.

But then they were partners in darkness and sorrow. They both had been dealt more than their fair share of agony and betrayal. Both had seen the worst of humanity and fey, and pulled themselves up from the brink of despair to soldier on in spite of that brutality.

It was something the scars of her body gave testimony to, the same as his.

And he winced as he saw the jagged stretch marks that still hovered over the beauty of her stomach from where she'd carried her son. Unlike him, she wore that agony on both the inside and outside of her heart. How could she stand to see such an obvious reminder of her loss?

Until now, he'd never realized how lucky he was that he'd been spared such a physical blow.

Such a brutal, constant reminder.

It said much about her strength and character that she'd carried on with the grace and determination she'd shown all these centuries past. That she'd remained sane through it all. Never had he respected anyone more.

And he was glad that for this one moment, and for whatever reason, she was with him.

Medea tugged at his shirt.

Eager to oblige her, he pulled it off.

She gasped audibly as she ran her hands over his tense arms. He clenched his teeth as his head reeled from pleasure.

The things her touch did to him . . .

It was incredible. Invigorating. It made him feel virile and feral.

Like the dragon he'd been born.

He was hard and aching. Most of all, he felt vulnerable in a way he'd never imagined.

But he couldn't pull back. Not now. He needed more of her. Needed to touch every inch of her body and to claim it as his own.

Medea felt a moment of panic as he removed the rest of her clothes from her. She was suddenly exposed to him. Not just naked.

Truly bare. In a way she'd never been before. He didn't just see her body. He saw her.

Her heart. Her soul.

Most of all, he saw her pain.

It was scary and strangely erotic. She couldn't recall ever being so exposed to anyone.

No one but Falcyn.

Her heart pounding, she stared at the large size of him and reached down to gently take him into her hand. The moment she cupped him, he growled with a look of supreme pleasure.

His eyes glowed vibrant red.

"Bet you terrify the humans with that."

He laughed and nuzzled her neck. "I've sent a few screaming for the hills."

Sucking her breath in sharply, she squeezed and reveled in the sensation of his hot skin sliding against hers. "Why do you smell like cinnamon?"

"All the better to entice you."

And it did.

He lay down on top of her and gathered her into his arms. Her thoughts scattered at the glorious feeling of his skin against hers. Of his heavy weight that felt good instead of oppressive.

Falcyn took her hand into his and guided it back to him.

"Never be afraid of me, Medea," he whispered. "You're the one person I would never hurt."

She nipped his chin. "I'm going to hold you to that promise, dragon. If you lie, your Amazon dragonslayer is the least of your concerns."

Medea ran her hand down his shaft before she gently guided him into her body. He kissed her again, then drove himself deep inside her.

Falcyn whispered sweet encouragements in her ear while he used his tongue to toy with the tender flesh of her neck.

Crying out in pleasure, Medea arched her back against him. She'd never imagined a dragon or any man could feel like this, but she was glad it was Falcyn who was inside her right now. Glad for the strength of his arms around her and the sound of his deep voice in her ear.

Medea wrapped her arms around his shoulders and buried her face against his muscled neck so that she could inhale the warm scent of him as she thrust her hips against his. Dear gods, how she wanted this. Wanted to share her body with him and have him fill her for the rest of eternity.

Falcyn ground his teeth at how incredible she felt. He wanted her in a way unimaginable. She surrounded him with heat and her breath against his neck sent a thousand chills straight to his soul.

In this moment, he never wanted to let her go.

Especially when she looked up with an adoring smile that set fire to every part of him. Inside and out. The sight of her lying underneath him, her body bare and joined to his . . .

It was the most incredible thing he'd ever seen. A wave of

fierce possession tore through him then, especially when he looked down to see them joined.

Suddenly, she bit her lip and scowled at him. "Are you growing larger inside me?"

Falcyn laughed at her question. It wasn't something they normally did.

Not unless they were extremely aroused. "Yeah. We do that sometimes." He thrust deeper inside her.

She gasped and sank her nails into his back. "I swear I can feel you all the way to my core."

He sucked his breath in at her words and the image they created. He liked to hear her speak of such things. "Can you?"

She nodded.

He pulled back, then thrust his hips against hers.

They moaned in unison.

"I'm not hurting you, am I?"

She wrinkled her nose at him. "Trust me, I'd be hurting you back if you were."

Even so, he gentled his thrusts, taking care with her, since he'd never done this with a woman before. He wasn't sure exactly how big he'd get.

"Oh that feels so good," she sighed.

His head spinning, Falcyn rolled over with them still joined. He sat her on top of him and watched her as she took over control so that he wouldn't have to worry about harming her while his body continued to expand.

Because honestly, he felt as if he was about to die from the pleasure of it. Especially when she leaned forward, whipping her pale hair over his chest while she rode him.

Her laughter rang in his ears while she nipped at his chin. "Does this make me a dragon-rider?"

He laughed, unable to believe the sound. Or that he could be so amused while having sex. "I'm yours any time you're so inclined, Lady Apollite."

His mind dazed from the feel of her naked skin sliding against his, he ran his hands over her body. "Tell me how I feel inside you."

"Hard and strong. I can even feel you pulsing here." She lowered his hand to her abdomen.

The sight of their joined hands stroking her stomach so close to the juncture of her thighs almost shattered his control. Instead, he bit his lip before he sank his hand into that mat of hair so that he could stroke her in time to her movements.

She cried out so loud that it echoed in the trees and ground herself against him in a way sublime.

Medea felt so strangely free with him. In a way she never had before. Not even with her husband. She ran her hands over the hard muscles of his chest and abdomen. It was so odd to see him lying there under her, between her spread thighs.

Her dragon.

She knew he wouldn't be like this for many. Not a dragon who hated to heel as much as this one did. It just wasn't in him.

He held her hips in his hands and guided her movements. But what held her transfixed was the bliss on his face. His cheeks were flushed, his eyes dark and unfocused.

She moaned as he ran his hands up from her hips to her breasts, where he toyed with their swollen nipples.

Had anyone ever told her she would ever sit on a full-blooded dragon like this and enjoy it, she would have called them a liar, and yet here she sat with his thick hardness inside her. And not just any dragon.

The son of Noir . . .

"What do I feel like to you, Falcyn?"

"Wet and soft."

"Have you been with an Apollite before?"

He stopped moving. "No. Why?"

She smiled at that. It made this moment all the more special to her. "I'm glad. I want this to be special between us."

Falcyn cupped her face in his hands. "Believe me, Medea, it is." He pulled her down and kissed her fiercely.

Medea trembled at the passion she tasted, at the way he teased her lips with his and twined his tongue around hers. His muscles bulged around her, making her tremble.

When he kissed her like this, she could almost believe him.

Please don't be lying to me. She'd hate to have to kill him for it. And she would kill him. Because if he was lying, she wouldn't be able to stand living with the pain of his walking away with such an awful deception.

It just wasn't in her to be that forgiving.

Not for anyone.

Falcyn pulled back from the kiss, then rolled over with her and took control again.

Medea arched her back as he moved faster. Harder. It was as if he were racing for something.

He was so large now that he was wall to wall inside her. Every stroke brought more pleasure. Every kiss and touch reverberated through her.

"Make me yours, Falcyn."

But in her heart, she knew he already had.

He claimed her lips again as he slammed himself into her even deeper than he'd been before. In that moment, she screamed out as her release came. Her body exploded with color and pleasure.

She wrapped her legs around his hips and let his passion sweep her away.

He lowered his head down to her shoulder and growled as he released himself inside her and he shuddered in her arms.

She drew a ragged breath as he collapsed on top of her and held her tight.

"Thank you, Medea," he whispered in her ear as he panted fiercely. Then, he kissed her lips again in a tender caress that sent chills through her.

He withdrew from her and rolled over onto his back and pulled her against his side.

She'd assumed he was through with her, so it surprised her when he spread her legs and touched the most private place of her body.

"What are you doing?" she asked.

"I'm claiming you the way a dragon claims his dragonswan."

"Excuse me?"

He smiled wickedly. "I've never once taken a woman as a dragon. Never found one who was woman enough for it."

That thought made her a little nervous.

"And what do you mean by that?"

"Do you trust me?"

Not really.

But . . .

Medea swallowed as his long, lean fingers delved deep into her body. She tensed a bit as they burned the tender flesh of her nether lips.

"I won't hurt you, Medea." Rising up on his knees, he pulled her back to his front and leaned her against him with her thighs spread.

Even though it wasn't natural for her to do so, she surrendered herself to him.

She felt him hardening against her buttocks as he rocked her in his arms. His breath teased her flesh while he played until she was breathless and hot.

He ran his long, tapered finger down her cleft. She shivered and jerked as every nerve ending in her body sizzled.

Cupping his hand to her, she arched her back and moaned. No longer able to speak, all she could do was feel each and every luscious stroke he gave her as he entered her body again. Only this time, something was different. He felt as if he was wrapped completely around her. As if they were truly one beast.

Who could have imagined? His breath was hot against her bared flesh as he stroked her entire body with his, inside and out.

With his head buried in the crook of her neck, he made love to her until she came again, screaming out his name.

Only then did he find his own release.

She expected him to pull away.

He didn't.

Rather, he sat back, holding her. "I can't pull out for a few minutes. Not without hurting you."

It was only then that she realized he was still swollen inside her. "That's impressive."

Closing his eyes, he hissed lightly. "Yes, you are."

Completely spent and weak, she breathed raggedly as Falcyn held her close. Medea smiled and snuggled into him, wanting to be as close as she could.

"You know, if the others stumble back on us while I'm naked, I'm slaying you, dragon."

He laughed. "You are so violent."

"And you love that about me."

"I do, actually. It's nice to be with a woman who understands my dark, happy go-to place." He kissed her, then lifted her gently from his hips. "Damn. You have the nicest ass I've ever seen." He nipped at her cheek as she rose so that she could begin redressing.

She brushed her fingers over his cheek and gave him a warm, sweet look. "You keep doing that and we'll never get out of here."

"Don't tempt me. Besides, we can't stay. We don't belong in this world. The balance would be disturbed."

That was true. One thing she knew about interdimensional travel, unless you had special permission or circumstances, you could visit, but only for a very limited time. In order to stay, you had to exchange places with someone else.

A soul for a soul.

That wasn't an easy thing to do. And if you didn't choose

or steal the soul for yourself within a specified time, the powers that be would do it—usually at the worst possible time.

That was the last thing anyone wanted, as they seldom chose the one you'd have picked. Rather they went after the one to cause you the most pain possible. Vengeful bastards, they always found a way to punish you for daring to thwart their wills.

Much like the Fates.

And the gods.

Sadness chased away her happiness with that thought while she dressed. As the gods and Fates had never once allowed her any kind of peace or real happiness. They seemed to take a perverse pleasure in ripping it away from her.

Tears choked her as reality came crashing back and that tiny glimpse of a future she'd had just a few moments ago died horribly. There was no chance of anything with Falcyn, or anyone else.

She was an Apollite damned over a curse her father had levied against her race because of the actions of a jealous bitch-queen.

Falcyn was a dragon damned for his own birth by a jealous bitch-goddess. As the old saying went, fire and gunpowder made for a very poor and extremely short marriage.

There could never be anything for either of them, except death and misery. That was all the gods would ever allow for them. All their enemies would let them have. And between the two of them, they had a frightfully long list of creatures wanting them dead.

Drawing a ragged breath, she relegated herself to a cold,

bitter reality. To an eternity of being alone. "We have to find the others."

Falcyn nodded. "I know."

As he withdrew, she saw the strange scroll marks on his lower back that she'd missed during their earlier play. She reached out to trace the ancient black swirls. "What's this?"

He glanced at her, over his shoulder. "Symbols of healing and protection that were placed there by my brother, Hadyn."

"They're beautiful."

He nodded. "He was incredibly powerful. One of the strongest Simeon Magi ever trained. A true manslaghe." That was impressive given that a manslaghe could not only take a life, they could destroy a soul.

It was what made them some of the most dreaded breed of god-killer. More so than even the Chthonians who'd been created to police the gods themselves.

"You fought together?"

"We did." Sadness darkened his eyes. "He saved my life during the Primus Bellum."

"Which side did you fight for?"

"It wasn't so much a side I fought for, as a person I fought with." He pulled his shirt over his head. "I served with the Sephirii. Protected their commander."

She paused while dressing to gape at him. Surely he was kidding. . . . "Jared? You protected *that* bastard?"

"No. Before him. His mother. Myone." A tic started in his jaw as if he shared her anger for Jared's behavior.

And when he spoke, she realized that he did, indeed,

understand why she harbored so much hatred for the former Sephiroth warrior. "I was there when Jared turned on his army and led them to slaughter. Whatever you did to him while your mother held him for Artemis, I don't care. As far as I'm concerned, he deserved it. I know he thinks he had a noble reason for his actions, but I can't forgive it. All I can say is that I'm glad his mother was dead at the time. It would have broken her heart to see him betray his oath."

"You're one of the few who feels that way."

"Because I was there for it. I saw the carnage." He fastened his pants. "There's so much I hate the gods for."

"Believe me, I resemble your pain."

Falcyn moved to her side so that he could brush his fingers through her hair. "I will help your parents. Not because of what we did just now. But because I'm tired of watching the gods destroy lives for no reason."

"Thank you."

He inclined his head to her. "No problem. You just have to find a way to get us out of here so that I can get to them."

"Well, that's easier said than . . ." Medea paused in her sentence as a strange sensation went through her body. Like someone or something had squeezed her soul. It was the most peculiar thing.

A deep, dark ache set in. One that made her strangely depressed and exhausted.

"Medea?"

"I'm so tired, all of a sudden. Can barely keep my eyes open." She sat down to finish dressing. "Just overwhelmed, I

guess. There's so much to do. I don't even know where to start."
Her heart sank at the thought of what lay ahead for them.
"What if we can't get to them in time? What if it's too late?"

"It's not."

"What if it is? What if we're underestimating Kessar and
Apollo? He's a god, you know. . . . How can we hope to fight
that?" She rubbed at her forehead as tears choked her.

Falcyn went cold as he saw a movement in the shadows to
his left. Something wasn't right and he had a bad, bad feeling
that he knew what it was.

"Medea? Look at me."

She did.

Cupping her chin in his hand, he studied her dark eyes. Her
pupils were a bit dilated. She had a funny glaze over them as
she continued to lament their situation.

Shit . . .

"Did you sit in a shadow?"

"What?" She frowned at him.

"Did one of the shadows get you? You're whining, and
that's not the psychotic Daimon I know so well. I'm thinking
you got hit by one of the SODs."

Her eyes were filled with uncharacteristic despair. "How
would I know? Oh, what does it matter? We're doomed anyway. Even if we succeed, we'll fail."

Oh yeah, that had SOD all over it.

"Dee . . . stay with me."

"I'm not going anywhere. Why bother? It's all useless, anyway."

Growling low in his throat, Falcyn tried to think of some way to get her back to normal.

It was hopeless. Like she said. Everything they did turned to shit.

Ah crap . . .

He now had it, too.

10

This was so bad, and on so many levels. Falcyn turned around slowly as he tried to think of how to combat the SODs. But like Medea, he felt an overwhelming sense of doubt in his abilities to do anything at all, and the ultimate despair.

Never had he known such.

I am drakomai!

Yeah, so what? So are a lot of dragons. . . .

What makes you a special snowflake?

He had to drive this shit out of his head

before he went mad from it. And from the depth of that madness, there was only one place he could think to go.

"Medea?"

She glanced up at him. "I hate this feeling, dragonfly. How do you fight it? I want something external that I can kill!"

So did he. This was so insidious. Like a madness eating away at his will and desires. He was so tired from it. As if a weight pressed down on not only his will, but his entire body.

He needed Blaise or Brandor to explain to him what the mortal enemy of these bastards would be so that they could use it against them and end this. "Everything has a weakness. We can find theirs."

"How? We can't even see them. It's hopeless. Impossible. We'll never win."

In that moment, he hated his brother Max more than he ever had before. Why? Because the next words out of his mouth came straight from his brother and he knew it. He could practically hear Max's voice over his own as he spoke the dreadful happy words that sickened him. "Nothing's ever hopeless."

Yeah, he wished he was back at Sanctuary so that he could beat the utter shit out of that ever-optimistic bastard.

How he hated Mr. Merry Sunshine.

As bad as Max had been before these past few weeks, he was twice as awful and sanctimonious now that he had his dragonswan and children with him. There were times when Falcyn was sure he'd puke from the saccharin overload of being around the lot of them. Only thing worse than Max was his kids and wife.

Especially that optimistic son Seraphina had dared to name after their brother Hadyn.

Dear gods, it was like someone had cloned Max.

He shuddered. And Hadyn would shit a brick to meet his happy Opie Taylor–acting namesake.

With a sneer, Falcyn tried to wipe the ick off physically with his hands, but it was no use. No matter how much he scratched at his skin or rubbed it, the sensation remained. "What drives away doubt?"

"Confidence," Medea said. "A leap of faith. Sledgehammer to the face of whoever made you doubt yourself. Personally, I like the latter."

He laughed at her surly tone and words that rang home to him, as he'd like nothing better.

Then he sobered. "That's it!"

"What? I get to sledgehammer someone? I'm game if you are. Just point the bastard out."

He quirked a grin at her sudden happiness and what had caused it. "As long as you're naked, you can sledgehammer *me* all you want."

She rolled her eyes at him and snorted. "Is that really your solution?"

"No, but now I have an image of you naked on top of me again and I completely forgot my original train of thought."

"Seriously?"

"Sadly, yes. You're terribly distracting to me. What was I saying?"

"Oh my God, Falcyn! Really?"

Screwing his face up, he groaned. "Yeah. Where was I going a minute ago? I seem to have lost my way in the deep valley of your shirt plunging between your breasts."

She popped him lightly on his stomach. "We were talking about driving away doubt. Remember? I said confidence and leaps of faith."

"Oh yeah . . . yeah! Had a thought about that. Leaps of Faith. You know?"

Medea scowled at him. He said that as if she should understand some arcane meaning behind that phrase. But it meant nothing to her. "Yeah? Okay . . ."

He deflated before her eyes, and shook his head. "I keep forgetting you're an Apollite. With no real experience among the fey."

"Sorry. We're not on their party lists."

"Trust me, you're better off. Last time they came out to play with your people, they made the Were-Hunter race."

She scoffed at his oversimplification of that major historical event. "Dagon wasn't a fey creature. And I do believe, as a Sumerian god, he'd be highly offended at your categorizing him as such."

"True. But as his brother, I'm morally obligated to bust his chops every chance I get. Which he'd appreciate if he were here and would return said insult with gusto. And probably a punch or god-bolt."

Her jaw dropped at something she'd been completely unaware of. "You're not really his brother, are you?"

"I am, indeed. Half, anyway. His mother's Hekate. But we share the same piece-of-shit sperm donor."

"Is that why he joined the Sumerian pantheon?"

"That was mostly a bad bout of teenage rebellion . . . or, more to the point, a bout of midlife crisis for a god." Falcyn paused to consider it. "Or maybe, given his current extreme old age, it would best be considered a prepubescent tantrum?"

She laughed at the way he summarized things. The dragon had a unique phrasing and perspective. "You have an interesting family tree."

"Says the woman related to Apollo and the king of the Daimons."

"And you're off point again. . . . I've noticed that you tend to do that. A lot." She gestured at the trees around them. "Leaps of faith? Where were you going with that?"

"Oh yeah. Sorry. Faith is a modern word for *fey*. And 'leaps of fey' was once a slang term for fresh, running water gathered in a stream, as opposed to a well."

"Okay . . ." She still had no idea where he was going with that.

"I'm thinking if we gather some, we can use it to get rid of them."

Ah! That made sense. Running water was often used to chase away malevolent spirits. Hence the propensity of throwing holy water for exorcisms. And why some paranormal species couldn't cross streams or rivers. "It's worth a shot."

"It's what I'm thinking."

"But what if we don't find any?" She sighed heavily. "What if it doesn't work? What if it's hopeless and we're stuck like this forever?"

He growled deep in his throat. "You're doubting me?"

Medea gave him a no-duh stare. "I'm possessed by the spirits of doubt. You think? Of course I'm doubting you. And thanks for this wonderful experience, by the way! So much better than a trip to Disneyland. I can't believe I left home for this."

He let out a "heh" at her continued sarcasm. "Just help me find some fey water."

"That doesn't explode when we touch it."

"Exactly."

Sighing, she followed him as they looked for a stream or brook. "I guess I should be grateful, all things considered."

"How so?" Falcyn asked.

She pointed up at the dim, gray sky. "At least I'm not bursting into flames in the daylight."

He drew up short at her words. "Do that a lot, do you?"

"Well, I was banned from it as a girl. After Apollo made his curse."

"But not anymore?"

"That demon blood you smelled in me?"

He nodded.

"It allows me to tap into their powers and shields me from his curse. With it, I can walk in daylight. Not for long. Just enough that it leaves me with a nasty sunburn and no exploding flesh. And I'm completely immune from his curse in other realms, like this one." She crossed her arms over her chest. "The demon blood at least gives me time to do some damage in the human realm to go after enemies where and when they're most vulnerable."

"You like being a villain, don't you?"

That was a no-brainer. "I played by the rules and what did it get me? A broken heart and murdered family. Busted body.

Fuck that. So yeah. I learned to harden my heart and give as good as I get. With relish."

He pulled her to a stop. "I know the feeling."

"I'm so sorry that you do. I would never have taken your son from you. Especially not like your brother did. If you want, I'll help you kick his ass."

With a tender expression, he brushed his thumb against her cheek. "And I would never have allowed the humans to harm yours, or you."

A tear fell from her eye as those sincere words singed her. "We will find your Maddor for you. You should meet him at least once in your life."

"I don't know if that's a good idea."

"That's the SOD talking."

"No. It's common sense talking. I'm sure he hates me for what my brother did to him. Hates me for not finding him sooner." He drew his brows together in deep consternation. "You're right. That might be the SOD talking and not me."

Rising up on her toes, she kissed his cheek. "You're adorable when you blush. Uncertainty looks good on you."

Falcyn savored the gentleness of her touch. "Why are you being so kind to me?"

"I have absolutely no idea. It's really not like me. I'm usually a major bitch to everyone." She smoothed down his collar. "But something about you makes me want to leash my claws."

He fingered her ear. "Yeah. I feel the same with you. There's a calmness inside me whenever you come near. And I don't understand it. Even now. Most bring out the beast in me. But you . . . you seem to bring out only the best."

Those words made her eyes water. Even stranger, they made her feel giddy like a girl again. Something she hadn't felt in countless centuries.

More than that, he made her feel safe in a way no one ever had.

It was so peculiar. Not unwelcomed.

But strange nonetheless.

"What are you like in your dragon's form?"

"I'm sure you don't want to know. It tends to terrify the natives."

"I'll bet you're beautiful."

He laughed bitterly. "Bet you'd scream."

"Bet I wouldn't."

"Never met a woman yet who wasn't a dragon who didn't scream at the first sight of me in my real body."

She boldly stood before him, hands on hips, to face him. "You never met me."

Growling low in his throat, he felt the dragon in him rise up. The beast was hungry and fierce. He expected nothing to come of it.

Yet this time, it worked.

In the blink of an eye, he changed into his shimmering red dragon's body.

Medea stepped back. Not out of fear.

Out of respect. He was a massive, dangerous beast. Even larger than she'd ever expected. His red scales gleamed as if they held speckles of gold in their red color. Long, bright gold talons and curved tusks protruded, reminding her that he was a predator of the top order.

Indeed, his head alone was larger than her entire body.

Fearless. Breathless, she approached him until she could lay her hand on his large snout.

"You are beautiful," she breathed, stroking his cheek, beneath his large serpentine red eye. She assumed his scales would be dry and cold to touch, but rather they were soft like rose petals, and yet as hard as warm steel. "Can you understand me?"

I understand you.

She laughed out loud. "You can still talk to me?"

I can.

"This is amazing! Can I ride you?"

His deep rumble washed over her. *You already did that, Lady Apollite. I told you that I'm always at your disposal.*

She shoved playfully at his snout. "Not what I mean and you know it!"

A saddle magically appeared on his back. *Climb aboard.*

Yet the moment she started for him, the shadows came closer. At first she thought nothing of it.

Neither did Falcyn.

Not until one snatched her back and they both realized it was a SOD. Wrapping around her, it forced her away from him and covered her body.

Furious, Falcyn changed back into his human's body.

But it was too late.

The fey demon had her.

11

Furious, Falcyn attacked the shadows, but it did him no good. Not even with his god powers. Because they had no solid form for him to strike and destroy, they couldn't be killed by conventional or any other means. Rather, they disintegrated as soon as he made contact, only to reappear as quickly as they vanished. Sometimes within nanoseconds.

Over. Behind. One even tapped his shoulder, just to be an asshole.

And all the while they laughed and mocked his efforts. Which only made him angrier.

More determined to find some way to do them harm.

How dare they! He punched and twisted, trying his damnedest to end them. Or at least wring a groan from their throats.

Nothing worked.

"Falcyn!"

Suddenly, he heard Blaise's shout, along with Urian's. But he didn't acknowledge them. Or let their voices slow him down in any way. He had to keep trying to fight and scatter his attackers and reach his Daimon. Nothing mattered past freeing Medea. He was consumed with a frenzied madness to save her, and drive these bastards away.

His blood pounded in his ears. He tasted bile and sweat. One minute the shadows were consuming her and in the next, she was finally in his arms, holding him. Bringing him slowly back to sanity.

She blinked, her gaze filled with total disbelief as she reached up to place her cold fingers to his chin. "Falcyn?"

He could barely breathe as he stared down into those dark eyes. Cupping her head in his palm, he pulled her against him and held her tightly. His breath came in ragged gasps. "Are you all right?"

She glanced about as if in a daze herself. "They were trying to infiltrate my mind . . . to take me over and make me think their thoughts. It was awful! I was sure they had me."

"I know. So was I."

"How did you get me free?"

Brandor rudely cleared his throat to indicate the bottle in his hand. "I threw fey water on them to make them solid, and he beat the utter shit out of them while they were weakened. We were trying to explain to him what to do. But he didn't listen."

"He didn't need to," Blaise added with a laugh. "Apparently, you can just wail the bloody buggers out of any wet body. Good old Falcyn. There's no problem so big that it can't be solved with an adequate supply of canned whup ass."

Falcyn reluctantly let go of Medea and snorted at the uncharacteristic term from Blaise, which showed that he'd been spending way too much time at Sanctuary lately. "You know, I've never really understood that expression. Seriously. If someone says they're going to open up a can of whup ass on you, it means that someone out there is actually canning whup ass. Truth be told, that's the guy I'd be most afraid of."

Urian laughed. "Valid good point. Next time Nick or Dev uses it, I'll have to bring it up to them." He jerked his chin toward Medea. "You feeling better?"

She cast a nasty glare at Brandor as she pushed herself to her feet. Dusting herself off, she grimaced at him. "Aside from the water some thoughtless bastard slung all over me, yeah."

With an amused grin, Falcyn used his powers to create a leather jacket that he draped around her shoulders. "If it makes you feel better, you'd win the Sanctuary wet T-shirt contest, hands down."

Scoffing as she shrugged it on, she turned her grimace toward him. "Don't go there. I've been told by the Charonte demons that roasted dragon is quite tasty. With or without the barbecue sauce."

"That threat would hold more weight if you weren't an Apollite who lives solely on the blood of your own kind."

"Yes, but I still hunt and kill for sport. Never forget that."

Blaise smacked Urian on the shoulder. "And here you were afraid they'd start getting along if left unguarded. Told you, you had nothing to fear. Falcyn pisses off everyone. Even without trying. He can't help himself."

Medea grew quiet as that remark hit a little too close to home. Not that Falcyn had ticked her off.

Rather that they'd gotten along a lot more than the others would ever guess. And the seductive scent of her dragon standing so close to her right now was warming her significantly more than the leather jacket he'd conjured.

Worse was the need she had to bury her face in the crook of his neck and breathe him in. Tongue that tendon that stood out just a bit along his collarbone and sink her hand in those soft, short curls.

Tease his jawline with her fangs . . .

It was all she could do to not give in to those urges that made her entire body burn.

As if he could read her thoughts, his cheeks darkened and Falcyn quickly changed the subject.

And to her chagrin, he also took a step to the right—away from her. "My changeling powers are back," he said to Blaise. "How are yours?"

Blaise quickly shifted into his dragon form. But he didn't stay long before he returned to his human body. Yet the expression on his face said that he wasn't happy to have the ability restored. "This isn't good."

His ire baffled Medea. Surely he had to be relieved to have those powers restored. "Why not?"

"I'm thinking if we can shift it could only mean one thing. . . . We need to get to my father's castle. Fast!"

"Lead on, brother. I've got your six."

Falcyn and Blaise returned to their dragon bodies. He lowered his wing for Medea to have access to his back while Blaise allowed Brogan and Brandor to mount on him for a ride.

The moment Medea slid into place, she felt Falcyn's sharp intake of breath as he shuddered between her spread thighs. Worse was the wave of desire that reverberated through her entire being. She quickly glanced to the others to make sure they didn't see it, and over her shoulder to ensure her brother hadn't picked up on it.

Luckily, no one seemed to notice. Yet her cheeks heated up anyway. It was so uncomfortable to know what thoughts were in her head and in Falcyn's. And she hated the power he had over her. Hated how little control she had where her dragon was concerned. Especially when he lifted the edge of his wing up to brush her face and she caught the heated look in those serpentine eyes.

Yeah, no missing *that*. Or the rumble that preceded a bit of fire that came out of his mouth before he stood up in all his dragon glory.

Unaware of where her wayward thoughts kept drifting, Urian situated himself behind her in the saddle while Brogan took up Blaise's reins.

Once everyone was secured, they took flight over the not-so-fun enchanted forest.

Medea quickly learned that she wasn't keen on air travel. At all. In fact, she loathed it with every molecule of her being. The only thing that made it tolerable was that Urian kept her anchored from behind while Falcyn flew low to the ground as soon as he realized how scared she was to be in his leather saddle.

She truly didn't care for this at all, and kept a death grip on his spiny ridges. How could anyone stand flying like this?

I won't hurt you.

She stroked the scales on his neck and projected her own thoughts to him. *I know. But I'd still rather have my feet safely on the ground.*

She was no dragon-rider, after all. At least, not in this manner. How anyone could ride them into battle and fight, she couldn't imagine. The rocking sensation combined with the dipping and rising, and the rushing wind, was nauseating her.

But luckily, it was only a matter of minutes before she saw the bright crystal castle that floated above the tree line, turning in a slow circle. Without a doubt, she knew this was where Emrys Merlin made his home. And as soon as it came into focus, it was obvious that something horrible had happened here.

Blaise had been right.

Tendrils of gray smoke rose up from the blackened towers. Animals and demons lay slaughtered about on the road, leading from the forest toward the cleared grounds and meadows. There had to be a thousand rooks lying on the ground in a twisted, macabre display.

The drawbridge yawned open to show a bright, gilded hall that gleamed in the dim light. Yet for all the ostentatious wealth, it wasn't inviting.

It was insidious against the blood-laden landscape. As was

the quiet that reverberated and was broken only by the sound of the dragons' flapping wings.

Blaise turned green as they surveyed the damage. "Who would dare attack?"

"Morgen, maybe?" Brandor suggested.

"No." Brogan's eyes glowed bright in the dimly lit mist. "Not even she would dare attack Nimue. Never mind Merlin. Not here in their stronghold."

"She's right," Blaise agreed. "Besides, there would be gargoyles, Adoni, and mandrakes among the dead had Morgen battled here. She isn't humane enough to see to the dead. She'd have left them wherever they fell."

After landing in a small clearing and making sure his passengers were safe, Blaise took off running across the narrow bridge that was suspended over a deep, dangerous ravine. Brogan and Brandor stayed back to check the bodies for life signs while Falcyn landed and helped Urian and Medea to dismount.

Urian went to help them.

Falcyn shifted back into his human body and rushed after Blaise, knowing what he'd find and that his mandrake kin would need comfort when he did. The fact that Blaise didn't even think to teleport said it all about how upset the poor boy was. He wasn't thinking straight.

Only feeling the pain of loss and despair.

And Falcyn knew the moment Blaise found their bodies. His anguished bellow echoed through the burned-out Great Hall, and made Falcyn's stomach clench tight. Never had he heard a more sorrowful sound. One that held the betrayal of the ages. He wanted to cry for him.

More than that, he wanted to ease the pain and knew there was no way to soothe what he heard. No words could undo this. No magick.

By the time Falcyn got there, Blaise was on his knees, cradling Emrys's body in his arms. He winced at the sight of them entwined, at the way Blaise wept while he held the man he considered his father. But what hurt most was the knowledge that his own blood would never mourn for him to that depth.

Yet Falcyn would be far more devastated if something ever happened to Blaise. That he'd been even more inconsolable after Max had divided him from Maddor. And that was what burned so deep right now.

He'd cried those tears for thousands of years. Had howled and cursed for his son, while his soul and heart had bled from a wound that no amount of anything could heal.

Damn them all for this!

Regretting his past more than ever before, he forced himself to kneel by Blaise's side and hold him. "I'm sorry."

"How can he be dead?" Blaise choked on the words. "He was so powerful."

Falcyn had no idea. But even the gods could fall. All it took was one misstep. One enemy more lethal. He glanced around at the destruction. From the remnants and smears of blood all around, it was obvious that Emrys had put up a vicious fight for his life. "Where's Nimue?"

That succeeded in distracting Blaise.

"She would never leave him to battle on his own." He laid Emrys down gently on the stone floor, then moved to search the room. "Nimue?"

They looked about for her body. There was no sign of her anywhere.

Until Falcyn heard a soft moan off in the distance.

Together, they ran to the small courtyard in the back. At first, they saw nothing. But then Falcyn realized that the light on the far wall wasn't really a light.

Nor was it a shadow.

It was Nimue encased in the wall. She appeared as a textured painting, or a thick fresco.

What the hell?

Scowling, Blaise went to stand before her faded image. "Nimue? Can you hear me?"

Opening her eyes, she choked as she saw the two of them. Blood dripped from the corner of her mouth. *I hear you, but I'm dying.* Her lips didn't move at all. For all intents and purposes, she appeared lifeless already.

"What happened?" Blaise ran his hand over her stony arm and sleeve as if seeking a way to break through whatever magick held her trapped in the wall.

Gallu came. We weren't strong enough to fight them. They wielded some form of magick we've never seen before. Something older than Merlin knew.

"No!"

A tear ran from the corner of her eye and froze halfway down her cheek to become a solid pebble on the wall. *Listen to me, Blaise. Merlin loved you . . . as do I. You were always considered as his true son. Just as Arthur. Now we need you to pull the stone from his ring and use it to free the dragons Morgen imprisoned beneath her castle.*

"I don't understand."

The dragon's breath of Camelot? It's made by them. The real dragons of old. The ones she used to make the mandrakes. If they are left unguarded, she can awaken them now that he's dead, and enslave them for her battles. Emrys is no longer here to protect them from her or to keep her from using them in her army. You must do this for him, otherwise the world of Man will crumble and all we have sacrificed for will be for naught.

"Why didn't he free the dragons?"

They would have killed him for what he did to them. He didn't dare risk their wrath. Please, dearest! You must . . . Her voice trailed off as she expelled one deep breath and froze completely.

"Nimue!" Blaise shouted, pounding his fist against the wall.

It was too late.

She was gone.

Falcyn shook his head. "She wants us to free a bunch of pissed-off dragons? Awesome."

Blaise didn't comment. He stood completely still as if he were catatonic from the loss, and that made Falcyn feel like a total insensitive shit. Wanting to comfort him, he reached out and pulled him into his arms.

The fact that Blaise didn't protest his hug told him exactly how much pain Blaise was in. In fact, he laid his head on his shoulder like a child—something he'd never done before.

Fisting his hand in Blaise's white hair, Falcyn held him with a knot in his stomach as he resented every year Igraine and Narishka had stolen from him and his child and grandchild. Damn them to hell for this. He should have been there for Maddor and

Blaise. Neither should have ever known a moment of mockery. A moment of pain. He'd have beaten the hell out of anyone who'd harmed them.

And damn Max for it all. . . .

It was so unfair. Closing his eyes, he felt his god powers surging in a way they hadn't done in centuries. Dormant powers he'd let atrophy because he hadn't cared what happened to himself. Hadn't cared what happened to the world or to Max. Everything he'd loved had been taken and so he'd learned to live in the state of Fuck It All.

Now, he felt a bitter rebirth as old emotions were awakened inside him.

Not with a gentle touch. But with an acid drenching.

And there was nothing he could do to stop it.

Medea froze as she came into the room and saw the anguish on Falcyn's face and the way he held on to Blaise. She blocked the door to give them privacy as the others started to enter the hall. They both needed this. Blaise to grieve and Falcyn to hold his child for the first time in his life.

It was several minutes before Blaise pulled away and wiped at his eyes.

"You okay?" Falcyn's voice was barely audible.

Blaise nodded as he cleared his throat. He blushed the minute he realized Medea was there and that she'd seen his weakness.

Wanting to comfort him, she walked over and kissed his cheek. "I would never judge you."

"Thank you." He went to join the others, who were finally coming into the ancient hall.

Her own eyes moist, she reached up to brush her hand through Falcyn's hair. "Are *you* okay?"

"I'm always fine."

"You really think I'm going to buy that bullshit?"

His facade cracked. A sudden light flickered deep in his eyes that betrayed his divine birth, and it sent a shiver over her. How odd. She knew the powerful origins of her father and grandfather. Yet neither of them had ever scared her.

But right here. Right now . . .

Falcyn did.

This wasn't the gentle dragon who'd made love to her. This was the ancient war god Veles that the fiercest ancient warriors had made blood sacrifices to before leading their armies into battle.

Something about him had changed in the last few minutes. He was a very different beast.

Even stronger than before.

More fierce.

Medea swallowed hard. "What is in your head?"

"That no one hurts my grandson like this with impunity. They want a war. . . . I'm here to give it."

Smoke actually came out of his nostrils.

Oh yeah, Kessar had awakened a sleeping beast in Falcyn. She arched a brow at that. "Nice trick."

"I don't scare you at all, do I?"

More than he'd believe. And a lot more than she was comfortable with.

"I command demons and corralled and held the Sephiroth

for thousands of years. What can I say? It takes a lot." But honestly, he did. She just wasn't the kind of person to ever admit it out loud. That knowledge gave too much power to others over her and that was one thing she'd never do.

Not for anything.

Without another word, Falcyn followed after Blaise.

Unnerved, she stayed back to watch. There was something eerie in the air. It left the hair on the back of her neck prickling her skin. Goose bumps ran along her arms.

Shivering, she glanced around the room. If she didn't know better, she'd swear someone or something was watching her. Not wanting any part of it, she rushed to follow Blaise and Falcyn to Brandor and Brogan.

They were all gathered over Emrys's body.

"How can this stone free the dragons?" Urian cocked his head to stare at it.

"I don't know." Blaise pulled the ring gently from the man's hand.

Which was so strange to Medea, as she realized how much younger Emrys Merlin had been than Blaise. "How is he your father when it's obvious you're at least ten years older?"

Blaise let out a sad laugh. "He aged backwards."

"Seriously?"

Nodding, he smiled. "Both he and Nimue. It was a spell."

"Damn . . . I need that magick. Any chance you know it?"

"Sorry, Dee. If I did, I'd sell it to Lancôme and retire on an island like Savitar."

Falcyn snorted. "Having been retired in such a manner I can

tell you not to bother. Some asshole always turns up, wanting a favor. Usually when you're at your most zen . . . or naked."

Now that was intriguing. "Spend a lot of time naked, do you?" Medea arched her brow to warn him he'd best be careful with that answer.

He grinned at her. "Only in my natural dragon body. Hard to find clothes that fit."

Rolling her eyes, she shook her head. "You're such a goof."

"I'm a goof? You're the one asking for aging cream when you don't age."

"Yeah, but I can sell it to the humans and make a killing."

Falcyn gave her a gimlet stare. "That Daimon humor?"

"Kind of."

"Har . . . har." His voice dripped with his sarcasm.

Blaise slid Merlin's ring onto his hand, then lifted his body and carried it to where Nimue was trapped in the wall.

Silently and reverently, he used his powers to place his father into the wall beside her. As soon as Merlin was a sketching like Nimue, his image reached across and took Nimue's hand into his. Then, expelling a breath, he settled into the wall and turned pale.

With a ragged breath, Blaise splayed his hand over his father's image. "They might have fought constantly, but they loved each other more than anything. I couldn't let them be apart. Not even in death."

Falcyn patted him on the back as he looked at the two serene frescoes. "They appreciate it."

A single tear slipped past Blaise's control to slide down his cheek. Without a word, he wiped it away. "I want Kessar's heart in my fist."

"I will hand it to you myself." Falcyn's eyes burned with his fury as he made his promise.

Medea cleared her throat gently to get their attention. "I don't mean to intrude, but I do have one question. . . . With them gone . . . how do we get out of here?"

They're in Val Sans Retour."

Narishka froze midstep at the last thing she expected to hear. "Pardon?"

The Adoni warrior who'd been serving her for centuries shifted nervously as he rethought his report. He actually took a step back into his two-man armed escort in the narrow hallway that was lit by the glowing entrails of the gutted demons who'd displeased the mistress they served. As soon as they parted and he collided with the wall, he grimaced and swallowed hard. "I heard it from the Sylph queen myself. They entered her realm a short time ago. A mandrake, a dragon, an Apollite, a Deathseer, and a man whose powers they couldn't identify. Apparently, they've befriended Brevalaer."

She cursed Morgen's lack of foresight for banishing her toy right into Emrys's treacherous hands. "A Deathseer, you say?"

"Aye, my lady."

That could only be the whore's sister that he'd been forever droning and whining about.

"Now there's a face for radio. Who pissed in your Wheaties, Narishka?"

Narishka turned a cold, harsh stare from the Adoni before her to the exceptionally tall blond man approaching them. Dressed in green and gold armor like the three Adoni who'd been reporting to her, Arador Pendragon still carried himself as a thief, and spoke in a peasant's vernacular. As Morgen's latest paramour and the king of her fey court and Circle, he thought himself the most lethal and capable warrior in all the world.

But he paled in comparison to the once-great Kerrigan, who'd ruled here before him. And not just because Kerrigan was the keeper of the sword Caliburn.

Nay, there had been much about Kerrigan's dark powers that few surpassed. And no one could touch the skills of her own treacherous son, Varian duFey. While Arador's merlin powers were impressive, they had a long, long way to go before he could ever begin to challenge some of the more ferocious members of the Lords of Avalon who opposed them.

Or her.

While she might not possess Arador's Stone of Taranis that could enchant any blade it touched and coat it with a poison so lethal it would bring instant death to anyone it scratched, she was no less dangerous. Indeed, she'd laid many men and women in their graves with a single kiss.

And a knife to their gullets.

Giving him a bow that galled her to the core of her being, she offered him a cold smile. "I didn't realize you'd returned . . . Majesty."

"Careful. That lack of vigilance here could cost you. Your beauty. Your position." He paused and raked a cool smirk over her body. "Your life."

She narrowed her gaze on him as that threat made her seethe. Yet she refused to let him know it. Instead, she smiled as if his words didn't bother her in the least. Because while they angered her, she didn't see him as a threat. No more than one would a buzzing gnat. "So what brings our king to our counsel?"

"Morgen summoned me."

"Ah."

"What's that supposed to mean?" Unlike her, he didn't have the wisdom to keep the anger from his tone.

She bit back a true smile. What it meant was that he was nowhere near the man Kerrigan had been. That rank bastard had never come at Morgen's behest. Rather, he'd driven her niece to distraction with his endless defiance. And it was one of the reasons why Kerrigan had lasted longer than any other in his reign here.

But Narishka had no interest in helping Arador hold on to his power. Not when it was in her best interest to dethrone Arador before he learned any more of his merlin's skills and grew strong enough to strike out at them. " 'Tis naught. You'll find her in her bedchamber with Apollo."

A strange light came into his eyes before he swept past her. "Arador?"

He paused to glance at her.

"To answer your question . . . yes, Apollo would love a threesome, and Morgen wouldn't mind it either."

His face went stark white. "How did you know what I was thinking?"

"You have your skills. I have mine." And he should *never*

underestimate hers. "Now, run along. Morgen doesn't like to be kept waiting."

Turning, he headed off.

The moment he was out of sight, she grabbed the Adoni knight behind her and snatched him closer so that she could whisper in his ear. "Fetch me Maddor. I don't care what whore you have to pry him off, bring him to me within the quarter hour or it's your balls I'll be dining on!" She shoved him away from her. "I'll be awaiting him in the study."

With those words spoken, she went to gather her own agents to plan her strategy for this next round.

The Adoni turned on his companions with a hiss. "You heard her! Fetch the mandrake!"

"Fuck you." Varian duFey slid his knife straight into the lung of the bastard in front of him and held him upright until he stopped struggling. Only then did he use his powers to remove all traces of the fey's existence.

"Damn, V. That's so cold."

Wiping the blood off on the sleeve of his jerkin, he sneered at his hellhound companion. "Oh, like you wouldn't have bitten his throat out, then licked your own balls."

"Probably the former, but never the latter. Too many others willing to do that for me." Kaziel grinned at him. "At any rate, killing an Adoni on an errand for your mother seems a bit reckless when we're supposed to be keeping a low profile. And to think, Aeron and Nick accuse *me* of being rash."

"You are rash, my friend. So rash, it's actually creeping down your neck."

"Those are the hives I get from being this close to you when you're doing something profoundly stupid." Kaziel glanced down the hallway to make sure no one else was around. "Damn shame to be this near to your mother and she didn't recognize you."

"You've no idea. But I wouldn't put anything past her. The main thing for now is that we find Blaise and let him and Emrys know what's going on. You take Beau and find them."

Kaziel hesitated. "What about you?"

"We still need more information for *our* Merlin. I'm after Maddor to see why my mother was so insistent on him. That's not like her. Which means there's something peculiar there, and I intend to find out what."

Kaziel inclined his head to him. As he started away, Varian grabbed his wrist and pulled him into a dark alcove.

They'd barely vanished into the curtained shadows before Morgen's two newest paramours came down the hallway, grumbling.

"I wish Brevalaer was still here. No one else can handle her when she's in this foul a mood. How did he manage it for so long?"

"Brevalaer? How did Kerrigan? I swear I can barely walk."

They paused right in front of their hiding spot so that they could examine each other. "You don't think we're infected, do you?"

The dark-haired Adoni bit his lip. "I hope not. They're feeding the infected to the gallu."

Cursing, they went on their way.

Varian didn't move for several heartbeats as he digested that news. "Morgen's working with the gallu? Why?"

"No idea. But I'm sure nothing good can come of it."

Something cold brushed against Varian. Quicker than he could think, he drew his dagger and lunged.

The shadow beside him solidified into a man who quickly disarmed him, and tsked. "Careful, coz. I require dinner before someone daggers me."

He rolled his eyes at the shadowborn demon. Just above average height and well built, Shadow had eyes of steel. And like his very soul, his shoulder-length hair that he wore pulled back into a short ponytail was neither light nor dark, but strands of varying shades that were trapped squarely between his two dueling natures. The man was fearless as a rule, hence his personal motto that he feared no evil, for he was the most evil thing that stalked the darkness and called the deadliest night home. "Careful, demon. You tread on treacherous ground to be sneaking up on me."

"Sorry about that, but your Merlin sent me to you with news. Emrys and Nimue have fallen."

Varian gasped at the last thing he'd expected to hear. "What do you mean?"

"Apollo bid his demons assault them. He's closing the noose around the dragons, trying to get to the dragonstone first. Meanwhile, you have to get the tablet from Morgen before she finds Falcyn's stone and resurrects Mordred. Otherwise, all is lost."

"That's what I was trying to do when you rudely barged in."

Shadow growled at him. "And saved your life. Let's not forget the good part."

"Are you done harassing me?"

"Not even close." He flashed a cocky grin at Varian. "She also wants you to hand over a portal key."

Varian laughed. Until he realized it wasn't a joke. "Is Merlin crazy?" Without a key, he'd be trapped here.

"Probably. She has been inhaling fumes again in her library. However, without Emrys around, the dragon and crew are stuck in the Valley and they have no way to walk through the portals, back to their world. She wants me to escort them through and make sure they're safe."

"Can't you get them through on your own?"

He shook his head. "Shadowalkers can only pass through alone. Without a key, they'd be trapped and forced to wave at me on the other side."

"Well, that sucks."

"More than you know." Shadow held his hand out. "Give it up."

Grumbling, Varian pulled the dragon key from around his neck and handed it over. "How am I supposed to get back?"

After pocketing the key, Shadow clapped him on the arm. "Sure you'll think of something. I hear that you're good in a crisis."

"You're such a bastard."

" 'Course I am. Suckled on the tit of all evil itself."

There was never any shaming the rank demon. He thrived on insults for some unknown reason.

Disgruntled and annoyed, Varian sighed. "And here I thought you were some master thief who could steal a key from anyone you wanted."

"I can. Unfortunately, they tend to miss such an item quickly and form a search party for it. Last thing we need is them finding our comrades before us. If Falcyn's stone falls into Morgen's hands . . . it'd be as bad as her finding a way to restore the Table."

There was that.

And Varian's stomach tightened at the thought. Shadow was right and he knew it. Arthur's Round Table was just one of several divine objects that had been hidden in the mortal realm and protected by a cadre of guardians who'd sworn a blood oath to keep them out of the hands of evil. To give their lives before they allowed their sacred objects to be used for destructive means.

While they'd won Kerrigan back from Morgen's Circle, Arador and his charge still remained in her hands. The last thing they could afford was to see any more of Arthur's mortal or fey objects taken by her members.

Which also made him think of something else. "Question?"

"Not an oracle, but you're free to attempt it."

"How is it the sharoc can't detect you?" Morgen's cruel allies and spies, the sharoc were shadow fey who thrived at Camelot. Varian had a hard enough time eluding their detection whenever he ventured here on his missions. He'd never understood how Shadow managed it.

"You want secrets I'm unwilling to give." He passed a gimlet stare to Kaziel, who was being unusually quiet. "The two of you aren't the only ones with pasts you don't want disclosed." And with that, he vanished.

Kaziel crossed his arms over his chest. "You trust him?"

"I don't trust anyone, other than my wife and children, but he's never given me a specific reason not to. Why?"

"Just thinking of something Aeron always says. I'd sooner trust my enemy than a friend, as I can afford to lose an enemy. But killing a friend over betrayal burns twice as deep and thrice as long."

"Your point?"

"No point, really. Just something about that demon makes my hackles rise."

Varian couldn't agree more. "Don't worry. Like you, my bite is much worse than my bark." And he'd taken enough lives to prove it. If Shadow betrayed them, Varian would have no compunctions about laying open his throat.

Still, there was an evil presence here, and for once it wasn't his mother or Morgen.

No, this was something far more insidious. Like a blackness trying to devour the world. Like Níthöggur gnawing at the roots of Yggdrasill as he sought to free himself from his prison.

For now it was contained, but his gut said it wouldn't stay that way.

Kaziel scowled at him. "What's wrong?"

"Just a bad premonition."

"Of?"

"What the world would be like if we fail to stop Morgen and Apollo."

Morgen watched as Apollo left her bed to dress. Exceptionally tall and golden fair from the top of his blond head all the way to his toes, he was exactly what one would expect of a god.

In and out of bed.

She pouted at him. "Why are you leaving?"

"It's taking too long to round up the dragon. I don't like this delay."

She scoffed at his worried tone. "My men will handle it. They know better than to fail me."

He rinsed his mouth out and spat before he turned toward her, patting his chin dry. "And I know my son. He was ever resourceful. Not to mention that bitch he serves. Apollymi hates me with a passion. As do her two sons."

That news shocked her. "*Two* sons? I thought her one and only son was dead."

"I wish." He let out a bitter laugh. "Nay, my evil fairie queen. Not dead. Acheron is hers by birth and conception. Brought back to life by my idiot of a twin sister who wanted to fuck him, and instead screwed the rest of us by her insatiable appetite for an ex-human whore. As for Styxx, he belongs to Apollymi by adoption. To that end, you can count my son as well. Indeed, she oft mothers Stryker more than she does her own."

"Really . . ." Morgen's mind whirled with this newfound information. "Any other brats I need know about?"

He dropped the towel and reached for his pants to pull them on. "You could almost count the Malachai. He is a direct descendent of her firstborn. Granted, a thousand times removed."

Four sons for Apollymi . . .

Morgen rose up to lean against Arador, who slumbered in her bed. Worthless prick had no stamina. "Does she consider the current Malachai as one of hers?"

"Not as far as I know. Her loyalty to that end seems to have died with her original son, Monakribos."

"And what of his father? Was Kissare not supposed to be reborn so that he could return to her?"

Apollo froze in the middle of buttoning his shirt. He blinked slowly before he answered. "He was, indeed." A slow, evil grin spread across his face. "Why, Morgen, dearest evil bitchtress, I do believe you've found something."

"So he was reborn?"

Laughing, Apollo crossed the floor to her bed and pulled her naked body against his. "I don't know. But I know who will."

The Fates.

He didn't say it, but Morgen knew the answer as well as he did. Those three whores knew everything about everyone.

"And if he does live," Apollo whispered against her lips, "we will find him and gut him at her feet!"

"I don't follow. Wouldn't that be a bit anticlimatic? What's the point?"

He kissed her lips. "The point is that the goddess of all destruction and darkness has only had three weaknesses in the whole of her life. Kissare, Monakribos, and Acheron." He nipped at her lips. "Given how frigid a bitch she is, I'm willing to bet that they had more in common than just their mother."

Morgen's eyes widened as she finally understood. "You're thinking that Acheron's father is Kissare reincarnated?"

He actually drew blood from her bottom lip with his fangs as he pulled back and nodded. "It would explain so much. . . . Archon swore he would never father a child with her and he went to his nebulous state claiming Acheron wasn't his son. Had Apollymi truly loved him, she would never have ended him as she did. God knows, she suffered much to protect Kissare and their offspring."

"Then who's Acheron's real father?"

"Only Apollymi knows."

Morgen smiled at this newfound knowledge and what it signified. "And the Fates."

"If they don't, they will learn it." He gave her one last kiss, then stepped away.

She frowned at his actions. "Where are you off to?"

"To find Kessar. I have another errand for him."

12

"Shake that moneymaker, baby! You go! Make that barrier pay! Kick it! Show us more biceps! Spank it till it bleeds! C'mon, you can do it. Pound it harder! Put some muscle into it."

Aghast and irritated, Falcyn turned around to glare at Medea as she sat on the ground beside Brogan and catcalled to them while he, Urian, Blaise, and Brandor sought some way to break through the barrier. Hands on hips, he narrowed his gaze at her. "Not helpful."

Medea put her hand up to her lips before she leaned closer to Brogan to whisper rather loudly. "Neither are their attempts, but notice it doesn't stop them from trying."

Brogan laughed.

Falcyn arched a brow at their misplaced humor. And it was then he was struck by just how different the two women were. Not only because one was blond and the other a brunette. Medea was dressed in black leather, tight T-shirt and jeans, and heeled boots with an innate I'll-cut-you-for-irritating-me aura that bled from every fiber of her being. Meanwhile, Brogan was much softer with her multi green and brown shimmery gauze that floated over her brown leather. Even though she was a powerful kerling with the abilities of a Deathseer, there was an air about her of serene gentleness.

How sick of him that he preferred Medea's rough fire and spirit to Brogran's much more subdued and quiet nature.

Yeah, he felt nothing for the kerling, but one look at Medea was enough to make him hard and aching for another taste of her lush, full curves.

Even while she insulted him in front of everyone.

"Instead of heckling, woman, you could try helping."

She flashed a grin to expose a hint of fang that for some insane reason he found adorable. "I am helping. I'm giving you encouragement, dragonfly."

His jaw out of joint, he turned toward Urian. "Would you consider *this* encouraging?"

"Coming from my sister? Yeah. She's not throwing things at you or directly insulting us and our parentage. Hell of an improvement, if you ask me. Makes me wonder what you've done to her that she actually located some semblance of humor and good nature."

Medea shot a blast at Urian, who deftly dodged it and laughed before returning it with one of his own.

"Hey!" Falcyn snapped, shoving Urian aside. "Play nice! You hurt your sister and I'll fry your ass. Ash or no Ash."

Medea righted herself from where she'd dived to miss Urian's blast. "You tell him, sweet cheeks."

Urian scowled. "Is she drunk?" He glanced back at Blaise and Brandor. "What did you throw on her again?"

"Water." Brandor wiped at his brow.

Medea scoffed. "I'm fine. We're just enjoying the sight of male stubbornness at its prime best, and wondering at what point the lot of you will cede defeat to the Penmerlin's shield." She glanced over to Brogan. "How long have they been pounding this poor defenseless shell now?"

"At least an hour." Brogan wrinkled her nose.

Blaise shot a sudden blast at it that ricocheted and hit Brandor squarely in the chest. The blast knocked him back fifteen feet and sent him head over heels until he landed on his side, in a smoking heap.

Medea burst out laughing again.

With a groan, he pushed himself into a seated position to glare at Blaise. "Really, mandrake? Really?"

Squeaking in fear for her brother, Brogan scrambled to her feet to check on Brandor and to make sure he didn't attack Blaise out of anger over his indignity.

Medea opened her mouth and rubbed her thumb against

her fang. "You know, Falcyn, I think that puts the wall over for bonus points on all your sorry hides."

"At least we're doing something. You could try your hand at it, you know?"

"Why? It's obviously not budging. If sheer force of will could open it, I'd give it to you and it would have surrendered ten hours ago."

"*One* hour ago."

"Tomato. Tahmahto." Leaning on her side, she propped her head on her hand and rested her other arm in the hollow of her narrow waist. "I should go ahead and take a nap while the lot of you waste your time."

He wasn't sure if it was the words or her new position, but right then a nap was the last thing he could think about.

Medea naked under him . . .

Yeah, that image was vivid and sharp. And it made his pants uncomfortably tight in the crotch.

Even more agitated, he turned his back to her and considered kicking the shield. It wouldn't do any good, but at this point, he'd be willing to throw a shoe just to get some satisfaction from the aggravating bastard thing.

At least that was his thought until a sharp light almost blinded him.

Summoning his dragonfyre, he was about to release it when the shadow took the form of a man he knew well.

One he trusted not at all.

The moment he saw the glow engulfing Falcyn's hand, Shadow drew up short and set fire to his own hands as if to retaliate. "Whoa, dragon! Down, boy!"

"What are you doing here?"

After allowing the fire in his hands to go out, Shadow tugged one of the three amulets he wore about his neck over his head. "I have a present for you." As he spoke those words, another form appeared by Shadow's side.

Since Shadow didn't react to the peculiar gargoyle with him, Falcyn assumed they must be allies as Shadow tolerated few to stand that far back in his peripheral where they might attack unseen. Especially since the gargoyle stayed back and crossed his arms over his muscled chest as if content to wait for them to finish their business.

Yeah, they were definitely allies of some sort.

"It's a portal key," Blaise said instantly. "I can feel it on him."

"The mandrake would be correct. Varian sent me to escort the lot of you out of here."

"We need to get back to Sanctuary." Medea rose to her feet. "We've wasted enough time."

"First we have to free the dragons at Camelot," Blaise reminded her.

Medea rolled her eyes. "They're statues, right? Been that way for centuries. What's a few more days? Meanwhile my people are dying even as we speak. We need to save them!"

Blaise approached her with angry strides. The fact that he could walk so assuredly while blind amazed Falcyn. It always had. Yet he stopped right in front of her so that he could speak in sharp staccato beats. "If Morgen frees the dragons, she'll tear through your Daimons. They'll die anyway."

"And Falcyn's sister is among those being held at Camelot.

She'll be the first Morgen will slaughter should she wake her. Would you condemn her, too?"

Falcyn arched a brow at Brandor's unexpected disclosure. He'd had no idea that Xyn was one of the dragons frozen beneath Camelot. And it stunned him that the fey courtesan would know of her presence there when he'd just learned it.

Shadow frowned as he listened to them arguing. After a second round of their escalating pitches, he whistled. "While this argument is really unamusing and unproductive, and I couldn't care less about the outcome, I feel obligated to mention something you might find interesting." He waited until all of them were facing him before he spoke again. "Why would Morgen summon Maddor for *this*? Seems a massive waste of his talents, if you ask me."

Falcyn felt the color drain from his face. "What delusions are you suffering?"

"No delusions, friend. Right before I left, they sent a guard after him. Knowing her, it wasn't for coffee or tea, or for an afternoon snack. While he does bear some similar characteristics with her past lovers"—he cut a meaningful glance to Brandor— "he's not her usual fare, and she normally keeps him on a short leash, at a long distance from her, as he hates the bitch with a desperate passion and is likely to tear out her throat one day. But neither of us could figure out why she'd want him. She usually only calls him out for war."

Medea cursed under her breath as a bad feeling went through her. Only one thing came to mind.

And the moment she met Falcyn's steely gaze, she knew he

held the same dreaded thought she did. "They're planning to use him to lure you, aren't they?"

Falcyn nodded. "He's walking into a trap."

By the expression on his face, she knew the pain in his heart. And what she needed to do.

"Urian?" She pulled the ring from her pinkie and held it out to him. "Go to Davyn and make sure he's all right. Tell him I'll be there with the dragonstone as soon as I can. Please keep him safe for me."

Falcyn gave her a puzzled stare. "What are you doing?"

"I'm not about to let you walk into that nightmare without someone at your back. God or whatever you are, you'll still need some support you can count on."

"What about your people?"

"They're not my son. But Maddor is yours." Tears blurred her vision. "For *that,* we march to hell itself."

His expression softened into the tenderest look imaginable. One that tugged at her heart. In two strides, he moved to stand before her and pulled her against him for the hottest kiss she'd ever known.

And when he pulled back, she saw the first spark of love in his eyes as he cradled her face in his calloused hands. He didn't say the words, but she knew what the softening in his eyes meant. It was the same look Evander had given her so many centuries before. One she'd missed so much that for a moment, it almost broke her, as she'd never, ever thought to have another man look at her like this. To feel the sudden primal rush through her body that wanted her to hold him safe and keep him close.

Forevermore.

With one ragged breath, she shoved her tender emotions aside and forced herself to remember her anger that kept her strong.

This was about blood. And oaths.

Family.

Today, they would fight. Tomorrow, she would feel.

Brandor cleared his throat as he nudged Urian. "I'm thinking they didn't just get lost in those woods."

"Yeah . . ." Urian dragged the word out. "Wondering if I should kick dragon ass now, or later."

Medea nipped Falcyn's chin, then turned to her brother. "Lay one finger on my dragonfly, brother, and you'll be missing vital body parts."

Urian snorted. "Not much of a threat, seeing how I never use them, anyway."

Medea frowned as she faced Shadow. "Do I know you?"

"No."

And still she had a strange sensation that they'd met somewhere. That she'd seen him. Something about him was unbelievably familiar.

She just didn't know what.

Falcyn stepped around her. "Shadow, get Urian back to Sanctuary. We'll—"

"Ah, no," Urian said, interrupting him. "We stay together."

Shadow exchanged a less-than-amused stare with his gargoyle. "Oh yeah, 'cause a large, unfamiliar motley group sneaking through Camelot would *never* get noticed. By anyone. Or get reported to Morgen and her bitches. Sounds like a great suicide plan to me. So glad Varian volunteered me for this happy venture into torture and hell. Bastard fey rat that he is!"

"Don't insult my father like that."

They all gaped at the indignant gargoyle.

The gargoyle glanced around them and their shocked expressions. "Well, obviously I'm adopted. While my father might have questionable morality, I promise he never got frisky with a rock."

Medea laughed at the last thing she'd expected. A rock with a sense of humor.

Shadow grinned. "Realizing belatedly that I should have introduced you all. Beau duFey . . . this is . . . *them*. Best known as the ones who are going to get us killed."

"Is he a member of the Stone Legion?" Medea remembered Blaise talking about them earlier.

"No." Beau tucked his wings down. "The Legion were all members of the Round Table. Knights who were cursed. I was born long after Morgen took Camelot from Arthur."

"In fact, he was born not too far from here."

Beau nodded at Blaise. "Uncle Blaise was there for it. Sort of."

Blaise made his way to the gargoyle. "And you should have spoken up earlier to let me know you were here with Shadow. I thought I felt another presence, but then you went still and I no longer sensed you."

Beau hugged him. "Sorry, Uncle. You looked busy and I didn't want to intrude."

Blaise clapped him on the back before he let him go. "That's the problem with all you natural-born gargoyles . . . not a very verbose bunch."

Falcyn draped his arm over Medea. "You sure about this? Shadow's right. Heading into Camelot with us isn't the sanest bet."

She nodded.

He leaned down to kiss her head.

As quickly as the tenderness had come, it vanished the instant Falcyn met Shadow's gaze. "All right then, demon, off to Camelot to see what trouble we can find."

Shadow let out a fierce groan. "Why do I always end up with the crazy ones?"

Urian winked at him. "Birds of a feather?"

Shadow sneered at him. "Now I remember why I don't like you." He swept his gaze to Blaise and Falcyn. "Any of you, as far as that goes."

With a deep breath, Shadow cracked his knuckles. "All right, kids. Last chance. Those who want a ticket to Sanity, raise your hand and we go out the portal to your home realm."

He waited a full minute before he let out an exaggerated groan. "Okay then, suicide it is. Buckle up, buttercups. Keep your hands inside the cart at all times and try not to get your heads chopped off. Thank you for choosing to ride The Grand Stupidity today, and for dragging me into this when I'd much rather be at home, sorting my dirty underwear and watching the grass grow."

"Oh stop your bitching." Blaise clapped him on the arm. "You love the excitement."

"Yeah, you keep believing those lies, mandrake, and inhaling those fumes." Shadow manifested a long rope.

Medea frowned as he stepped toward Brogan with it. "What are you doing?"

He paused to give her an irritated grimace. "Well, punkin, if we march in through the front doors, Morgen's entire Circle will descend on us like vultures on nummy roadkill. And while I do have more stupidity than the average man and a certain flair for theatrics, I can really do without a thorough gutting. Fact is, I'm doing my best to avoid the experience for the entirety of my exceptionally long life." He knotted the rope around Brogan's waist.

"You plan to take us through the Shadowland." Brogan's voice was scarce more than a whisper.

He nodded. "If we teleport into Camelot, Morgen will know instantly. Only safe way in or out is my realm."

Medea was even more confused as Shadow moved to loop and tie Brogan to Brandor. "And so I ask again . . . why the rope?"

"Keeps you from getting lost in the dark, princess." Shadow moved next to Blaise.

"Remember the SOD?" Brandor asked her.

"Yeah."

Brandor double-checked the knot at his waist, which told her how serious this was. "We're going into the world that spawned them."

Her heart stopped beating as she finally understood. "The thread between the worlds?"

Shadow nodded. "Home sweet fucking home. The rope is

to keep anything from snatching one of you away from me while we move through it."

Because to get lost there was to never be seen again. The darkness was ever hungry and sought any nourishment it could find.

Life being its number-one sustenance.

Shadow tied in Urian. "Keep your fear in check. Anger more so. Remember that the shadows are only a mockery of the shapes and feel of what they're attempting to duplicate. Nebulous and transitory, they lack all substance and form. They scatter in fear at the first sign of light, because they know they can't hold their own. Trickery and deception are the primary weapons the shadows use to distract the unwary and fool them into thinking they're something they're not. But in the end, those shadows are nothing more than dancing tricks that prey on unsuspecting minds, unable to differentiate the lie from the truth. When all is said and done, the shadows are swallowed either by the rays of the burning sun or the dark that eats them whole."

He paused in front of Medea. "Are you afraid?"

"Truth never scares me. I was here before time began and I will be here long after your shadows are forgotten."

Smiling, he inclined his head in respect for her fight and bravery. But when he moved to reach around her waist, Falcyn stopped him.

"I'll take care of Medea and myself."

Shadow tsked at him. "Careful, Veles. Been a long time since I've seen this side of you."

"Yeah, and I haven't forgotten what a mercenary bastard

you are. As you said, shadows are deceitful things, indeed. Ever more likely to lie than to tell the truth."

Unabashed, he smirked at Falcyn. "We do what we have to, to survive, isn't that right, brother?"

Something dark and vile passed between them in a single look. An acknowledgment of their pasts that they each knew about one another, and yet didn't want shared with anyone else. It was so intense that for a few seconds she expected Falcyn to attack him.

Finally, it settled down to be nothing more than a tic in Falcyn's jaw. "Why don't you go hug a wall?"

"That's my plan."

Falcyn rolled his eyes.

As Shadow turned away to double-check everyone's knots, Falcyn caught a strange image at the sight of Shadow's profile. It was so peculiar. His mind transposed a memory of Maxis over Shadow's face. But not a current one. It was of Maxis from the ancient world when he'd been adorned in furs and paint.

Strange . . . he'd never realized before how much Shadow and Max favored.

Even the way the demon moved.

Shadow paused as he caught Falcyn staring at him. "Please tell me that you're not thinking of asking me out, dragon. Or worse, for a booty call."

Falcyn sneered at the mere thought of being intimate with someone as treacherous as Shadow. "I think I just threw up in my mouth. Trust me, if I were to bend my tastes in that direction, it wouldn't be *you*."

Medea arched a brow. "Why do you hate him so?" she asked Falcyn.

"Ever wonder how Jared was able to switch out the swords for his army?"

Shadow froze as an agony so profound even she could feel it darkened his eyes. "You know *nothing* of what happened that day, dragon." His breathing ragged, he glared at Falcyn. "You judge me, you bastard . . . yet you know nothing of my past."

"I know enough."

"That's what they all say right before they pick up the stones to slay a victim for being a part of a crime they never wanted any part of. Wallow in your misery. Whine and bitch, dragon. It's what you're good at. Some of us were never allowed a haven where we could give in to such tantrums."

And with that, Shadow moved to tie in Beau.

Beau stopped him. "I can walk in the front gates of Camelot and no one will notice or be the wiser." He winked at Shadow. "No offense, gargoyles don't do well in the Nithing. I'll be waiting for you in the South Tower."

"Be safe." Shadow patted him on the arm.

Beau spread his wings. "And you." He launched himself into flight and vanished quickly into the dark, gray clouds.

His expression grim, Shadow turned back to them. "Remember to avoid the SODs. Don't listen to anything and stay focused on your goal. Let nothing distract you."

Yeah, that tone wasn't creepy at all.

Medea was about to ask Falcyn about it when Shadow lifted his arm and drew a series of symbols. He reminded her of an orchestra conductor, directing a band only he could hear.

Then he began a melancholic humming from deep inside his chest. Haunting and thrumming, he picked up the crescendo, and as he did so, the air around them stirred.

One moment they were standing outside, and in the next they were in a blurry, swirling world of dark sepia. It was like being trapped inside an old nickelodeon machine. Everything had a jerky, surreal feel to it. One that left her disoriented, and a bit queasy.

Medea stumbled. Falcyn caught her and held her against his side.

"It'll take a few minutes to get your bearings." Shadow's voice sounded as distorted as the scenery.

"Why is everything so weird here?"

"You're in the lining of the worlds. Think of it like a hollow realm." Shadow held his left hand up and a small porthole appeared to show them a bright sunny park where children played a game of chase. "From here, you can venture anywhere. Past. Present. Future. In all the worlds." He closed the porthole and opened one on his right that showed a storming sea.

It was both beautiful and terrifying.

Shadow walked forward, slowly, drawing more windows for them to see different times and places.

"You grew up here?"

He glanced at her over his shoulder. "Not as romantic or spectacular as your voice makes it sound. For all the beauty, it's fraught with nightmares."

A howling sounded off in the distance.

Shadow leaned his head back and answered with a chilling, bloodcurdling battle cry.

Medea started to summon a god-bolt, but Falcyn caught her hand and stayed it. "It's a skatos."

She scowled at a term she'd never heard before. "A what?"

"Guardians," Shadow breathed. "To make sure you belong here. If you're an intruder with no business in this realm, they unleash the Fringe-Hunters on you."

"You're not alone, Shadow. . . ."

Brogan let out a squeak at the dark, hooded figure who appeared beside them and uttered those disappointed words.

"Leave off, Mairee."

She tsked. "You dare to flout the rules? Even a prince must answer when he crosses the line."

"Then bring *them*. I dare you."

The woman floated over to Medea and it wasn't until she was even with her that Medea realized why Brogan had gasped out loud. Half the woman's face was missing. What remained was twisted into a garish nightmare.

"You're not afraid of me?"

Medea snorted. "Something a lot scarier than you tucks me into bed at night."

Mairee moved to hover near Shadow. She studied him intently for several minutes. "Where are you off to?"

He kept moving forward. "I've no time for you. So find another to annoy."

She leaned in to whisper, but her voice carried plainly. "Fear the shadow of the hawk when he flies, for his talons bite deep."

Shadow shoved her away. But she didn't go far before she began to sing a haunting ditty. "Into your life, the hawk will creep . . . sing, my child, sing. Let your voice to the heavens fly. . . . But remember there's no one to save you when you die."

"Enough!" Shadow roared. And when he did, his eyes turned bloodred. They glowed an unholy fire in the darkness.

And still she tsked. "The Shadow Hawk bellows and all the world kneels. . . . For bow you must or your life will he steal."

"I swear on my rotted and damned soul, if you don't leave, Mairee, I will finish what the Sakers started!"

"Temper, temper, Lord of Shadows and Dark. There was a time when you begged for my smile."

"That was before you betrayed me."

"Do your friends know what they follow? How quick you are to turn?"

Shadow let out a bitter laugh. He started for her, then stopped. He turned toward them then and cursed. "Brogan!"

Medea looked over to see that the howling wind was masking the sounds of the Crom's horse as he rushed toward them.

And he wasn't alone.

What appeared to be a hundred shadow dogs followed in his wake, with yellow eyes glowing.

Medea felt the blood drain from her face as she realized they had no way to fight that number.

Shadow handed the rope to Falcyn. "Stay on the road. Move forward and I'll join you as soon as I can."

"What are you—"

"Go!" he roared at Falcyn. "Forward. Don't stop! If the barking dogs get to you, you're finished."

Falcyn rushed forward, dragging them in his wake. They ran up a small hill and turned back just in time to see Shadow overrun by the demonic dogs he'd sought to hold back from their heels.

Medea's eyes widened at the horrific sight. "We're so effing dead."

13

Falcyn, Urian, Blaise, and Brandor took positions between Medea and Brogan as the rabid dogs approached them. Medea held her breath, waiting to be overrun and swarmed the same way they'd done to poor Shadow.

There was nothing left of where he'd been.

Not even a drop of blood. It appeared as if he'd been completely devoured by them. Every last bit. Body and soul.

Louder and louder, the barking and snarling grew. Brogan reached out and took her hand.

While she stood bravely with her jaw locked in silence, there was the slightest tremor in her hand to let Medea know just how frightened the woman was.

Then, just as the twisted demonic dogs reached them, the shadowed earth shot up at a right angle, forming a wall between them and the demonic beasts. They slammed into it and howled out in agony. Swirling and twisting like smoke, the ground formed a giant hand that sent the animals scattering and running off into the dark.

The Crom came in the next wave, on his eerie ghost steed. Rushing and snorting fire, the beast seemed every bit as determined to add them to its menu. Just as it would have reached their position, the hand bent around and curved up to form a huge beast of a man.

"You have no power here!" Though the voice was distorted in its inhuman growl and pitch, Medea still recognized it as Shadow's.

The Crom pulled his horse up short, causing it to rear and paw fire at the hand. "This kerling belongs to me!" The rasping voice came from Brogan.

Medea gaped as she saw that Brogan's eyes were now milky white with no iris or pupil whatsoever. Her skin was ice cold to touch.

The Crom had obviously taken her over completely so that he could speak through her.

Blaise growled low in his throat as he must have realized what was going on. "You're not taking her!"

"B-b-b-b . . ." Brogan choked, then fell to her knees to clutch at her throat. It was obvious the Crom was commanding her to speak Blaise's name and she was refusing to give him the power of death over the mandrake.

Throwing her head back, Brogan let out a blood-chilling screech. She pounded the ground until her fist was bloody and bruised.

"Stop it!" Blaise shifted into his dragon's body. He let loose a blast of fire toward the Crom.

Engulfed by the fire, he laughed through Brogan's throat. Then threw his whip of bones and skulls toward Blaise. The head at the end of it opened its mouth as if it were screaming silently at the mandrake.

Shadow caught it and threw it back toward the horse and rider. "Leave here or I will dine on you both!"

Yanking his whip free of Shadow's grasp, the Crom snapped it in the air, shooting sparks of fire in all directions. Sulphur choked Medea and burned her throat.

"I demand my property!" He cracked his whip for Brogan.

Shadow caught it again and yanked the Crom from his horse. Faster than Medea could blink, Falcyn was on him.

He grabbed the Crom and pulled him up from the ground. "Renounce your claim on the kerling. Here and now. Give her her freedom or I will rid you of your essence for all eternity!"

The Crom struggled for several seconds until he realized that Falcyn wasn't about to give. More than that, he came to the startling and truthful conclusion that Falcyn indeed had the means and ability to carry out his not-so-empty threat. "Very well, my lord. I give the kerling her freedom."

No sooner did Brogan speak those words than she fell forward to lie in a heap. Blaise returned to his human form so that he could rush to her side and pull her into his arms.

"Ro?" His voice quivered from the strain of his fear. "Speak to me! Say something!"

Brandor knelt beside them. "Brogan, please don't leave me alone!"

Still, she didn't move. She didn't even appear to breathe. Her face turned pale, then blue.

Fearful tears choked Medea as she feared what they did. That the Crom had freed Brogan by killing her. Though she'd just met the woman, she felt for her and didn't want to lose her any more than the men did.

Blaise cupped her cheek and cradled her against his shoulder. "Speak to me, my lady. I cannot live knowing I caused you harm."

When she didn't respond, Blaise choked on a sob and lifted her up. Her head fell back while Brandor took her hand and kissed it as if it were unspeakably precious. Tears fled down his cheeks. This was pure brotherly love and it made her chest tighten in sympathy for all of them.

Medea's gaze swam from her own unshed tears, especially when she saw the agony on Urian's face. Without being told, she knew he was reliving the death of his own sister. And more than that, his beloved wife.

His most precious Phoebe.

That tortured look made her stomach ache for him. And it brought out the memories of her own loss. Made all those old wounds fresh and new.

For a moment, she feared she'd give in to the agony of the past and be ruined by it again.

Falcyn wrapped his arms around her and held her back to his front as her vision blurred from unshed tears. She felt his jaw tic as he whispered, "I can't interfere in this realm. My powers won't work here."

"What?"

Falcyn ground his teeth. "I can't save her from this."

His eyes flaring at those words, Shadow swirled past them to Brogan and lightly touched her cheek.

No sooner did he withdraw his hand than her eyes fluttered open. Lost in their grief, neither Blaise nor Brandor saw it at first.

Not until Brogan pulled her hand from her brother's grasp and sank it deep into Blaise's pale hair. "They can take me by force and break every bone I have, but only you will ever have my heart, Blaise. For it alone is mine to give."

Laughing and crying, he pulled her to his lips so that he could kiss her.

Brandor quickly withdrew from them. And though it was obvious he didn't like to see his sister in the arms of another man, he didn't say a word as he moved to stand beside Medea. Facing the opposite direction.

Like Urian.

Snorting at their ridiculous actions, Medea wiped at her eyes. She drew a ragged, grateful breath.

Urian glanced at her with Falcyn, then over to Brandor. "Don't we feel like the odd ones out?"

Shadow manifested between them and draped his arms

around their shoulders. "I feel your pain, my brothers. I'm always the oddest of the odd." He darted his gaze around them. "So which of you assholes destroyed my rope?"

Medea let out a half laugh. "That's your concern? Seriously?"

"I like my rope. Comes in handy for all kinds of things. And we still need to get the whole lot of you out of here. Mairee is only one of a number of treacherous bitches who can summon all manner of hell down upon us."

That made her think of something else, other than their near miss. "She called you the prince of shadows. Why?"

He let out a long sigh. "This dimension is its own world. With its own predators. Its own rules. And as with all things in the shadow realm, the title is both one of respect and one of shame. Neither all good nor all bad. Always something between."

She didn't understand. "How so?"

"Because I reign here as the supreme badass, and at the same time, it's a reminder that my mother abandoned me to the beasts who used to rule this land when I was a child, to be preyed upon." He cut a sinister glare to Falcyn. "You had your sister and brothers to rely on. I had no one. My brothers don't even know I exist. What actions I took during the Primus Bellum to survive, I took to protect the only family I've ever known. And instead of protecting me for my loyalty, they stripped my powers and sent me back here, where it took me a thousand years to regain all I'd lost in the blink of an eye. You judge me when you know nothing of who I am or what I've been through. And you know even less about Jared. Instead of holding grudges for what you *think* happened, maybe you should spend five minutes learning the truth. Open your eyes and engage the brain the gods gave you for something other than watching porn and jumping to conclusions that even a three-year-old would see were stupid lies."

With those bitter words spoken, he turned and lifted his cowl to cover his head. His charcoal-gray armor clanked in the darkness as he strode with his hand on the hilt of his sword. "Follow me or don't, it's entirely up to you. But unless you wish to build home property in this hellhole, I suggest you pick up the pace."

Falcyn fell silent as he watched Shadow moving ahead. He went to help Brogan and Blaise so that they could all follow after Shadow.

Urian and Brandor remained quietly behind them.

Medea took Falcyn's arm. "Okay, I get that, like you, he's older than shit and fought in the Primus Bellum. Whose side was he on?"

"His own. He started out with the demons, fighting for Noir and the Mavromino. For reasons unknown, he switched to fight with the Kalosum . . . until he helped Jared slaughter his army for Noir."

"And no one knows why?"

Falcyn jerked his chin at Shadow as those words haunted him and he tried to understand them. Nothing in that war had been simple. Even less had made sense. Especially not the sides they'd each chosen to fight for. Or the reasons why. "I'm sure he knows his reasoning. Jared might know it, too."

And yet as they walked, details of the past played through his mind. Things he'd forgotten completely.

Or perhaps the correct reality was that he'd chosen to bury them more than simply forget about them.

Shadow had come in early to speak to Caleb, who had led one of their largest bands of demons against the Mavromino. Falcyn and Adidiron, one of their Arel commanders, had stumbled into that meeting quite by accident.

To this day, he could see the sneer on Shadow's face as he raked a cold look over Adidiron's body, taking in his golden armor and wings.

"Watch your back, Caleb. Those who profess good too often practice evil in its name."

"Why are *you* here?" Adidiron wore the same expression as someone who'd just stepped in a flaming pile of horseshit.

"Slumming." Shadow stood slowly.

Adidiron rolled his eyes. "Go back to the whore shadows where you belong."

Shadow had shaken his head. "Careful, Arel. Lest you learn one lesson too late."

"And that is?"

"We are never punished for the sins we commit. Rather we are punished *by* them."

Those wise words haunted Falcyn to this day. They'd never been far from his mind.

But then what had been his sin where Maddor was concerned? Seeking love? That was the only reason he'd allowed Igraine to lie and seduce him. He'd been so desperate for a kind touch that he'd ignored all common sense and reason.

And what of Medea? Her sin had been in trusting humans not to harm her child and husband.

Were those sins so great that they had to spend the rest of eternity paying for them? Seriously?

No one should have to bleed to the bone for loving or trusting another.

"Where are you, dragonfly?" Medea's voice brought him back from the darkness of his thoughts.

Lost and cornered. At least that was what it felt like.

Still, he refused to let her know that. "I'm here."

"You say that, but I can see in your eyes that you're off somewhere else."

He would tell her that he was thinking of the future. Yet why bother? He didn't believe in a future. Didn't believe in anything at this point. Other than misery and hell.

Betrayal. That was what the world had taught him.

Just how black the souls of the rest really were. And how often others condemned innocent people for their own misdeeds and rotten acts they couldn't stand about themselves. Because it was easier to see them in someone else and hate them for it than it was to hate yourself and go to the effort of trying to fix it. After all, people were less likely to see it in you if their attention was being diverted by the guilty pointing the finger of distraction toward those who couldn't defend themselves because they were innocent and couldn't even contemplate the sins being cast upon them.

Sick, really.

But luckily, he was spared having to answer as Shadow slowed down. "We're here."

With his powers, he cut another hole through, into a small room from his shadow realm into that of Camelot. Shadow stayed back while they walked through. Then he joined them and sealed the rupture tightly closed.

Medea screwed her face up at his actions. "How do you do that?"

"That's like asking me how I breathe. I don't know. I just think it and it happens." Shadow gave her a sarcastic grin. "It's magick."

Rolling her eyes at his sarcasm, she shook her head at him. "You're a sick bastard."

"Always." As he stepped away, Medea frowned.

There was a smear of blood on the floor. Even though there was no color in this room where they were—everything appeared as shades of black and white, like an old movie—she knew the looks of it. The smell of it.

And it took her a few seconds to realize the source.

"You're wounded?"

Shadow paused at her question, but didn't answer.

Then she saw it. The huge, gaping wound in Shadow's side that was partially concealed by his cape. "Shadow?"

His eyes rolled back into his head as his legs buckled. He would have hit the ground hard had Falcyn not caught him and lowered him slowly to the floor.

Yet no sooner did he pull back than the door opened to show a small group of Adoni who weren't their allies.

The rasping of metal filled the air as the Adoni unsheathed their swords.

An instant later, they attacked.

14

Alone in the stone tower with her prisoner, Narishka watched as Maddor attempted to reach her so that he could kill her. Luckily she had the mandrake quelled. Though the term was becoming more a hope than actual reality as the mandrake continued to fight against the magick she was using to imprison him.

"Let me out of here!"

She tsked at his furious tone. All in all, she'd give it to the huge feral beast. Like his father, he was a handsome one. With black hair and eyes, he bled an innate, raw masculinity that drew others to him. And though she'd never had a taste of his lush, sexy body, she suspected he was incredible in bed. At least that was what all the rumors of him said.

Again, just like his father. Oh for the days when Falcyn had been much more reckless and nondiscriminating. When he hadn't cared who ventured to his bed or where he found himself in the morning.

What he drank . . .

But that was for another day to test the boundaries of Maddor's tastes.

Right now, she had to keep him caged.

And far away from her throat he was so desperate to tear out.

"Don't make me drug you."

Drugging a mandrake was a very tricky thing that killed about half of them. And if Maddor died, Falcyn would rip out her heart and force-feed it to her. Little did Maddor know, their profound fear of Falcyn's temper was the only reason the beast was still alive.

"Why am I here?"

She shrugged. "Why are any of us in this thing called life? That's a question for the ages and for philosophers. Is that really what you want to discuss?"

"No. What I want is to feast on your fetid heart, bitchtress!"

Aye, she knew that fiery, hate-filled glare in those dark eyes. How no one had ever guessed that Maddor was the single, true son of Veles she couldn't imagine. They were so similar in temperament and mannerisms. Even more alike in words and actions. They might as well be the same person. Only a fool could miss how similar they were to one another.

"Is that any way to speak to your aunt?"

He scowled at her unprecedented and unexpected disclosure.

One that succeeded in taking a degree of his bluster and fury from him. "My what?"

Folding her arms over her chest, she cocked a brow at the beast she'd finally subdued. "Aye. Seems we've kept a few things from you over the centuries you've been imprisoned here. The least of which is that your birth mother, Igraine, was my true blood-born sister."

Maddor froze. By his expression, she could tell he was debating whether or not to believe her. "You're lying. Just like you always do."

"Truth, dearest nephew. Absolute, stinking truth. There is no reason for me to lie over this. And I have another bit of information you might want . . . that mangy beast you hate so much—"

"Kerrigan."

Oh, she'd forgotten about that one.

Come to think of it, he had a long, torrid list of those he hated to the marrow of his bones. So much so that if she continued to play this game, they'd be here for weeks.

She shook her head. "Nay, the beast who serves him . . . Blaise."

"What about the worthless wretch?"

Scoffing at his tone, she approached his cage ever so slowly, wary of any sudden move he might make against her as she prepared herself for the most fatal blow to his mind that she intended to give him.

Aye, this would take her fair mandrake down a few pegs.

And cause him to hate the others for all eternity.

"There's something you need to know about our dear Blaise . . . *and* how he's related to you and your *real* father. Brace yourself, boy . . . this is going to kill you."

More than that, it would make him kill his own father.

Medea manifested her sword and charged it with her powers before she caught the first Adoni's blade with her own. She parried his thrust and drove him back while the others moved around her to battle their individual opponents.

Brogan stayed by Shadow's side to defend him as they dealt with this newest assault.

Of course the Adoni sounded an alarm. 'Cause keeping quiet would just be too much to ask. Wouldn't it?

Damn villains. Unlike her, they didn't have a code they followed. Mannerless pigs.

Urian cursed. "Well, this wasn't how I saw these events unfolding."

Falcyn snorted at his sarcasm. "I knew better than to get involved with Daimons and Dark-Hunters. What I get for coming out of my hole."

With a grimace, Medea lopped the head off her Adoni opponent, then turned toward Falcyn before she engaged another enemy and sought to end him, too. "Stop whining, dragonfly!

Why don't you shift and set fire to them? Make this a little easier on us? Eh?"

"Simple spatial awareness. If either Blaise or I change right
now, we'd kill the lot of you, as we'd take up this entire room
and you'd be crushed beneath us. Still want me to shift, love?"

Oh. Medea flashed him a grin as she kicked her opponent
back. "Please, don't."

"Thought you might feel that way."

Just as they finished off their Adoni and began to make sure
there weren't more, the door flew open.

They turned as one solid group to face this new onslaught.

As tall as Falcyn, the newcomer was swathed in the gold and
green armor of an Adoni guard. A thick leather hood covered
his head. Muscled and fierce, he stood with the cocksure stance
of a warrior who knew how to fight to the bitter end.

Yet he didn't draw his sword.

Rather, he held his hands out to his sides as if amused by
them and their predicament.

Medea braced herself for a psychic attack. Or one born of
magick. That was what someone like this usually went for.

Instead, laughter greeted them. "Bet if I sneezed right now,
I'd send the lot of you jumping straight to the ceiling like a glaring
of cats."

Falcyn growled deep in his throat. "Varian, you worthless
bastard! Get in here. Shadow's down."

The humor died instantly while the man shut the door, then
lowered his hood. Medea arched a brow at his unexpected
handsomeness as he brushed past her with a predator's lope to
check on their fallen friend. Though, being Adoni, his degree of

superior gorgeousness shouldn't have surprised her. Yet even by their stellar standards, the black-haired fey was exceptionally formed. With pointed ears and sharp, perfect features, he was absolutely exquisite—the pinnacle of masculine perfection.

"What happened?" Varian knelt by Shadow's side.

Falcyn joined him there to help tend Shadow. "We were cornered by dire wolves."

"Dire wolves or gwyllgi?"

"Gwyllgi," Blaise answered, making her wonder how the mandrake knew the difference.

Varian cursed. "Was the Crom with them?"

Blaise nodded without further comment.

Growling low in his throat in a manner eerily similar to the one Falcyn had done on his arrival, Varian used his powers to strip Shadow's leather armor away. Then he lifted the linen shirt to inspect the damage.

Medea cringed at the sight of the festering wound and all the other deep, ridged scars that marred Shadow's cut and ripped abdomen and chest. That armor had hidden quite an impeccable body. For a creature who inhabited a nether realm, he spent a great deal of time in the gym with weights.

Or he worked out by bench-pressing gargoyles.

Again, Varian cursed—this time, more lewdly. "Damn, Shade. Can't you ever do anything halfway once in a while? No, you don't get a little wounded. You've got to get practically gutted."

Falcyn sat back on his heels. "If you hold him, I can heal him."

Varian stopped Falcyn. "If you're planning to tap what I think you are, don't. Morgen will feel it and jump all over you the minute you try." He worked to stop Shadow's bleeding. "I've got this. You have a mission to complete. But I should warn you . . ."

Falcyn's gut knotted. He knew the Grail Knight's words before Varian spoke them.

"Narishka has Maddor, and he's furious." Varian's gaze went to Blaise before he met Falcyn's stare. "I also know what I doubt you want made public."

Yeah, that gave Falcyn's ulcer a baby and a friend to chew on.

Varian sighed heavily. "I didn't want you to walk in there until you had all the facts. Narishka told Maddor everything about his past and parents. And I do mean *e-v-e-r-y-t-h-i-n-g*." He pulled the key from Shadow and handed it to Falcyn. "There's a stairwell at the end of the hallway that will take you down to the catacombs. Be careful. They're expecting all of you to come here and be stupid."

"Then far be it from us to disappoint them." Falcyn saluted him with the key. "Thanks." He rose as dread continued to gnaw his confidence and erode his sense of purpose. As Varian had noted, this was a fool's errand. Yet one look at Blaise and he knew they had to see it through. "Lead the way."

Hesitating, Blaise took Brogan's hand. "Is Shadow going to be all right?"

She cocked her head as a faraway look darkened her eyes. "Aye. I don't see his death nearby. And it's definitely not imminent."

Falcyn's hackles raised at a note she had buried in her voice. "What aren't you saying?"

She pressed her hand to her forehead. "I see death all around me, all the time. In everyone. In everything. To me, the world isn't a beautiful place. It's a graveyard, filled with walking corpses. So when I'm asked to look more closely at the ghouls who haunt me, it feels like it steals a part of my soul." She drew a ragged breath. "That was all I was saying."

Medea moved to stand by her side. "I'm sorry, Brogan. Sadly, there are too many things in life that feel that way."

Brogan reached out and touched Medea's hand. With a sad smile, she turned it over and pointed to the lines on the side of Medea's palm. "Did you know you'll have four more children to love and hold?"

Medea's features turned as pale as her hair. "Pardon?"

Brogan opened Medea's palm and, using her fingernail, traced the lines that bisected her skin. "Your heart is broken, but healing. And while you'll never forget what's happened to you, you can and will move past it. Brave in all things. That's you, Medea. Your scars don't define you. They are merely silent testimony to your resilience and inner beauty."

Medea squeezed her hand. "I'm not the one who's beautiful, Brogan. You are. I don't understand how you can be so gentle after everything you've gone through. I envy you that. You're like a fine steak that's been tenderized while I'm steel that's been tempered."

A sad smile tugged at the edges of her lips. "Don't. I would give anything to be the fighter you are, and to have the same sharp edge to me. But alas, I've been worn down too far by the blows I've taken. There's nothing left anymore except a memory of the girl I once was and the woman I used to hope I'd be." She took a ragged breath. "That is the bite, isn't it? That day when we wake to remember what our future once was and can never be."

Medea tightened her hand against Brogan's. "Never, ever beat yourself up, love. Not when there are so many others willing to do it for you. See the gentle beauty that you are. Not the sharpened dagger I've become."

Falcyn moved so that he could lean down to whisper in Medea's ear. "And I think you're perfect just the way you are. There is nothing about you I'd change."

Those words melted her. Worse, they brought tears to her eyes, as they were the sweetest thing anyone had said to her in so long, she couldn't remember ever hearing anything more precious.

So used to anger as her constant state of being, she wasn't sure how to deal with these tender emotions Falcyn touched so effortlessly.

Damn him for it!

And damn her heart for letting him in against her wishes.

She didn't want to care about anyone. But when he looked at her like that . . . When he spoke in that rich, deep timbre that sent shivers over her . . .

How could she resist him?

You can't lose someone you love again.

The thought of having more children and a spouse . . .

That was what gave a grown Daimon nightmares. At least in her case. Medea could imagine no worse horror. No worse tragedy than to spend every day in terror of losing it all again.

No. She wouldn't do it.

She *couldn't* do it.

Falcyn saw the panic flaring in Medea's eyes a heartbeat before she turned on her heels and ran from the room like the hounds of hell were nipping at her soul.

"What did you say to her?" Urian asked.

"Nothing that should warrant *that* reaction."

Blaise scoffed. "I don't know. Frightening women and small children, and making grown men piss their pants, is kind of your specialty, brother."

Falcyn ground his teeth. "It's a good thing I like you." And with that, he went after Medea, who was quickly heading toward the fey court.

"Honey, you might want to slow it down before you burst headlong into Adoni central. You might make *their* day, but it'd probably ruin yours. . . . Then again, knowing you, it might make you smile. Provided they don't take you by surprise."

That at least succeeded in making her slow her hell-bent pace. "What?"

He nodded, then jerked his chin in the direction she'd been headed. "That's where the Circle parties down. Bad idea for us to break in on them. Unless you want roasted Adoni for dinner. That I can arrange."

She snorted. "You're not funny."

Nearing her side, Falcyn cupped her face in his hands as he sought to comfort her. "So what was that about, anyway?"

"What?"

"Your running off in the middle of our moment. What's going on?"

Her eyes darkened with so much torment that it hit him like a fist to his gut. He couldn't stand seeing her in pain. "Brogan may see death, but the future she described for me is more than I could cope with. It terrified me."

The magnitude of her confiding in him wasn't lost on him. He understood exactly how rare this was, and he didn't take it for granted.

Floored and humbled by it, he stroked her cheek before he smiled at her and sought to lighten her mood. "Yeah, domestic hell is something I've done my best to avoid. It's that whole suburban lifestyle. Little ranch house. White minivan. Block parties and lawn mowers." He shuddered. "I'd be funneling Drano within a weekend."

That succeeded in easing her pain. "I don't know. You'd be cute in an apron."

He grinned even wider. "What can I say? I might be able to make mom jeans look sexy."

She burst into laughter. But only for a moment before the sadness returned to her dark eyes. "Why can't I be normal, Falcyn? Why did I have to be born so cursed?"

His heart breaking for her, he pulled her against his chest and held her close. "Trust me, we all feel that way. Many times I think either the Fates have a major grudge on me, or I'm just their favorite whipping boy and punch line."

"Exactly."

Kissing her forehead, he squeezed her. "C'mon. We need to get out of here before we're seen."

Medea allowed him to take her hand so that he could lead her back to the others. But with every step they took, she couldn't stop the overwhelming fear that weakened her in a way she hated.

Worse was the premonition that something bad was about to happen.

Something more than Shadow's injuries.

A lot worse.

All right, Chicken Little. Stop waiting for the other shoe. Breathe and let it go.

She smiled at the memory of Davyn's favorite thing to say to her whenever she started with her doom-and-gloom scenarios. He said it so much that he'd even begun to call her Chicken Little as a nickname.

Only Davyn could get away with that without her murdering him for it.

Oh shit, I am attached to someone.

She loved that crotchety little Daimon. He was her family. And she would be devastated if anything happened to him. It was why she'd come out on this quest and strong-armed Urian into this venture.

Davyn wasn't just her right hand, he was her best friend. The only confidant she had. Loyal to a fault, he was the least judgmental and easiest to get along with person she'd ever met. Nothing got him down.

Not even this plague.

Well, better me than you, right? That was how he viewed the world.

And while she had the blood of thousands on her hands, it was only the death of a tiny handful that haunted her. Davyn would be one of them, should he ever fall.

No, he wouldn't haunt her.

Davyn would destroy her. She couldn't stand the thought of losing him, too. No matter what, she had to save him.

With that thought foremost in her mind, she glanced up at Falcyn while he walked. "So how do you use your dragon-stone?"

He flashed an annoying grin at her. "With great caution. It's a deadly thing when used by a non-dragon. It's moody and irritable."

"Like me?"

"Didn't say that." His eyes glowed at her.

"Yeah, you did. I heard your voice in your own head. Spoke so loud, I thought it was my own inner voice screeching."

He snorted. "Nice trick, Savitar."

She fell silent as they drew near their *friends*. Though that seemed a peculiar word to her. Urian was her brother and she wasn't sure why she considered Blaise, Brogan, and Brandor that way when it wasn't in her nature to do so. Trust had never come easy to her. Yet there was no denying the innate fondness she had for them. For no known reason.

Strange, indeed, for someone who trusted no one. Not even her own parents. While she loved her mother dearly, she wasn't blind to Zephyra's flaws. End of the day, her mother was a vicious survivor who wouldn't hesitate to kill or torture to get what she wanted. And while Medea didn't think her mother could turn on her, she'd seen her mother do things that made her never want to put her mother to the hazard for fear of learning a harsh, bitter truth.

Same for her father. Even though Stryker was a bit more moderate—"bit" being an interesting word in this scenario. But at least her father had a screwed-up sense of honor that her mother lacked.

Her mother was a firm believer in *kill them all and the gods will sort them later*. And if you could torture information out of them first, all the better.

Yeah, sympathy and empathy weren't on her mother's list of virtues. Therefore, Medea didn't delude herself into thinking that her mother would ever be above selling her out for the right price.

And that terrified her most of all.

Trying not to think about it, Medea followed the others down a narrow, winding tower. As they continued on, it began to feel as if they were descending into hell itself. It kept getting colder, darker.

More sinister.

And that, too, made her wonder if and when they'd betray her. What price these strangers she dared to call friend would put on her life.

"Where does this lead?" Medea asked.

"Morgen's garden." Blaise's tone was flat and emotionless in the dim light.

"I don't understand. A garden underground?" No sooner had she finished the question than they slowed down.

Falcyn used his dragonfyre in his hand as a torch so that they could see what was around them.

The moment he raised his arm over his head and the light chased away the heavier shadows, she gasped. The garden was massive and lined with giant dragon statues that went on in an endless, eerie display.

In every direction.

"Holy shit," she breathed.

Falcyn nodded. "Holy shit, indeed. The light fog down here is from their breath. At least by that we know they're still alive even if they are frozen by Merlin's spell."

"I don't understand. If they're frozen, how can they breathe fog?"

Though he was blind in his human form, Blaise glanced toward Brogan and then Medea before he answered. "The gas we exhale. It causes that. Even when we're locked in by magick. Not sure why. Just a peculiar by-product."

Okay, then. Sometimes there was no rhyme or reason to magick. She knew that better than anyone.

Of course, ultimately there was rhyme and reason, it just wasn't readily apparent.

"Do we have to free them all?" she asked.

Falcyn headed for the largest beast over on his right. "It's the safest thing to do. That way, Morgen won't have any to rouse and use against us."

Blaise left Brogan's side as he felt his way through the darkness. "I'm not sure how to use my father's ring to awaken them. Do you know?"

Falcyn reached out to take it from him.

Just as their fingers brushed, the dragon nearest them opened its eyes and growled.

15

Falcyn pulled back, ready for war, as the beast by his side rose to do battle. He stepped away from Medea, intending to change into his own dragon body to fight.

Blaise took his arm and fisted his hand in his sleeve to stop him. "Don't! *That's* Maddor."

Those words froze him to the spot. His heart started racing at the sight of the largest dragon.

This was his son. Close enough to touch.

To hold.

The one creature he'd always wanted to meet.

And he was standing beside his grandson, who continued to hold on to him. For the first time in his life, he was with his children. Both of them. The magnitude of the moment overwhelmed him as he struggled with emotions he couldn't even begin to define. Twisted pain. Heartache.

Inexplicable joy and pride.

Unbelievable love.

These were *his* boys. His own flesh and blood . . .

Feelings slammed into him and left him reeling until the entire lot of them settled down into a rage so profound that it was all he could do not to go straight back to Sanctuary and gut Max for what he'd done.

For what he'd unknowingly cost his children.

And yet—

"Maddor . . ." The name came out in an anguished breath as he stepped forward, wanting to embrace him.

Urian splayed his hand against Falcyn's chest to stop him from approaching his child. "They have him pinned." He jerked his chin toward the chain that held Maddor in place. "I'm betting if you free the dragons, it'll kill him."

It took Falcyn a moment to realize that Urian was right. The chain ran straight into Maddor's chest and no doubt through his heart. That was the kind of cruelty Narishka and Morgen specialized in.

Damn the bitches for it.

And that wasn't all. They had him muzzled, too.

That combination of cruelty made Maddor insane. Falcyn couldn't blame him in the least. No dragon did well in captivity.

Not even a mandrake. They were meant to roam free, not be bound in such a manner.

Stepping past Urian, Falcyn reached to touch his son's scales. "Maddor, calm yourself. We're here to help."

With a fiery hiss, Maddor lunged at him so that Falcyn couldn't make contact. *Fuck you!*

There was no missing that angry voice in Falcyn's head. Maddor lashed at Blaise with his tail.

Falcyn barely pulled Blaise back before Maddor pierced him with a spike. "Stop! You don't want to harm us."

Of course I do. It's your fault I'm here! I intend to kill you both!

Falcyn winced at a truth he couldn't change. "I know, and I'm sorry for that."

You're about to be even sorrier those three seconds before I kill you!

Falcyn ground his teeth, needing some way to reason with an unreasonable temper. Why of all the things his son could have inherited from him did that have to be the primary one?

Then again, it could be worse.

He could have inherited his mother's.

Yeah, Igraine's temper had made a mockery of his own. And right now, that double dose of bad genetics was palatable.

Suddenly, the floor rumbled under their feet. Like a 6.0-magnitude earthquake . . .

Confused by the cause of it, he reached for Medea. But it was hard to remain standing. "Blaise? What the hell is going on here?"

"No idea. Flying hell-monkeys, maybe?"

They should be so lucky. Instead of dramonk demons being unleashed, the cracks in the stone widened and a greenish smoke spiraled out. It was as if the entire dungeon was alive and moving.

No, not moving.

Breathing. That was exactly what it felt like. Smelled like. The way the floor and walls moved was in time to someone's intake of breath. In and out. Seismic. Rolling.

Jarring.

Urian sneered as he caught a whiff of some foul sulfuric stench. "Someone tell me these are vapors like the Delphian oracle used to get high on before she mumbled gibberish."

Medea shook her head. "Sorry, little brother. I actually visited her once. This ain't it."

True to her prediction, the smoke coiled into fierce warriors, complete with armor.

And swords.

They had a *lot* of swords.

What the hell?

"Man!" Urian snapped. "We cannot catch a break."

"Hey, I gave you an easy way out," Falcyn reminded him. "You could be home right now, watching *Survivor*. But no, you chose to be here."

"What can I say? I'm an idiot. I'd blame it on the fact that I come from a long line of them, but my mom and dad would kick my ass for the insult. So I'll blame Stryker for raising me among them." Urian used his powers to conjure a sword. "Anyone have a clue who and what these assholes are?"

"It's the dungeon."

They turned to stare at Brandor.

"What did he just say?" Urian's tone was filled with disbelief.

Brandor nodded. "There are two sections to the chambers down here. La Mort à Jamais—the Eternal Death, where Morgen and Narishka place those they want to torture without fear of killing them. It's enchanted to ensure their victims will live no matter what's done to them. Once they're finished with the torture, Morgen has the lifeless body taken and added to the catacombs. But the by-product of that cruelty and magick is that the dungeon absorbs the tortured soul and holds on to it forever. It makes the soul a part of it. After a time, *l'âme en peine* bonds with the others that are trapped here until they become one single entity."

"Okay." Falcyn glanced around at the forming warriors. "So they're ghosts?"

He shook his head. "No. The nature and strength of the residual magick combines with the souls. Instead of making individual ghosts, they become one single beast. Lombrey de la Mort."

Falcyn let out a tired breath at the words that meant *Death Shadow*. "Are you telling me that we're facing Shadow's evil twin?"

Brandor laughed. "His prince underling, actually. If Shadow were here, he could control Lombrey and force him into retreat. Or at least order him to stand down."

Why did those words make him sick to his stomach?

"Without him?"

Glancing around at the numerous warriors the darkness

was spawning, Brandor sighed. "We're screwed. Lombrey's a nasty bastard. Filled with the screams and righteous agony of a million innocent victims. They say it's driven him mad and so he attacks everyone who comes into his domain. Indiscriminately."

Medea scowled. "Then how does Shadow quell him?"

"Hell if I know. For that matter, no one knows for sure. Only that he goes without fear into wherever it is that Lombrey lives and emerges victorious."

Falcyn growled in frustration. "Well that's . . . fucking useless." They had to find some way to get Maddor free without killing him. Awaken the dragons.

And stop Lombrey from attacking them.

Or killing them.

But how could anyone fight a shadow when they weren't a shadow? When they couldn't drag his soldiers out, make them solid, and beat the hell . . .

Wait a second.

Yeah, that was it!

Falcyn licked his lips in expectation of the fight to come. But as he prepared himself mentally, he had a radical idea.

Mad radical.

This was crazy, but just insane enough that it *might* work.

He glanced over to the women. "Um . . . Brogan? Can you do us a favor? Summon the Crom."

Eyes wide, she turned to gape at Falcyn. "Beg pardon? Are you out of your mind?"

"All the time. But strangely, this isn't total lunacy." Well, *total* being the operative word. "It makes complete sense." If one was insane.

Blaise cleared his throat. "I'm with Brogan. I think this is a profoundly bad idea."

"Good thing I'm bad to the marrow of my bones." Falcyn shot a fire blast at the spiraling shadows headed for them. "You might want to coo to the Crom, love . . . Sooner rather than later."

Medea attempted to fight off an attacker, only to learn what he already knew.

It was an impossible task. They were too quick and noncorporeal. A bad combination in a fight.

Brogan's voice echoed off the stone walls as a large shadow peeled itself away to approach them.

"Scream. Scream. Loud and clear." His voice was haunting and raspy. "Anguish is the sound most dear." He laughed. "Tell me now of every pain. Until no life here shall remain."

"You're a twisted bugger." Falcyn shot a fireball at their new *friend*.

The light broke through the darkness to show an ethereally handsome face. At least one side of it. The other was concealed by a black hood. With haunting eyes of gold, Lombrey stared at him. His caramel skin glistened before he faded back into the recesses of the wall.

The floor buckled again as the ground continued its rhythmic pulsing.

"Hear me, Crom, I bid you ride," Brogan breathed. "I need you now, by my side."

Lombrey hissed at her chant. "What are you doing?"

She didn't respond to him. "Of darkest sin and mighty power. Let your fiercest wrath reign and shower."

"Stop that!" Lombrey growled.

It was too late. A swirling vortex twisted in the air, sending debris all over them, and scattering the shadow warriors Lombrey had conjured.

"What is this?" Medea asked.

"The Crom rising." Falcyn jerked his chin toward the light that spiraled in dizzying circles. A horse neighed in the distance.

Then they felt him. That heavy, rhythmic thrumming of demonic hooves. They pounded in his chest like a second heartbeat.

Until the Black Crom and his horse leapt from the portal and reared before them.

Brogan shrank back with a shriek while Blaise ran to protect her.

Falcyn smiled. "Brogan? Tell him Morgen, Narishka, and Mordred."

Her eyes widened. "Pardon?"

"He wants the names of victims. I can't think of any better. Or more deserving of his wrath."

A slow smile curved her lips as she finally understood what he was asking her to do. With a tilt of her chin and a wink, she let out a small laugh.

"Master of life and silent death. I call upon you with my sacred breath. Hear these names and so pursue. Morgen, Mordred, Narishka are the ones meant for you."

The Black Crom shot his skull whip toward Brogan so that it could open its mouth as if catching those names, and laugh at her. *To them all I will ride. And never spare them my homicide.*

Suddenly, Medea began to chant in a language Falcyn couldn't identify.

As she did that, he began his own incantation. It was something he hadn't done in a long while. Something he'd once been *real* good at.

The air around him sizzled as he called on his arcane powers. The kind that only a god could command. Every hair on his body stood to attention.

Goose bumps ran from his neck, down his back, and across his arms. The aether whispered in his ears. The voices of a billion people and those of his parents and those of other pantheons.

He heard the lifeblood of the world. The universe. Even the stars whispered in his ears. Power rose up inside him. Crackling. Snapping. Sizzling.

Without being told, Falcyn knew his eyes had turned a serpentine yellow. Something confirmed as Medea looked at him and gasped.

Falcyn ignored her as he came to the most dangerous part. Should he lose focus now, Maddor would die. It took a lot of care to remove a soul from a body, especially against the will of the owner. Most couldn't even begin to do this, as all souls had to be given and gently coerced.

But he was older than those laws. Back in the day, his father had commanded the souls of all humanity. He'd bartered and sold them like a child with a set of Pokémon cards.

Lombrey froze.

As did his warriors.

It's working. . . .

Any moment now, his son would have a new home. Maddor might hate him for it, but at least it would get him away from Morgen's clutches.

Falcyn whispered faster.

Louder.

The Black Crom screamed. Lombrey cursed and writhed as he fell to his knees.

Something dark and cold passed through Falcyn. It rose up like a wave and came crashing down. Electricity roiled through his body, making his hair fly up and out. For a full minute, no one moved.

No one breathed.

No one dared.

Falcyn turned toward Lombrey, expecting to see Maddor.

The shadow warriors faded into the walls of the dungeon, where they hung as motionless shadows. "What have you done?" Lombrey asked.

"I freed you from Morgen."

Lombrey laughed. "I was never enslaved by that bitch."

Confused, Falcyn turned toward Blaise for an explanation. "I thought Morgen owned all the mandrakes."

"She does."

His brow arched in question, he turned back toward Lombrey, who stared at him with a frown of utter bewilderment.

"What do mandrakes have to do with me?"

A bad feeling went through Falcyn. He'd pulled Maddor's soul out of his body. He'd felt it. There was no mistaking that sensation. Granted, it'd been a while since he'd last done such, but still . . .

He returned to the "dragon" Maddor's side.

The dragon who for all intents and purposes appeared to be

Maddor could no longer speak. He glanced about the room as if every bit as disoriented and confused as Falcyn felt.

That bad feeling deepened inside him. *Please tell me I didn't.* . . .

With a knot in his stomach, he glanced around at his companions. Yet no one seemed to be different.

Who the hell had his son's soul?

"Maddor?"

Brandor took a step back. "Why are you looking at me?"

He pinned an inquisitive stare on Brogan.

"What?" she asked.

"Urian?"

"Yeah?"

Ah, God, please tell me it's not . . .

Falcyn swallowed hard as fear gripped him with an icy hand. "Medea?"

"Yes?"

Relief poured through him so fast that he saw stars from it.

Okay, everyone seemed to be the same.

And that was not helpful. He still had no idea what had happened to his child.

If Maddor wasn't Maddor, and everyone else was who they were supposed to be, what could have happened to his . . .

His thought trailed off as the one and only answer dawned on him.

Fuck me.

Stunned and more fearful than he'd have ever thought possible, he turned toward the only rational explanation.

Dear gods no . . .

And yet, there was no other option.

Maddor was the Black Crom.

Demonic laughter echoed around them. "Took you long enough to figure it out, dragon. Thank you for the upgrade."

16

My son is the Crom. Falcyn cursed himself for the spell that had gone all kinds of wrong.

In all his evil glory, Maddor reared his black horse before them. Pawing in the air, the horse screamed and blew its demonic fire. Maddor uncoiled his whip and cracked it at Falcyn.

Instinctively, he grabbed the bony spines that wrapped around his forearm, biting deep in his flesh, and leaving a bleeding welt. It took everything he had not to snatch his son from the back of the horse and drag him over the ground to beat sense into him.

No one attacked Falcyn with impunity.

No one except his son and grandson. For them alone he would bleed.

Medea saw the bloodlust in Falcyn's eyes. She fully expected him to jerk the Crom off and beat him down. So when he let go of the whip and stepped back, her jaw went slack.

From what little she knew of her dragon, retreat and mercy weren't in him.

"What's going on?" she asked.

"I was only trying to save him." Falcyn's voice was barely audible.

Meanwhile the Crom made no move to leave and go after the ones Brogan had named earlier. "Why can't I kill you?"

"You're not tasked with it." Brogan approached him slowly. "The Black Crom can only take the lives I decree. No others."

He started to charge her.

The horse threw him to the ground before it snorted fire and shook its head to let him know it would have no part in what he'd intended. Maddor rolled and landed in an undignified heap.

Brogan scoffed as Maddor rose up in front of her and again recoiled off an invisible wall that prevented him from assaulting her. "You can't harm me in *this* realm. At least not physically. It's why I wanted out of the other one so badly. You can only do me harm in our home. I'm your voice, though how it is that you can now speak on your own is beyond me. No Crom should have that power, in *any* world."

Lombrey solidified in front of them. "When you broke the seal, you mingled their lives. He's neither a mandrake nor a true Dullahan now."

"He's *other* . . . like me." Urian sighed.

Nodding, Lombrey bit his lip. "So it would seem."

Maddor cursed. "I want *my* body back so that I can kick your ass, old man!"

"And people in hell want ice water." Brandor smirked at him. "Guess we're all screwed."

Maddor lunged at him.

Snorting, Brandor sidestepped his attack and tripped him since he couldn't harm Brandor either. "Though I can't say as I blame you. 'Cause no offense, Maddie, you looked a lot better with a head on your shoulders than you do like this. You were always a freak, but never more so than what you are right now as you search about for that little head on a whip."

Falcyn grabbed Maddor to stop his advance as he moved for Brandor's throat. "I'll get this straightened out."

"How? You're the one who screwed it up!"

"I am, but I'm the best chance you have."

With a fierce scoff, Maddor shoved him away. "And why would you help me? Why didn't you just kill me?"

Medea wasn't sure which of them was the most stunned by his question.

Falcyn snapped his head back as if he'd been physically slapped. "You're my son. Why wouldn't I?"

Now it was Maddor's turn to act stunned—at least that was what she assumed. Though to be honest, it was hard to tell when he had no head or facial expressions to judge by. Rather, he stood there, stock-still. "What? Bullshit! You're not my father! You're lying!"

Falcyn was completely baffled. "You said Morgen told you everything."

"Aye! She said that you murdered my mother for protecting me, and left me to die!"

Falcyn's jaw went slack. Those words cold-cocked him. "I killed your mother when she came to gloat to me about selling you, *our* child, *my* son, to Morgen to torture me over what she'd done to you! Think about it. How else would I've had access to her, since I've been banned from this realm since before you were born?"

Deflating before their very eyes, Maddor stepped back in uncertainty. "I-I don't understand."

"It's true, Maddor. At least I think you're Maddor. Falcyn sent me here to watch over you. I'm the one who goaded her into going to Falcyn, hoping he'd be able to get to you and help you out of here. I didn't count on his overreaction that would result in her death. Guess I should have."

That unexpected, sweet, lilting voice went through Falcyn like a knife.

No.

It couldn't be. . . .

His heard pounding, he turned to see Sarraxyn. Pale and standing on unsteady feet, she had one arm braced against the wall nearest her.

"Xyn? Is it really you?"

She gave him a wan smile. "Greetings, brother."

His own limbs shaking, he crossed the room to gather her into his arms. "How?"

"I don't know. One minute I was frozen, and then I was *here*. Wherever this is."

Closing his eyes, Falcyn fisted his hand in her long, flame-red hair that parted to show off her pointed ears. Her translucent, vibrant green gaze seared him. And she was still one of the most beautiful women he'd ever seen. "I never thought I'd see you again."

She clutched at his back. "I know." Kissing his cheek, she pulled back to stare at Maddor. "He is your father, Maddor. Just as Blaise is your son."

That sucked every bit of the air from the room and had the same impact as a nuclear bomb detonating in their midst.

Blaise stumbled back. "W-w-w-what?"

Falcyn ground his teeth at the way she told him something he'd have been much more delicate with.

Xyn nodded. "I was there when you were born. Your mother was furious, thinking your albinism had to do with Max's curse."

"What curse?"

Falcyn winced as she unwittingly spilled the beans. "I never told Blaise the truth, Xyn." For a reason—as the last thing he'd wanted was to hurt him.

Her jaw went slack. "I'm so sorry. I assumed he knew."

Falcyn shook his head. "By the time I learned about his birth, he was grown. I didn't have the heart to tell him then. Thanks, sister. You were always good at ratting me out."

Maddor sat down. "Blaise is my son? How?"

Xyn sighed. "Ormarra. She hid her pregnancy from you and was hoping to parlay Blaise's birth to her advantage."

"When I was born deformed, she tried to kill me."

Brogan moved to hold Blaise. "You're not deformed!" Her low tone was punctuated by Falcyn's shout of the same words.

"And I killed her for her actions against you," Xyn said. "Everything you were told, Blaise, was a lie concocted by Morgen to hurt you. You were still wet from cracking open your egg when I took you to Emrys to raise. The only truth you knew was that your father was the leader of the mandrakes."

He'd just assumed it was the mandrake before Maddor, because only a tiny handful of fey knew Maddor was the first of their breed.

Another lie Morgen had kept so that no one would know she was related to their race.

Maddor growled at Xyn. "You should have told me about him!"

"I was planning to once I knew he was safe, but Morgen caught wind of my intentions and trapped me here before I had the chance."

With a fierce roar, Maddor started for Xyn, only to be stopped by some unseen force.

"You can't harm her," Brogan reminded him. "I haven't given you her name."

"I hate all of you!" he roared.

Falcyn flinched as Medea moved to stand next to him so that she could offer him comfort. But the guilt he felt over his son didn't last long. It gave way to a profound fury while he raked his gaze over Maddor's former dragon body and then his new one as the Black Crom. "How dare *you*! Feel free to hate me all you want. I deserve it. Blaise, however, has never done anything to deserve your animosity for him. He's your son. One you've treated like hell and mocked over the centuries for no reason whatsoever. You owe him an apology."

Maddor scoffed at Falcyn. "You're daring to lecture *me* on parenthood? Seriously?"

"Yeah, and I'll bust your ass, boy! Don't ever think I can't take you in a fight. I promise you, I've eaten much tougher hides than yours and used their scales for shoes. If you want to act like a child, then I'll treat you like one."

The real Crom made a noise deep inside the dragon's body.

Falcyn turned toward him at the sound, curious as to what was causing it. "What's going on, Brogan? He about to spew?"

She shook her head. "It's the strife between the two of you. It feeds him. Makes him—"

The Crom broke free and stood up.

"Stronger," she finished with a squeak.

Blaise took her hand and pulled her behind him. "What's he doing now?"

"Not sure." Falcyn put his hand out to stop Medea from engaging the beast as she moved in for an attack.

Because the Crom wasn't the only dragon rising.

All of them were, and he wasn't sure what that signified. But with their luck, it wasn't a good thing.

"Maddor?" Falcyn glanced to his son. "You want to return to your real body?"

His whip sizzled as he turned a slow circle to survey the

number of original dragons who were now a little more than just plain pissed off. And since they had no other target, they were circling the only enemy they found in the room.

Them.

The whole group. And that included their mandrake leader that they couldn't identify as a dragon since he was in the Crom's body and had no head.

"Yeah, I think I do."

Falcyn couldn't blame him there. Judging by the mood of the newly animated dragons, anything not one of their scaly clan was about to get eaten.

Summoning his powers, Falcyn felt his hands heating up as he began the process of reversing what he'd done to change out Maddor's soul.

Lombrey rose up in an effort to block the dragons, but they passed right through his noncorporeal form.

Urian rolled his eyes. "Good to be a shadow, huh? Makes me wish I was one." He drew a sword and prepared to attack.

And just as Falcyn began the incantation, a bright light flashed near them. It was intense and searing. So much so that it temporarily blinded him.

Until his sight cleared enough to see the last creature he'd have ever expected to appear in their midst.

Simi Parthenopaeus.

Dressed in a short purple skirt, black-and-red-striped leggings, and a matching corset, she was the Dark-Hunter Acheron's . . . something. No one was quite sure what, and Acheron was never big on giving details, on Simi or anything else.

She drew up short as she surveyed everyone around her. Her

red horns sprouted on top of her head as a tail came out from underneath her short skirt. A set of leathery bat wings sprang out, letting him know the Charonte Goth demon was ready to battle. Otherwise, her wings would have been of soft black and red feathers.

Urian's eyes widened. "Simi? What are you doing here?"

"Akri done told the Simi that you'd be acting all weird and funky lately, and that the Simi should be keeping her eyeball on you, Akri-Uri. So . . . your heart rate picked up during my commercial break. Since I knew you wouldn't be with no heifer cow-like redheaded goddess creature doing things that make the Simi go blind, I thought you be troubled. So then I thought, Simi, you best be checking on that old ex-Daimon to make sure he okay and not about to get et by something not friendly."

She scowled as she put her finger to her cheek to consider her words. "No, that be wrong. Be *in* trouble." She grinned widely, flashing her fangs. "You in trouble, Akri-Uri? Can the Simi eat your troubles? 'Cause I don't think these dragonlies be on the Simi no-eat list. Pretty sure Akri won't mind if the Simi eats them up." She bit her lip with a childish enthusiasm that almost made Falcyn smile. Especially as she reached into her coffin backpack and pulled out a bib and a bottle of barbecue sauce to prepare for her meal.

The moment she did, the dragons actually stood down. Some even gulped audibly.

And that made Maddor nervous as hell. "What's going on?"

Xyn laughed. "No one is dumb enough to tangle with a hungry Charonte. Don't you know?"

Simi gasped. "Say it no so! The Simi so-o-o-o-o hungry! It been a whole twenty minutes since the Simi ets her last diamond. . . ." She pouted as she turned around, looking for a meal.

As she stepped forward, the dragons stepped back.

"Yeah!" Urian blustered at them. "That's right! I've got a Charonte here and I'm not afraid to unleash her. Hah!"

A dragon sneezed beside him, blowing out fire that came a little too close to Urian.

Urian dashed to Simi's side, putting her between them. "Are you fireproof, Sim?"

"Bomb proof, too." She belched and shot out a stream of fire that caused several dragons to scramble for cover. "See!"

"Ah, you bunch of hatchlings." With his hands on his hips, Falcyn finished putting Maddor back into his body.

The moment the Crom was himself again, he picked up his whip and went straight to Brogan.

They all tensed in expectation of what he intended to do with her, especially Blaise.

Brogan held her hand up to let them know that it was all right. After a few seconds, she nodded. "Peace to you, Crom."

With a curt jerk of his coat, he flashed himself onto the back of his horse and vanished.

"What did he say?" Blaise asked.

She smiled warmly. "That he never wants to be a dragon again. You can keep your smelly old body."

Blaise snorted. "Can't blame him there."

Her eyes twinkling, she took his hand. "And he said he'd see about my list that I gave him. I'd hate to be Morgen right now."

"Not too sure I want to be us." Medea glanced around at

the restless dragons, who were still eyeballing them a little too closely for her happiness.

Xyn held her hands out in an arc. "How long have we slept?"

"Centuries," Blaise and Falcyn said simultaneously.

An unhappy murmur ran through them.

"Simi eat them now since they all grumbly?" Her wings twitched with expectation.

The dragons quieted immediately.

Medea laughed. "Nice to know you don't just scare Daimons, Simi."

Simi pressed her finger to her lips and cocked her head to an adorable expression. Yeah, that made no sense to Falcyn. How could such a lethal creature be so uncommonly charming? The dichotomy of the Goth demon had never failed to amaze or surprise him.

She scowled, then smiled at Medea. "The Simi knows you! I's seens you lots and lots. You're the evil princess who libs with the Simi's akra in Kalosis!"

"She's also my sister."

Simi gasped at Urian's words. Then caught herself. "Oh yeah. I should have . . . but wait. Your daddy is fake-akri." She pressed her hands to her eyebrows. "The Simi is so confuseled!"

Urian laughed. "So am I most days."

Sobering, he gently pulled one of her hands down until she opened her eyes to look at him. "It's just like your daddy, Simi. I was taken out of my mother's womb before I was born and put into the belly of another. So the Apollite who birthed me wasn't really my mother. And Stryker wasn't really my father. Styxx is my father and Bethany is my real mom."

"Ah! Like Simi you're adaptable!"

Urian's grin widened. "Yeah."

"Wait . . ." Brandor scowled. "Does she mean adopted?"

"No, silly!" Arms akimbo, Simi rolled her eyes. "Even though we both were adopted, the Simi meant adaptable, 'cause Akri-Uri had to libs with people not his people. He not really a Daimon, he a demigod. Which is better. Sometimes, anyway." She tsked as she looked back at Urian. "I'm sorry, Akri-Uri. That why you have sadness besides Phoebe-sadness?"

His eyes darkened. "No, Sim. Mostly I just have Phoebe sadness."

She held her barbecue sauce out toward him. "Wanna eat a dragon? Make you feel all better. Give you warm and fuzzies in the belly."

And that succeeded in driving the dragons toward the shadows and Lombrey into a fit.

"No! No! No! You're not to hide in my domain! Get out, mangy beasts!"

Brandor cleared his throat to disguise his laughter. "You know, with all this noise, Morgen is bound to realize what's happened. We might want to think about getting out of here before she sends something or someone to investigate."

Falcyn nodded to his sister. "Granted, she should be a little preoccupied with the Crom after her, you still should take them to my island. Just to be safe."

She arched a brow at his order. "*All* of them? You really plan to tolerate us in your personal space?"

He tried not to be agitated at the thought of that many en-croaching on his territory, but . . . "It'll be the safest place for them."

Xyn kissed his cheek. "Love you."

Falcyn tried not to let those words weaken him. But they always did. Only his sister had ever said that to him, and meant it. "You, too."

She scoffed at his response. "I live for the day, *Veles*, when you can say that word without choking on it." And with that, she gathered the dragons and left.

All except Maddor.

"Aren't you joining them?"

"How can I?" His tone was as bitter as the light in his eyes. "I'm bound to Morgen. As are all mandrakes. Thanks to you. Bastard."

Falcyn cursed himself for not remembering that. "I should have left you in the Crom's body."

"I didn't want to be there." There was no missing the fury in his voice.

"Maddor—"

He brushed past Falcyn. "Don't say anything. There's noth-ing left between us." His eyes betrayed his torment as he neared Blaise. "I should never have tried to kill you. That was wrong of me. Had I known you were mine then, I would have pro-tected you." With those whispered words, he vanished.

"What kind of apology was that?" Falcyn wanted to beat his son. Yet he couldn't blame him. Not really. It was his own ass, and Max's, he wanted to thrash most.

Blaise sighed. "For Maddor, it was major. Believe me. That's as close to an apology as I've ever heard him come." He swallowed hard. "I can't believe you've kept this secret for so long. Damn."

"It was never easy." Falcyn braced himself as he asked the question he couldn't avoid. "On a scale of one to ten, how mad are you?"

"I don't know. . . . Eighty."

Falcyn winced.

"But strangely, not at you."

That shocked him. "How can you not be mad at me?"

"Don't know. I want to be. I feel that I should be, but then I remember all the times you've been there, and . . . I still want to kick your ass."

Falcyn snorted. "I am sorry."

Simi pursed her lips. "Don't be so sad, dragon people." Her wings rippled, then feathered as she walked over to Blaise to hug him.

Needing comfort, Falcyn slid his hand into his pocket where he kept his dragonstone.

His heart stopped as he realized that Maddor hadn't left empty-handed.

"What is it?" Medea asked.

"That bastard. . . . Maddor stole my dragonstone!"

17

Alone in his room, Maddor opened his hand to study his father's dragonstone.

His father.

That knowledge pierced him like a lightning bolt. He still wasn't sure how to handle it. All this time, he'd thought himself abandoned. Unloved. Had imagined a total bastard who'd screwed his mother and then left him to die.

Then Morgen had concocted a much more sinister tale of a bastard who'd rejected him, then killed his mother. In his mind, his unknown father had taken on an even more horrific persona.

Now he knew the face of the dragon who'd created him.

And a whole different story. One he'd never dared dream existed.

Not a bastard after all, if Falcyn's lies were to be believed.

Part of him didn't care. None of it mattered, and most likely every word out of his mouth had been a lie.

Either way, it damn sure didn't change his past.

Yet . . .

I have a father who's alive.

And a son.

He tried to get a handle on the moment, but none would come. Worse was the knowledge that he held a vital part of his father in his hand. A vital part of the world itself.

With this, he could destroy him.

Much like Excalibur, the dragonstone was able to take life and to give it. The power of it emanated and vibrated through his hand. Through his whole body.

This was rare, primal power. The kind that could take out Morgen and the whole of her Circle.

Forever.

With this, he could rule not only Camelot and Avalon, but the entire world.

All worlds.

And it was now under his control alone. *I could rule everything and everyone.*

"What you doing, dragon-man?"

He jumped at the singsongy accent of the Charonte demon he thought he'd left behind with his father. How the hell had she gotten into his room?

"Who let you in here?"

Shrugging, she approached him as if he were nothing to be concerned about. A foolish thing, since . . .

Well, he couldn't really kill her. He wasn't sure what, if anything, could kill her species. Those damned things were terribly hearty.

"Don't nobody be telling the Simi *no* excepting for her akri, and you not Akri. You cute like Akri, but only Akri is Akri. No other exceptions are accepted by the Simi. Excepting for Akri-Styxx and then only sometimes . . . and maybe Akri-Bas. And sometimes Akra-Kat and Akri-Lexie."

"You shouldn't be here."

"Then gimme what you took and the Simi will leave." She held her arm out with her palm open and tilted toward him in a very childlike gesture.

She was so honest and trusting. He couldn't imagine ever being like that. His life had never leant itself to such.

Part of him was angered by it. Another, curious.

But he wasn't dumb enough to act out against her. His survival instincts kept his temper in check and he decided the best course of action was to feign ignorance with her. "Don't know what you're talking about."

She wagged her finger. "Yes, you do. 'Course you do. Now be a good boy dragon." She pointed at the stone. "Akri-Falcyn is all upset 'cause you tookted his toy. He say he needs it and so I'm here to get it. 'Cause the Simi don't want him sad. Didn't anyone ever tell you not to steal? You don't take what don't belong to you! Now gibs it over."

"What about my childhood he stole?"

Simi tsked. "Don't be blaming others for you bad acts. Or trying to justify thievingness when it wrong, no matter how you slice and dice it. No need to even try for julienne fries. Or waffle cones neither. You know you didn't make the stone 'cause you not a woman demon and you know you tooked it from your daddy's pocket. Now gives it!"

"Or what?"

Pursing her lips, she cocked her hip and rested her hands on her narrow waist. "You really want to go there? 'Cause the Simi could use some barbecue. And dragon meat is most yummy. Just saying."

Maddor started to tell her where to shove the stone and to continue denying that he had it. But the moment he opened his mouth to speak, the full pain of it all hit him like a physical blow.

All the years of his brutal childhood and his humiliating subservience to Morgen. All the times he'd wanted a kind hand to touch him. Someone to tell him he wasn't what they said.

Now . . .

Overwhelmed, he choked on a sob.

Simi let out an anguished noise. "Oh no, Mr. Dragon Human. Did the Simi break you?"

Yes, but it was only his heart that was shattered as memory after memory tore through him. Even though he lived the majority of his life as a man, he'd never been treated as a human.

Only an animal Morgen was afraid would piss her rug and chew on her favorite shoes.

Even now, he could see himself in the cage where they kept him. Hear the mocking laughter that was never far from the surface of his pain.

King of the mandrakes you might be, but never forget who holds your leash, boy! The hand that feeds you can quickly become the hand that ends you.

Maddor winced at the images that took turns assaulting him without mercy. He hated life. He always had. Every fucking heartbeat was nothing more than another chance for someone else to tell him how worthless he was. How much they hated him.

And his father thought a simple apology could rectify that. Yeah, right . . .

With a stricken expression, Simi sidled up to him. "Don't be so sad, dragon-man. It okay. You see! Just 'cause you're mad at your daddy don't make him a mean, nasty dragon. Even the Simi can tell that he lubs you. You should talk to him."

"You don't understand."

"No, I don't. I get the mad. I get the sad. But when you have a choice of someone willing to love you and being all by your lonesome, seems to the Simi that being loved is always better than being alone. My akri even forgibbed Akri-Styxx and Akri-Styxx forgibbed my akri. Akri-Styxx forgibbed me for killing him. If they could learn to be friends and to forgive, I know you can, too. After all, your daddy didn't kill you."

That was true, he supposed. "You make it sound easy."

"It is." She reached up to cup his chin and squeeze his cheeks.

"I'm sorry. It okay. Didn't mean to be a douchy. See? Easy, peasy with extra cheesy."

He scowled at her deepened tone where she faked his voice. Damn, the Goth demon was charming.

Her frown melted to a sweet smile. "See! That's all you have to do."

But it wasn't as simple as she made it out. "If I give it to Morgen, she'll free me. And I can leave here."

Simi made a peculiar sound, almost like a horn. "Will she? You sure about that?"

He cringed as Simi voiced his own doubt. Morgen wasn't exactly known for keeping her word or for her integrity.

Screwing people over . . .

Lying when she could tell the truth . . .

That was definitely her forte. Hell, the bitch was known for going out of her way to screw others.

Literally and figuratively.

He clutched at the stone.

"Do the right thing, dragon-man. Gibs it back and apologize to your daddy. Makes it right so that he can love you and not feel all bad and gooey that he lubs you."

The only problem with that? He didn't know what the right thing to do was. Protect his father.

Or protect his own ass, since no one else ever had.

Medea felt horrible for Falcyn. All these centuries, she'd thought the worst thing in the world had been to lose her son. Watching Falcyn now, she realized that wasn't the worst.

A living child who hated you was far more cruel.

Blaise and the others had gone back without them. Torn between her family and Falcyn, she'd decided to stay here in Camelot with him.

He needed her more.

Falcyn was alone and the misery in his eyes kept her by his side even though she knew she was needed in Kalosis. Besides, there was nothing she could do for her people without his dragonstone.

Her heart breaking for him, she pulled him against her and held him tight. The fact that he didn't protest told her exactly how wounded he was by it all. He was weak, and she knew from Urian that it was a state this dragon wasn't used to.

The least she could do was comfort him.

Closing her eyes, she breathed in the scent of him as she ran her hands through his hair.

Falcyn choked on his unshed tears and the swell of unfamiliar tenderness Medea awoke inside his dead heart. The dragon in him wanted to carry her away to his den and keep her there, protests be damned. Hence the legends of old about his kind. It'd been their loneliness and abject misery that had caused his species to kidnap mates and force them to their isolated lairs.

Yet he'd never done such. Never had he wanted to.

Until now.

As far back as he could recall, he'd been reclusive in a way no other dragon had. The only time he'd ever been weak had been after Hadyn's death. Unable to cope with losing his brother, he'd allowed Igraine to seduce him for Morgen.

He'd deluded himself then. And he'd known it. He just

hadn't cared. Anything to keep from being alone with his guilt over his brother's death.

Now he'd screwed up not only his life, but Maddor's as well.

And Medea's. Because of this, her people would die. Most likely her parents, too. Yet she didn't curse him for being stupid or careless.

Rather, she stayed by his side.

The woman was so strange and made no sense whatsoever to him.

"Why are you being so kind to me?"

Medea let out a soft laugh. "No idea. I'm all kinds of stupid."

Burying his face against her neck, he inhaled her sweet scent and shook his head. "You're never that."

"'Course I am. Otherwise I'd be gone already. Only an absolute idiot would be here in their enemy's domain for no good reason." Medea toyed with Falcyn's belt. She really shouldn't be with him now and she knew it. Yet she couldn't bring herself to leave him and she didn't even know why.

This felt right. She needed to be with him in his hour of need. To give him comfort when he had no one else he'd accept it from.

And she couldn't take her eyes off him. Or her hands. It'd been too long since she'd felt like this. Since she'd wanted to be with someone.

And by the size of his obvious erection, he was definitely interested, too.

"What are you thinking, princess?"

Medea bit her lip as fear consumed her. "That I should be going."

He gave her a lopsided grin. "I'd rather you stay."

Taking a deep breath, she pulled his shirt over his head, then her own. "We are two entirely different species. This will never work out."

Falcyn couldn't breathe as she hesitated. Oh man, this really was cruel. "Don't tease me, princess."

With a slowness that was sheer torture, she unbuckled her belt and kicked off her shoes. He swore his heart stopped beating as he watched her open that belt, then slowly part her fly.

The way she wiggled her hips to slide her pants down hit him like a fist in the gut.

He expelled an appreciative breath at the sight of her naked body. She wasn't skinny, but rather she had lush, full curves that were perfect and mouth-watering.

Medea knew she should be heading back to Kalosis to care for the others, but she couldn't. She needed this time with Falcyn. It was an imperative urge she couldn't deny. The entire world could burn for all she cared.

He hesitated before her, so close that she could feel the heat of his body. Smell the scent of his skin. It was all she could do not to step into the warmth of him. To press her body against his . . .

Frozen to the spot, she didn't move as he bent toward her and drew a deep breath against her neck. He pulled back ever so slightly. "You smell like lilies."

And he smelled like darkness and all masculine skin. Her breasts tightening at the thought, Medea turned her head and before she knew what he was doing, he lowered his lips to hers. She moaned at the decadent taste of him.

He cupped her face in his hands as his tongue hungrily

explored every inch of her mouth. She shivered. This dark dragon lord certainly knew how to kiss. Her head swimming, she buried her hands in his thick, wavy hair.

Falcyn's heart pounded as he tasted her lips. He drank in her passion and was lost to it. Lost to her. Between the sensation of her hands and the heat of his own needs, he was sunk and he knew it. He pulled back only a tiny bit to nibble the corner of her delectable mouth.

Growling, he dipped himself down so that he could pick her up and carry her away to a small cushioned alcove.

Medea felt a wave of giddy joy as Falcyn caressed her breasts. Every part of her burned for his touch.

And then he did what had to be the most tender thing a man had ever done to her. He wrapped his arms around her and just held her close with his head on her shoulder while he rocked with her. Something inside her shattered and melted at the feeling of being held like this . . . as if she were precious to him. His alone.

Falcyn closed his eyes as he reveled in the sensation of her warm, naked skin against his. Her breasts were pressed flat against his chest while her thighs hugged his bare hips. God, it'd been so long since he'd just had a woman hold him, and never had he held one so sweet.

Most of the women he'd slept with would be clawing at him by now, wanting satisfaction. But Medea merely held on to him as if they were something more than strangers. As if he were something more than a tool for her to use to satisfy her needs.

He pulled back to return to her lips before he took her hand into his and led it to the part of him that was craving her the most.

She nibbled at his lips as she gently explored the length of his cock with her graceful fingers.

"You are so beautiful," he whispered against her ear.

Medea moaned as Falcyn rolled onto his back and pulled her against him. It felt so good to be with a man again. To be held, even if they were barely more than strangers. For some reason, he really made her feel beautiful. It didn't make sense, but she did.

Wanting to please him, she straddled his hips before she slowly slid her body onto his.

He hissed before he bit his lip and lifted his hips to drive himself even deeper into her. The look of pure pleasure on his face thrilled her. She couldn't remember the last time a man had been this happy to be with her.

Unlike the others she'd been with, he wasn't nervous at all. He was relaxed and calm.

Her equal.

Medea took his hand in hers and held it close. She understood that she meant nothing to him and that when this was over, he'd probably walk away. The thought hurt and yet she still couldn't bring herself to stop this.

She didn't know why, but she really wanted to be with him, even if it was only temporary.

Falcyn sighed as he teased her lips while her pale hair fell around them in a soft curtain. Oh yeah, this was what he'd needed in the worst sort of way. No woman had ever felt better

than Medea did. She rode him slow and easy, at least in the beginning. But after a few minutes, she quickened her strokes.

Sensing what she needed, he rolled over with her until she
was beneath him.

Medea arched her spine as Falcyn leaned back and thrust
himself deep inside her. He moved faster and faster, spurring her
pleasure on until she couldn't take it anymore. When she came,
her orgasm was so fierce that she screamed out from it.

Fire shone in his steel blue eyes as he smiled down at her.
He moved even faster until he joined her in that perfect moment
of bliss. And he let out a fierce cry of pleasure. While he shuddered in her arms, she cradled him with her whole body, and
she drifted back from the rippling edge. He felt so wickedly
good while she ran her hand over the muscles of his back.

She hadn't felt so at peace in a long, long time, and for that
she was truly grateful. Overwhelmed by the feeling, she pressed
her cheek to his so that she could feel his prickly whiskers
against the smooth skin of her cheek.

Completely content, Falcyn laid himself against her body
while his racing heart slowed its frenetic beat. For the first time
in years he felt a deep-seated peace and he didn't even know
why. There was something magical about this moment. Something magical about her.

He lay on top of her, unwilling to move while she played
with his hair and ran her other hand along his spine. "I'm not
too heavy, am I?"

"Definitely not," she said dreamily. "I like the way you feel."

Growling as another wave of desire hit him, he wiggled his

hips against hers, driving himself in a bit more. "I like the way you feel, too."

Medea smiled at him as he traced small circles around her breast. "I don't ever want to get up from here."

"Neither do I." But no sooner had he uttered those words and lifted himself up to kiss her, then he felt the air around him stir.

Unsure of who would dare invade his domain, Falcyn manifested his clothes on his body, and held a cover to shield Medea while she quickly followed suit.

He stepped away from her to confront the newcomer and he was grateful that he hadn't hurt her when he withdrew so quickly from her body.

A few feet to his left, a shadow began to materialize. Shock caused him to freeze as he met Maddor's hostile gaze the moment his son solidified in the cavern with them.

For a full minute, no one moved. Not until Maddor came forward and, to Falcyn's utter surprise, handed him his dragonstone. The heat of it singed Falcyn's palm.

His jaw slack, he glanced from it to Maddor. "I thought you'd given this to Morgen."

Maddor let his hand linger before he withdrew into the shadows. "I know better than to put my trust with her. With you . . ." He shrugged. "At least kill me before you betray me."

Falcyn clenched the stone in his hand as he met his son's wary gaze. "I won't betray you. Ever. Bastard I might be, but I'm ever loyal. Even to those I want to put through a wall."

Instead of comforting him, those words brought even more

torment and sadness to Maddor's eyes. "I'm not used to having anyone catch me when I stumble."

Simi tsked as she appeared behind him, and then pushed him forcefully with both hands.

Losing all balance, Maddor stumbled into Falcyn's arms. Instinctively, he held his son against him.

"There now!" Simi grinned. "Sometimes we all just needs a bitty push." Satisfaction shone in her dark red eyes. Her feathered wings flapped.

Falcyn would have snorted at her, but right then . . . all he could do was hold his child.

For several seconds Maddor was tense and rigid in his arms.

Until he melted to embrace him back. "You really didn't abandon me?" His voice was scarce more than a hoarse whisper.

"I tried everything to get to you. Damn my brother for it. Morgen had me locked out completely."

"I still hate you."

"I hate me more. Trust me."

Maddor ground his teeth against Falcyn's shoulder before he patted him on the back and took a step away.

Falcyn didn't miss the way his eyes glistened in the dim light. Clearing his throat gruffly, Maddor forced himself to look stern. "You need to get out of here before Morgen realizes that I'm not bringing her the stone. You don't want to have that here in her realm. She'll tear you apart."

"Come with me, then."

"Can't. I'm locked in here."

"Maddor—"

"It's all right," he said, stopping Falcyn. "I'm used to it. Take the stone and help as many as you can with it. If Morgen uses that to release Mordred, all hell will descend on the world again. As bad as I hate her, I hate that little prick more." He handed Falcyn a small, round amulet that was engraved with a dragon.

"What's this?"

"Key to the portal. With that, you can leave this realm."

Falcyn clenched it in his hand. "I will return for you. I swear it. And I will demand Morgen's head if she argues."

He smiled sadly. "I won't hold my breath. But it's nice to have someone finally offer." And with that, he opened a portal. "Think of your home and it'll guide you to it."

Simi stepped forward to hug Maddor. "You a good dragon-man. The Simi will help them dragons get you free! That a promise. And the Simi never breaks her word."

"Thanks, Simi."

Falcyn waited until the women went through before he jerked Maddor into his arms. "I love you, Maddor."

Xyn would be proud of him. He hadn't choked on the words at all.

As expected, Maddor didn't repeat them. He merely pounded him on the back, then shoved him through the portal.

Hard.

But as he was sucked through the dimensions, he heard his son's faint voice. "Love you, too, you worthless bastard."

Falcyn wanted to return to his son, but it was too late. The vortex sucked him straight to Sanctuary. Back to the room on the third floor where all preternatural creatures were drawn to because of the shields here that the bear family had put up to ensure no human would accidentally be exposed to their supernatural powers.

Colt Theodorakopolus stood up as soon as he saw Falcyn entering. Tall and dark-haired, the were-bear Sentinel was a regular on staff who worked as a bouncer and played guitar for the house band, The Howlers.

"Ah, it's you." Disinterested, Colt sat back down and returned to his e-reader.

Falcyn grimaced at him. "Where's Medea?"

He jerked his chin toward the door and reached for his beer. "She headed off to see Max as soon as she came through."

That thought caused his stomach to shrink. What in the world could she possibly want with his brother?

Unless . . .

Ah, shit. He knew that answer without asking.

A bad feeling went through him. He could only think of one reason Medea would seek out Max.

Terrified by the mere thought of the shit she would start, he teleported to Max's attic room to find Medea tangling with Max's Amazon wife, Seraphina.

Yeah, just what he'd figured.

"Hey!" He grabbed Medea straight up in his arms and pulled her away. She kicked her legs in the air, but strangely didn't kick at him.

When Sera started forward, Max grabbed her to keep her from reengaging in the fight. "Thank the gods you're here."

With Medea still thrashing in his arms, Falcyn growled at his brother. "What's going on?"

Titian-haired and Rubenesque, Sera gestured at Medea. "She went to attack Max!"

Falcyn arched a brow at Medea. "Seriously?"

She stopped squirming and waited until he set her back on her feet before she answered. With an indignant tug, she straightened her clothes. "Payment due you for what he did to you and Maddor."

It took everything he had not to smile at his wild Apollite. Only Xyn had ever protected him in such a manner. And before he could stop himself, he cupped her face in his hands and kissed her.

Max gasped.

Medea hissed at how good her dragon tasted. Fisting her hands in his shirt, she wished they were alone. A good fight always got her blood up, and that combined with his scent was all she needed to want to nibble on him all night long.

Sadly, he swept his tongue against hers, then stepped away to face his brother. Yet she didn't miss the fact that he wedged himself between her and them.

She kept her hand on his muscular back as she realized that the only thing he really had in common with his brother was the fact that they were both exceptionally handsome. However, Max was as fair as Falcyn was dark. Max's blond hair framed chiseled features and a pair of silvery gold eyes.

Yeah, he was nothing like Falcyn.

At least not until he cocked his brow into an expression that was identical to the one Falcyn used whenever he was irritated. Now she saw the similarities.

As Max glanced at his wife, she had a new epiphany about the dragon.

Holy shit.

Literally. No wonder the two dragons were so different. It all made sense now.

"Max is part Arel." The words flew out of her mouth before she could stop them.

All three of them turned to gape at her.

"What makes you think that?" Falcyn asked.

She gestured at the beast. Aside from the fact that he looked like one . . . "He reeks of their stench. Just as I know you're part demon—and something a lot more treacherous. You can't mistake it. He bleeds their blood. It oozes from him. Everything about him betrays his breeding."

A tic started in Max's jaw. "We don't speak of my father. Ever." He narrowed his gaze on Falcyn. "Just as we don't speak of *his*."

Maybe not, but at least she finally understood why Max had done what he had where Maddor was concerned. Stupid Arel bastards. All of them. They were nothing but sanctimonious prigs.

Worse? They would *never* put their blood first. It wasn't in them.

Rolling her eyes, she tugged at Falcyn's shirt. "We have to get Maddor out of Camelot."

"I know. But first let's see to your parents."

Max sputtered. "You intend to help the Daimons? Are you out of your mind? They're Daimons!"

Falcyn shrugged. "My stone. My rules."

"They're Daimons," Max repeated.

Falcyn leaned forward to whisper in his ear. "And you're the one who personally caused all the Were-Hunter races to be damned by the Greek gods to an eternal war against each other, Dragonbane. So do not lecture me on right and wrong. Especially not where they're concerned. I do what I want, your rules be damned." And with that, he took Medea's hand and flashed her from Sanctuary to Kalosis.

Something Medea thought was a good idea until they manifested in her father's great hall in the center of the Daimon kingdom.

No sooner did they appear in front of Stryker's empty bone throne than a loud, thunderous roar went up. Never had she heard such a clamor. And definitely not *here*. This was where everyone came when they first journeyed to Kalosis. It was set up so that her father could monitor them.

It'd been that way as far back as anyone knew.

Apollymi always sat in the center of her stone garden, where she kept watch over the world of man by way of her black pool that mirrored the world of man.

Today though, everything changed.

The moment she and Falcyn materialized before her father's seat, Apollymi was there in her full goddess majesty. Her white-blond hair whipped around her thin body. Her long black gown was plastered against her as the silent winds whipped through the hall and sent every Daimon there scattering for cover. Her swirling silver eyes turned bloodred as her wrath contorted her beautiful face into the visage of ultimate rage.

"How dare you!" she growled.

Falcyn didn't so much as flinch. Rather, he faced the ancient goddess without fear or anger. "I've come with good intention and in peace, Braith. There is no ill for you in my heart." He held his hands up with his palms facing him to show her that they were empty.

Still, she didn't back down. "How can I trust *you*?"

"How can I trust you, dearest aunt? But if I'd wanted to hurt you, I'd have struck you in the heart . . . where you're the weakest. And I wouldn't have done it here in your stronghold. But out in the world where you have no reach."

That succeeded in calming her. "You wouldn't dare."

"I don't fear you, Bra. Honestly, life is a burden I can do without. But I'm not my father, and I would never do to you what he did to me. I came here only to help."

The wind finally died down.

Her eyes returned to their familiar swirling silver as her hair settled back to her shoulders. By its own accord, her hair coiled into an impeccable and intricate braided chignon around her face. "It's hard to trust a former enemy."

Falcyn arched a brow at that. "I was never *your* enemy." That had been his parents. Never him.

She met Medea's gaze. "You brought him here?"

"I did."

"Then I hold you responsible for his actions. You'd best pray that he behaves."

Falcyn scoffed at her bitter tone. "Same old Braith. I see time hasn't mellowed you any."

"How could it? When all I have is bitterness to keep me company?"

"Then we have much in common, don't we?" He inclined his head to Medea. "Where are your parents?"

"In bed, I would assume."

"Take me to them."

Without a word, she led him down a long, dark hallway.

Apollymi followed after them, as if she didn't trust him in her domain, at all. It'd be funny if it didn't piss him off.

Falcyn glanced at her over his shoulder. "Afraid I'm going to abscond with something?"

"You might. Never could trust a dragon. Last time one of you was here, he pissed my rugs and cracked the ceiling."

"I'll try to contain myself."

"Please do so, as I have no desire to redecorate with anything other than your entrails."

Falcyn growled as Medea opened the door to a bedroom and he saw the large tester bed where a woman who bore a striking resemblance to her lay in sickened misery. The moment the door opened a man shot to his feet to confront them.

Then he hit the floor where he, too, writhed from his own illness.

"Papa!" Medea rushed to his side to check on him.

With a fierce groan, he forced himself up so that he could face Falcyn. Though he didn't pose much of a threat in that condition. Worst thing he could do was vomit on him.

"Relax, Stryker. I'm here to assist." Falcyn moved toward Zephyra, who was so weak she could barely open her eyes. No wonder Medea had been terrified. He doubted they'd have made it another day in this condition.

She'd been right. Apollo had sent one hell of an illness for them.

As it was, Stryker was forced to sit back on the bed.

With Medea's help.

"How long have you been gone?" His voice was weak.

"A day."

Stryker swallowed. "Are you ill?"

"No."

"Then you shouldn't have returned. You should have stayed where the illness couldn't reach you."

"I couldn't leave you sick like this."

Stryker reached for his wife. "She's been so strong until about an hour ago." A tear ran down his cheek.

Falcyn pulled the cover back to see an angry rash that covered Zephyra's pale skin. The blisters had opened to festering wounds. "I won't let her die. Don't worry."

For the first time, he felt Apollymi approach him with something more than hatred or suspicion.

She actually put her hand on him with a tenderness that was completely unexpected. "Can I help?"

"Take Medea from here so that she can't be infected while I work."

Nodding, Apollymi held her hand out toward Medea. "Come, child."

Medea hesitated. "Falcyn—"

"Please . . . I can focus better if you're safe."

As much as she hated to go, she inclined her head and let go of her father's hand, then followed Apollymi from the room.

Chewing her lip, Medea hesitated at the door to look back

and listen as Falcyn chanted quietly under his breath. He cupped his dragonstone in his hand and turned it over and over. A powerful glow from the stone shot between his fingers to illuminate his face with shadows.

Apollymi pulled her from the room and closed the door.

"He'll heal them, right?"

"Yes, I think he will."

Then why was her gut so tight? Why did something feel so wrong? She was home now.

Yet . . .

Medea was so unsettled.

Apollymi hesitated as if she heard her uncertainty. "Are you all right, child?"

"I don't know."

Apollymi glanced back toward the door and sighed. "I should have known Apollo would do something like this. He was ever a treacherous bastard. They all were."

She caught the heavy note in the ancient goddess's voice. "They?"

"The Greeks. Upstart bastards. The whole lot of them. I blame Archon for their rise. Lying piece of shit. They all should have been drowned the moment they first crawled into being."

Archon had been the king of the Atlantean gods, and Apollymi's husband. "Why did you marry him if you hate him so?"

"He lied to me. I thought he was my Kissare returned to life. But he wasn't. Too late, I learned it was a trick played on me to keep me under control."

Apollymi's eyes swam from unshed tears. "Too often we let our hearts lead our heads, and ignore signs that are sent to warn us of the truth. I wanted my Kissare so badly that I saw his face when it wasn't there. And then when he was back, I'd been so badly burned that I didn't believe in him or anything else, anymore. And especially not in something as cruel as love." She drew a ragged breath. "The saddest part, Medea? Our worst hells are always made by our own bad decisions."

And that was what terrified her the most. "How do we know when we're making a bad decision?"

Apollymi laughed bitterly. "That's the cruelest blow of all. We don't. It's only when we look back that we see clearly where we went wrong."

"So is it wrong to love?"

A crystal tear rolled from Apollymi's eye and froze to her flawless cheek. "That was the question I asked when I was told that my love was the cause of a war that should never have started. Not once. But twice."

And with that, she headed for her garden, where she could mourn for her son whose birth had been cursed and who'd been torn from her arms by the prejudices and vindictiveness of others.

Life was cruel. Medea knew that better than anyone. It made no sense. There was no rhyme. No reason. Misery spared no one. Injustice baptized everyone equally, without prejudice or mercy. Sooner or later, death would come calling. Pain would stalk all hearts.

That was the nature of the beast.

Yet, she still had hope and she didn't know why.

It made no sense to her. Truly, it didn't. If anyone had a reason to lie down and surrender to the utter despair that was life, she would be the one.

And still . . .

She blamed Davyn for this stupid optimism that wouldn't perish or go away.

And speaking of, she wanted to go check on him. If for no other reason, she suddenly felt a deep compunction to kick his ever-cheerful ass.

Yeah, that would definitely make her feel better. His neck in her hands . . .

In fact, every step that carried her closer to his room . . . and his throat, brightened her spirits. Along with the thought of beating him senseless.

As soon as she reached his door, she knocked on it. "Hey, Dav?"

Without thinking, she pushed it open, then drew up short as she saw that he wasn't alone.

He was with a woman. Which was really, really, *really* strange.

Because Davyn was completely gay. In every sense of the word. And not only was Davyn naked in his bed with the woman on top of him.

The unknown woman was happily *feeding* from his thigh. In fact, she was so giddy, she was smacking.

Dumbfounded and horrified, Medea started to back up and leave them in peace. But just as she did so, she caught the slight, barely audible squeak from Davyn.

"Help me," he breathed.

Yeah, that sounded more like a safe word or phrase.

Medea clutched at the doorknob, unsure if she should intervene or not. "Davyn?"

The woman looked up and hissed at her with a pair of glazed, feral eyes. Blood dripped from her chin and fangs.

Pale and weak, Davyn didn't seem to be enjoying it. Rather, he appeared more like someone turning gallu.

Okay, this was all kinds of wrong.

"Get off him, she-bitch!" Medea rushed forward, intending to kill his attacker.

As Medea grabbed the woman's arm and pulled her back, Davyn caught her hand in a surprisingly strong grip to keep her from making a lethal strike.

Stunned, she gaped at him. "What are you doing?"

The woman broke free of her grasp and scrambled for the door.

His breathing ragged, he shook his head. "You can't . . . kill her."

"Why ever not?"

"It's Urian's Phoebe. Kill her and he'll never forgive you!"

18

Those unexpected words floored Medea and leashed her claws as she stared at the open door through which the Daimon had just vanished.

Urian's Phoebe?

It couldn't be. There was no way.

Davyn staggered away from her to reach for a blanket so that he could cover himself while that name sunk in past her sudden stupor.

Stunned beyond belief, Medea stood there, gaping.

No ...

SHERRILYN KENYON

Wasn't possible.

Lots of women were named Phoebe. Right?

Yeah, but he'd said Urian's *Phoebe.*

"You don't really mean Urian-Urian's Phoebe."

Pale and shaking, Davyn wrapped the blanket around his lean waist. His caramel skin had a grayish tint. Obviously shaken, he sat down on the bed and raked a trembling hand through his tousled blond hair. "I don't know how, either. Like you, I thought I was dreaming at first . . . but it was her. I'd know her anywhere. Saw her many times over the years. It was her, beyond all doubt."

Her thoughts reeled. "It can't be. My father killed her." That was what everyone had been told.

Everyone.

"That's what I thought, too. It's what we were all told. Yet I know what I saw, Medea. I met her when she lived in the commune. Many times when I went there with Urian." He wiped at his thigh, smearing the blood over his skin. "I swear to the gods, it was Phoebe. I know it was. I even felt her scrambled thoughts while she fed from me."

She sank down on the bed to sit beside him. "Was she brought back somehow?"

It could happen. In their world? Weird was normal. Impossible doable.

"I don't know. I mean how could they? We disintegrate on death, right? But that was *her* body. Not someone else's they used to host her soul."

Yeah. Daimons turned into a gold dust that quickly scattered whenever they died. While their souls could be brought back from the grave, they required a new body to house them in. It was impossible to put them back into their disintegrated body, since it was gone.

To her knowledge, not even the gods could do that.

Scowling, she looked over at him. "Are you okay?"

"I don't know, Chicken Little," he repeated. His features were even paler now. His expression turned sinister. "This will destroy Urian when he finds out. There's no telling how he'll cope with the news."

She wasn't so sure about that. "Will it? All he wants is Phoebe back."

"Yeah, but that wasn't her. I mean it is. But . . ." He ground his teeth. "She's not right anymore. That wasn't the same woman he knew."

"Gallu?"

He pulled the blanket back so that she could see the bite mark on his thigh. "I don't think so. Wouldn't I be turning into one by now if she was one of them?"

She had no idea. That wasn't her pantheon, so she didn't know what rules governed their species. "I need to get you to Falcyn. He'll know the answers."

"Falcyn?"

"He's the one I brought here to help us. Get dressed. He's with my father right now, healing them. I'll take you to him and we can ask. If anyone knows about gallu, he will."

After all, his brother, Dagon, was part of their pantheon and Falcyn was older than dirt's second cousin. Surely he'd been around when the gallu were originally active and fighting against the Charonte and gods.

Her thoughts skipping and dancing over this new turn of events, she went outside the room while Davyn pulled his clothes on. Yet while she waited, only one thought kept playing in her head on an endless loop.

Phoebe is alive.

It boggled her mind. This changed absolutely everything. She had no idea how Urian would react to this. He'd hated her father for so long now because they'd all been told Stryker had killed Urian's wife in a fit of anger.

But what if he hadn't. . . .

What if something else had happened to her. Something Stryker couldn't stop?

Damn.

What would Urian do then? Who would he hate more?

Sitting at a small round table at the Café Du Monde in New Orleans, Dikastas looked up from his coffee and beignets as a shadow fell over him and blocked his view of the pedestrian mall where he liked to watch the tourists while they shopped and strolled along the busy street.

It was even worse than what he'd initially imagined for the interruption—some poor panhandler begging for spare change or an annoying ass wanting directions.

A pouting Girl Scout peddling some overly sweet cookies.

Oh no, those nightmares would be far preferable to this pestilent beast who brought with him a sickening sensation that caused Dikastas's jaw to fall slack. Indeed, he wouldn't have been more shocked or stunned to find Apollymi herself standing there, glaring hatred at him.

He choked down his bite of the sugary confection and took a drink of coffee to clear his throat. "Apollo . . . to what do I owe this . . ." He searched for an appropriate word.

Honor definitely didn't fit.

Horror, not really.

Inconvenience would be the most apropos, but since Dikastas was the Atlantean god of justice, moderation, and order, he had a bit more tact than to say that out loud, as it would cause conflict and strife. So he left it open to the Greek god's interpretation while he wiped his mouth with a paper napkin, then gestured at the small metal chair across from him.

Apollo accepted the invitation without hesitation. "What a peculiar place to find you. I actually thought Clotho was lying when she told me where you were living these days."

Little wonder that, given the fact that the vast majority of his pantheon was currently frozen as statues beneath Acheron's palace in Katateros—the Atlantean heaven realm. Because Dikastas had had the good sense to not cross Apollymi's wrath or Styxx's sword arm, he was one of the extreme few who'd been left free to roam the earth after Styxx, Acheron, Bethany, and Apollymi had broken buck wild on them all a few years back. "And how are my dear half-Greek nieces?"

"Worthless as always."

Dikastas didn't comment on that. Mostly because he agreed about the three Fates. What with their great stupidity and rash actions, they had accidentally damned the entire Atlantean race and pantheon in the blink of an eye. Jealous words spoken in a moment of fear against Acheron that had played out with devastating consequences for all the rest of them, especially the triplet goddesses.

He cleared his throat and pinned Apollo with a cool stare. "You still haven't told me why you're here."

After all, they weren't friends, or even friendly. In fact, they hated each other with a fiery zeal. Their pantheons had been mortal enemies, back in the day. And the only thing the two of them had in common was their blond hair.

Literally.

And even it wasn't the same shade. Apollo's was far more golden and his tended toward brown.

"I want information."

Dikastas cocked his brow. "The Fates couldn't give you what you wanted?"

Apollo snorted. "As I said, they're basically worthless. What I need to know predates their births by a number of centuries and has to do with Apollymi and Kissare."

Interesting . . .

A waitress came up to ask Apollo for an order.

He sneered at her. "Do I look like I eat or drink shit? Begone from me, mortal scum!"

Dikastas sighed at his angry words. So much for Apollo being a god of temperance. "That was unnecessary."

"So is wasting my time!"

Yet Apollo had no problem intruding on his zen and wasting his. Typical. But then Apollo had always been a selfish prick that way.

All that mattered was his life and *his* wants.

Everyone else could go to Kalosis and rot.

Leaning back in his chair, Dikastas sipped his café au lait. "Well, if that's what you're after, the person you really want to talk to is Bet, as she'd have the most . . ." He trailed off as Apollo gave him a harsh stare and he realized the total stupidity of what he was suggesting.

"Ah," Dikastas said with a snide smile. "Guess you can't go there, can you?" Not after Apollo had screwed Bethany over in not one, but two separate lifetimes. The Atleantean goddess of wrath and warfare wouldn't take kindly to Apollo going to her for anything other than a full disembowelment.

Followed with a thorough denutting.

And the sun itself would freeze over before she'd ever help the bastard who'd killed her beloved husband and cursed her to lose her baby.

"She wouldn't have been there when Apollymi set up the Atlantean pantheon anyway. She hadn't been reborn yet, right?"

Again, courtesy of Apollo's *first* brutal betrayal against her and her husband. . . .

Dikastas set his coffee cup down and reached for another beignet. "Correct."

Crossing his arms over his chest, Apollo stroked his chin as he thought about something. "So how did Archon convince the frigid bitch of all time to marry him and establish a pantheon with him as its king so that he could play ruler?"

Dikastas snorted at his assumption. "Apollymi isn't frigid. Therein is the problem. Her passions run deep and dark. She's ruthless and bloodthirsty, but that doesn't make her cold. She's as fiery as a volcano and even quicker to erupt, and far deadlier when she peaks."

"You still haven't answered my question. Why *him*? Why *then*?"

Dikastas shrugged. "Simple. Someone gave Archon the intel that Apollymi was awaiting the return of her precious Kissare and she mistook the dull god as her Sephiroth come back to be with her. The spy fed Archon enough information that he was able to dupe her into thinking that he was her betrayed lover reborn as a god. That was why she agreed to set him up as her king and allowed him to rule over her. At least for a time."

"Are you sure he wasn't?"

"Yeah. Very much so. Kissare loved Apollymi. He gave his life for her and for their son. There was nothing altruistic about Archon. He was much like *you*."

Apollo's eyes narrowed. But he chose to ignore the dig. "Who was he working with?"

"No one knows. Archon refused to betray his informant. He was too grateful to be the king of his own pantheon to ever give over the name of someone Apollymi would have surely gutted."

Apollo considered that for a few minutes. "Was Kissare ever reborn?"

"Again, no one knows. But I'd say he must have been."

"Why?"

"Because someone fathered Acheron. Knowing Apollymi as I do and how she is, I would lay my money and life that Kissare was the father of both her sons. You find out who Acheron's real father is and you will find out who Apollymi really loves."

"You think he's still alive?"

Dikastas cradled his coffee mug as he considered it. "That would be the question of all time, wouldn't it?"

Chewing her nail, Medea was beside herself as she and Davyn made the long walk back to her parents' room. In fact, this was the longest walk of her life. Neither of them spoke. Which was rare for them. She even forgot that she was aggravated at Davyn.

By the time she reached their room, she'd forgotten a lot of things.

Until she pushed the door open to find both of her parents completely restored. Relieved and grateful, she rushed in with tears in her eyes to embrace her mother, then her father.

But it was Falcyn she kissed. "Thank you!"

He smiled at her. "You're welcome."

Her father cleared his throat gruffly. "What's this? Leave room for the imagination between the two of you! Now!"

Falcyn snorted at his tone. "Don't even start with me, old man. Or I'll put you right back like I found you."

She smiled up at her irascible dragon, yet she didn't miss the fact that he was a bit pale for his efforts. "Are you all right?"

"Fine." He cut a nasty glare toward her father. "Better with a little Daimon blood to soothe my mood."

She popped him on the arm. "Then take it from Davyn."

"Hey! I think I resent that!"

Laughing, she turned toward her father, and sobered. "We have a problem."

Her father groaned. "What now? Apollymi in another foul mood? Or is Apollo back?"

"Neither. I found Phoebe Peters in Davyn's room, feeding on him."

While her father paled, he took the news a lot better than she'd have thought. In fact, he wasn't nearly as shocked as she'd been or that he should be, given how incredulous this was.

Neither was her mother.

And that sent a chill up her spine. "Father? Is there something you want to tell me about this matter?"

He glanced at her mother.

Her bad feeling tripled. She knew that look they were passing between each other—as if trying to figure out who would take the blame for whatever problem had cropped up.

"You knew?" she accused.

His features blanched even more. "It's not what you think." Yet that tone said that it was.

Oh dear gods! He really *did* know. Sick to her stomach, she exchanged a shocked stare with Davyn.

She turned back toward her father. "How is it not?"

Stryker drew a deep breath before he answered. "She was sick, Medea. Infected by the blood she'd been feeding on."

"Gallu?"

He shook his head. "Worse."

What could possibly be worse than the bite of a gallu that would turn them into mindless zombies?

Davyn cursed under his breath as if he understood it. "Anglekos."

In that moment, Medea cringed, too. Then she felt stupid for not realizing it on her own.

She hadn't even thought about that.

Yeah, that would do it. It was why she avoided preying on psycho humans. That tainted blood could overwhelm and taint a Daimon. Those corrupt souls were so evil that they had a nasty tendency to infect the Daimon who tried to feed on them, often turning the Daimon into a psychotic killer. There were some strong enough that they could handle taking souls like that.

Urian had been one. Davyn another. In fact, Davyn only fed on those souls, as had Urian when he'd been Daimon. In a way, they kept humanity safe by removing those members from society.

However, it wasn't an easy thing to do, and after she'd taken one once, it'd been enough for her to know to leave them well enough alone.

Stryker let out another long, tired sigh. "She was always weak. More human than Apollite. Never really a Daimon at all. It's why she couldn't kill for herself. The blood Urian had fed on mutated her. Driven her insane. We weren't the ones who attacked the Apollite commune in Minnesota. *She* was."

"What?" Davyn scowled at him.

Rubbing his hand over his face, Stryker winced. "It's why I had you keep Urian occupied that night. Trates and I got the call for help. I knew Phoebe was living there. Had known about her for a long time, contrary to what Urian thought—they'd told me about it not long after he set her up with an apartment. I just felt so betrayed that Urian had taken Cassandra and Wulf there, too. I didn't mind that he'd converted Phoebe. I could almost respect that. It was the Dark-Hunter I resented him for. That he'd lie and shield our enemy from me when he knew how much

I wanted that last bitch dead. And Kat. That was the bitterest pill. He even married them!"

Tears glistened in his eyes. "Even so, I couldn't let him know about Phoebe and her killing spree. When I saw what she'd become, I knew Urian would blame himself for it. Hate himself for the monster she'd become. I didn't know what to do."

"So you killed her." Davyn had a sick expression on his face.

He shook his head. "I started to, but I couldn't. I'm not as cold as you think. Instead, I brought her back here and locked her in the catacombs. Originally, I was going to tell Urian and let us deal with it together. Then when we were in *Dante's Inferno* . . . and Acheron showed up in all his arrogant, prick glory. The Dark-Hunter was there with that stupid demon disguised as a baby, and one thing led to the next . . . my anger got the better of me. Next thing I knew, I'd cut his throat and left him there to die." A tic started in his jaw. "Just like Phoebe, he was never really one of us either."

Medea gaped at her father. "And in all this time, you didn't think to tell him the truth? To tell *any* of us the truth?"

"To what purpose? The deed was done. Besides, you saw her. She's not his wife anymore. She doesn't know herself. Wouldn't know him. For all intents and purposes, she might as well be gallu. And it's not like he's going to forgive me at this point, anyway."

"You did cut his throat, Father."

"I know, Medea. I was there. Believe me, I've relived that nightmare more times than I care to recount. It's never far from my thoughts. Even when my eyes are wide open. That night is one of the few things in my life I would give anything to do over and do differently."

Her mother moved to hug him and offer him comfort.

But sadly, like Urian, Medea couldn't quite forgive him for his actions. As a mother, she'd never be able to harm her child. Not for any reason.

Even betrayal against her. Having lost her child, there was no way she'd be responsible for the loss of her baby's life.

And it made her wonder if Urian wasn't right. If one day her father would do the same to her.

How could she trust anyone? Ever?

Yet when she met Falcyn's gaze, she saw in him a promise of faith. A blood oath.

Like her, he'd known bitter betrayal. Pain.

Loneliness.

Lies.

And he wouldn't do that to another. Because he knew the bitter taste of it.

She was nothing more than the product of broken dreams and broken trust. Of heartache and sorrow.

But in his eyes, she finally saw a future. And for the first time, it wasn't bleak.

Against her better sense, she reached out for him.

Falcyn saw the torment deep in Medea's eyes and he recognized it for what it was.

Fear. Misery. Crushed dreams that hurt so deep down inside that she'd had no choice except to deny that they'd ever been there.

He felt them, too. Had buried them beneath an apathy that had left him unable to feel anything for so long he'd begun to believe the lie of it all.

That there was nothing inside him. No emotion. No sentimentality of any kind.

And there was the irony. He'd actually convinced himself he was numb and unfeeling. Uncaring when the truth was he cared so much that he'd been forced into denial so that he could remain sane when faced with the madness of a brutal world that constantly assaulted him with its insanity and pain.

Now . . .

He could no longer pretend. Damn it to hell. Against all his carefully constructed shields and safeguards this little Apollite had slid in past his defenses and carved her name into his dead heart. And he would never be the same.

Because now that he knew her name and her face . . .

Her touch . . . she was as integral to him as breathing.

Shit.

Falcyn didn't need his dragonstone to live.

He needed Medea.

Grinding his teeth, he searched his mind for something to say to her, but words failed him. There was nothing he could say to adequately convey what he felt for her.

Nothing.

So he took her hand into his and pressed her open palm to his lips, then to his heart so that she could feel the fact that it beat solely for her and no one else.

Medea swallowed as she saw the tenderness on Falcyn's face

and felt the strong beating of his heart beneath her fingertips. "Is that it, dragonfly? Really?"

"You know me, princess. If I speak, chances are, I'll say the wrong thing and piss you off. Ninety percent of intelligence is knowing when to shut the fuck up."

Laughing, she stepped forward to kiss him. "Then that makes you a genius."

Suddenly, a loud rumble shook the walls around them. Medea pulled back with a frown.

Falcyn cocked his head at the sound as a weird fissle went down his spine. One he hadn't felt in a long time. Surely that couldn't be what he thought. It would be impossible for Apollo to infiltrate Apollymi's domain.

Wouldn't it?

The sound returned. Even louder.

Harder.

"What is that?" Zephyra asked with the same note of panic in her voice.

Falcyn narrowed his gaze on the doorway. "It sounds like . . ."

"Strykyn," Stryker finished for him in a breathless tone as the cacophony of rushing wings grew louder and louder.

Closer and closer.

Like a tornado across a vast field. It rumbled all around, shaking the ground and walls.

An instant later, the door burst open to admit the giant black war owls of Ares.

19

Medea was frozen by the unexpected sight of the massive ancient Greek warriors who came through the door, first as gargantuan black owls. Then as armored soldiers. Armed with spiked shields, oversized pauldrons, and swords, they meant business and were here for blood.

Their blood.

The woman in her could appreciate their handsome, ripped bodies, but the demon warrior who'd survived countless battles didn't welcome them in her domain. She saw them for the threat they were, and wanted them dead or gone.

Their choice. Either option was fine by her. The bloodier, the better, because with what they would be bleeding, she'd get a free meal out of it.

She licked her fangs in expectation of a most satisfying dinner.

Stepping back, she manifested her own sword and made ready to send as many of them as she could to whatever god they worshiped if they chose to fight.

This was bullshit and she wasn't about to sit back and let them have her family. Not without it costing them life and limb.

Falcyn moved in to protect her. "What are you doing here?" he demanded of them.

"We're here for your stone, dragon."

Falcyn tsked. "Ah, see, you don't want to be going there, guys. You come for my stone and I'll be handing you yours instead. Now before the massive geldings commence, I suggest you take yourselves back to whatever moron sent you out on this suicide quest and bitch-slap them with my deepest regards."

Medea rolled her eyes at his sense of irony while Davyn made an indefinable noise that landed somewhere between humor and horror. Her father actually laughed.

Her mother applauded. "I like the way your dragon thinks, Medea."

"I knew you would, Mum. Knew you would."

The strykyn moved in to attack, but before they could get near them, a murder of Charonte overran their group like a school of starving piranha.

Medea ducked as one of the Charonte almost took her head off in his enthusiasm to chow down on the nearest strykyn.

They howled as the Charonte tore into them with glee.

Falcyn screwed his face up. "Guess they're not on Acheron's Charonte no-eat list."

Obviously. Just as Apollymi must still be looking out for her Daimon army, as well. Nice to know the goddess of destruction hadn't abandoned them in their hour of need.

Made her feel almost warm and fuzzy inside.

Or maybe that was the sudden weird nausea caused by the hungry demons.

Medea cringed as one of the female demons moved to rip a strykyn apart. "Wonder if they taste like chicken?"

"Ew, Chicken Little! I know we're cannibals, technically, but still. . . ." Davyn nudged at her. "You've been hanging out with the dragons too long."

"Actually, Simi." Worse? This was making her crave barbecue. Yeah, she was sick and she admitted it.

But then, that was what made her the villain. And what made her appreciate the darker side of Falcyn.

Which terrified her. She'd spent centuries alone, never thinking about being with someone else. Never considering the possibility of ever being part of a couple again. She'd become relegated to the concept. Complacent.

Now . . .

Dare she trust Brogan's prophecy?

Her own feelings?

For so long life had given her more kicks than it'd withheld. And that made it all the harder to trust. All the harder to believe. How could she have faith when all she knew was betrayal and pain?

Then again, two negatives did make a positive. And no one and nothing was more negative than Falcyn and her.

Together . . .

He scowled at her as he caught the look in her eyes. "What's *that* mean?"

"You wouldn't believe me if I told you."

Falcyn snorted. "You must be thinking something good about me then."

"I was."

"Yeah, you're right. I don't believe it."

She popped him playfully on his arm. "Told you."

Shaking his head, he whistled at the Charonte. "As much as I'd love to see a bloody banquet ensue, and that it pains me to put the brakes on your feast. But . . ."

The Charonte actually whimpered.

"Yeah, we might need the war birds, so could you stow the condiments and hang on to the poultry for a few?" He walked over to the strykyn leader and literally plucked him from the hands of the Charonte who'd been one bite away from his jugular. "Who exactly sent you?"

With an audible gulp, the strykyn rubbed at his bite wound. "Morgen and Apollo."

He draped his arm around the warrior's shoulders and pulled him away from the demon. "And how loyal are you feeling to them at the moment?"

The strykyn glanced around the room to the faces of his men and the Charonte who were begging him to be loyal to the

Greek god and fey queen so that Falcyn would allow them to finish their meal in peace. "Um . . . Not very."

"Good answer. Which means I'm going to not feed you to the Charonte."

There were more protests from the disappointed demons as they begged harder for him to reconsider.

"–Quite yet." Falcyn held his hand up to quell them. "There's always later. However, I'm feeling uncharacteristically charitable at the moment. So I would urge the lot of your friends here to not try my patience, or that of Apollymi's. And definitely not tempt the Charonte, who have no restraint whatsoever, and an insatiable hunger. Pack your wings, strykyn, and fly home, empty taloned. What do you think?"

The strykyn didn't hesitate with his answer. "I think your stone looks good on you, my lord."

Falcyn patted him on the cheek. "Thought you might feel that way, punkin. Now take your little owlkateers and vamoose."

Medea waited until they were gone. "You think you can trust them?"

"Hell, no. But I think I can trust their fear of our friends here." Falcyn looked down at her and frowned. "However, that's not what really concerns me."

"No?"

"Nope. What rates highest on my shitometer at the moment is just how the hell they got into Kalosis to begin with. I mean, think about it. Breaching the portal . . . not an easy feat. We know Mama Polly didn't open it. We didn't let them in." He glanced to her parents. "Lucy, want to take this?"

Her father turned pale. "He's right. The number of people who can open a bolt-hole is finite and small."

Medea went cold. "There's a traitor among us."

Davyn's eyes widened. "Who would dare?"

Only one name came to mind.

She arched a brow at him as they both knew that Davyn had dared in the past, but that had been for Urian's benefit alone. And while she knew he'd carried information to her brother, she didn't suspect him in this. It was one thing to help out his friend. Quite another to help out an enemy who'd betrayed them all.

An enemy and god no one could stand.

No. Davyn would *never* have helped Apollo against his own race. A race Apollo had cursed to die.

Only a rank idiot would be so stupid. So who among them was that said idiot?

Her mother crossed her arms over her chest. "We will find them and eat their entrails."

The Charonte perked up at her words.

"Yes," her mother said, louder. "I will personally hand-feed them to you, my demons. With barbecue sauce."

"Find the traitor!" they chanted as they rushed from the room to begin a search.

"Wow." Falcyn let out a nervous laugh. "Charonte are some scary beasts. Basically flying piranha, except piranha aren't nearly as . . . hungry."

"No kidding. Makes you wonder what the Lemurians were thinking when they created them."

"That they hated the Atlanteans."

The four of them stared at Falcyn for his flat-toned response.

"What? I was there . . . ish. It was what they were created to attack."

"Then how did they end up enslaved to the Atlanteans?" Medea was dying to know.

"Same way you ended up with a dragonstone."

She scowled at his answer. "Huh?"

"The queen found the only set of chains that could hold a truly feral beast. She captured the heart of their leader. Took him deep into her lair, warmed him with her fire, and made it so that he never wanted to leave her side ever again."

Those words melted her as she understood the underlying meaning and what he was saying not just about the Charonte, but about himself. "And is the dragon tamed?"

"Never, my lady Daimon. Like a Charonte, you can never tame so savage a beast. Only make him crave the fire where you are more than the cold where he used to live."

Her father laughed. "I would be angry over this, but I can't help thinking that having our own dragon can't possibly be a bad thing."

Falcyn scoffed at her father's words. "Unless you piss me off, Stryker, I wouldn't advise doing that."

"Ditto."

"Then do we have an accord?"

Stryker dropped his gaze to Medea. "So long as you treat my daughter with all due regard and like the queen she is, we will have no problems, you and I."

"Then we will never have a problem."

"Except for the god who is still out to end us." Medea

scowled as she met Falcyn's gaze. "This isn't over. Apollo's not finished with us, as the strykyn proved. You've saved my parents. But we still have a traitor to find."

Falcyn shook his head at her, then glanced over to Davyn. "Chicken Little?"

"Always. She can't help herself."

And he still had his son to free. Somehow.

Overwhelmed and losing hope by the second, Falcyn sighed. "I need to see to my sister. Make sure she's all right with the others."

Medea stepped forward. "I'll come with you."

"You sure?"

She nodded. "Just don't let me burst into flames."

"I'll do my best on that, as it would ruin my best day, and I'm sure it wouldn't make yours, either." He held his hand out for her. The moment he felt her touch, a strange flutter went through his chest. He wasn't sure if he'd ever get used to having such tender feelings for someone else. To having a living weakness.

Honestly? He didn't like it. It was hard to know that she was an easy means to his destruction. That alone made him want to push her away and deny her. He hated the feeling of vulnerability she wrought.

She narrowed her gaze at him. "You okay?"

No. He had a new, profound respect for her as he realized just how much strength she possessed. The fact that she'd been able to survive without her child and husband . . .

His only solace over the centuries had come from the fact that he hadn't known Maddor. His son had been a concept for him. Not a reality. He hadn't held him or known Maddor at all.

Not the way he knew Medea.

Now . . .

She was a part of him.

The best part.

And the thought of something happening to her was crippling.

"How did you survive after Evander?"

Her eyes turned dark and haunted. "One breath at a time. Some days, that was all I could manage to get through."

That was a sobering thought he didn't want to even contemplate. Terrified beyond rational thought, he pulled her into his arms, and teleported her to his home. "I will *never* let you go, Medea."

"I'm counting on that, dragonfly."

Taking her hand, he led it to his lips and kissed her palm, then stepped back so that she could inspect his island home.

Medea gasped at the beauty that was Falcyn's "lair." No wonder he'd been so defensive when she'd accused him of living in a cave. This was absolutely breathtaking. Open and airy, it was technically a cavern.

Just a very large, spacious one with an ocean view that took her breath. The enchanted walls were crystal clear, so that he could look out, but not be seen by anyone else. Their transparency made them shimmer and sparkle from the daylight that burned her eyes, yet not her skin.

"How long have you lived here?"

"Forever and a day." He winked at her.

Shaking her head at his humor, she turned a small circle to survey everything. Outside the cavern, the landscape held ancient ruins of some Greek city and temple. Inside, it was a bit cramped by the number of dragons. She could see why he'd balked a bit about having them here.

Still, without them, it would have to be lonely. Such a large space with no company . . .

Yeah, that wouldn't make her happy.

But then she'd never really been alone. She'd always had her mother and then her husband.

Unlike Falcyn. Never had she been forced to live by herself. Family had always been a part of her life.

His sister came over to them. "Like the new decorations? Wall-to-wall dragon?"

"Ha ha. I hate you so much." Yet there was a light in his eyes that said he appreciated his sister's teasing.

And Xyn knew it, too. "Ah, you're not fooling anyone. I know you missed me."

Falcyn made a disgruntled face at her.

Medea pressed her lips together to keep from laughing. It was so strange to see this side of him. He was so protective with his brothers. Protective with her and Xyn as well, but they saw the much less serious part of him. While he could be flippant and sarcastic with Blaise and Urian, it was a different kind of humor than the more vulnerable one he showed the two of them. He was softer and kinder to the women in his life.

"So what do you plan to do with all of these beasts, Xyn? I'm not planning to let them move in, you know. Definitely not comfortable with them here."

"Why not? It's rather cozy." Xyn smiled.

Falcyn let out a sound of supreme disgust. "You know why.

And don't start on me. As the old saying goes, door's in the wall."

"Oh relax, you old mangy beast. They're not planning to stay, anyway. We're just messing with you."

His relief was tangible.

Xyn met Medea's gaze and shook her head. "How do you put up with him?"

"I think he's hilarious."

She blew a raspberry. "This one's a keeper, brother. You better not let her go."

Before he could comment, the light dimmed near them.

Medea braced herself for another battle, then relaxed as she saw Shadow manifesting near Xyn. Yet for the life of her, she couldn't imagine why he was here, given the condition he'd been in when last they'd seen him. She would have thought he'd have been out of commission for a while.

At least laid up for a month or more.

But apparently, nothing kept the being down for very long.

Inclining his head to them, he approached Xyn and spoke to her, letting them know that he must have been assisting her for a bit now. "I've found a few more homes."

Falcyn let out an audible sigh. "Shadow . . . you're my man."

Shadow let out a nervous laugh. "Since when?"

"Since I saved your ass. How are you feeling?"

"Like I had the hell beat out of me . . . And you're welcome."

Crossing his arms over his chest, Falcyn's expression said those words chafed him. Yet the gleam in his eyes betrayed his amusement. "How has Varian failed to gut you all these centuries?"

"Not from lack of effort on his part, I assure you. I'm just quicker than he is."

Falcyn shook his head. "Anyway, I'm glad to see you back on your feet."

"Glad to be back on my feet. Especially without Varian hovering over me like some great hairy mother. And I heard you made friends with little brother, Lombrey."

"Yeah, you can keep him."

"Hmmm, so everyone keeps telling me. He's actually not so bad. Get him liquored up and laid, you can get about five or ten minutes of peace before he's in your face again."

"So that's your secret."

"Basically. I find it works on most people."

Falcyn laughed. "And why is it that I think there's a little more to it than you're letting on?"

"Again, he's not so bad. You just have to understand where he's coming from. We're all creatures of the hell that birthed us. Are we not?"

Medea would give him that.

"True." Falcyn stepped back as one of the dragons approached them.

"Are the sanctuaries ready?" he asked Shadow.

Shadow nodded. "Merlin's preparing them. We should be able to transport more of you before much longer. Kerrigan and Merewyn said they'd come to assist you as soon as they're open."

"Thank you."

"Our pleasure."

"Kerrigan?" Medea vaguely recalled the name, but couldn't place it now. She remembered that Merewyn was Varian's wife.

Falcyn let out a bitter laugh. "The former Pendragon of Morgen's Circle. He was the one who took Arthur's place to lead her knights."

"Now he fights with the Lords of Avalon." Shadow smiled. "War and love make strange bedfellows."

That was certainly true, but it made her wonder one thing. "Why did he change sides?"

Shadow jerked his chin toward Blaise and Brogan. "Kerrigan was the merlin charged with the sword Caliburn. His wife Seren was the merlin for the loom of Caswallen that Morgen demanded he and Blaise capture. In the process of taking it from her, the Lady Seren won Kerrigan's heart. He couldn't hand her over to Morgen any more than Blaise was able to hand over his Brogan to the Crom. So Seren and Kerrigan, and their son and daughter, now live in Avalon with the others, where they continue to fight against Merlin and her fey court."

Medea glanced to Falcyn. "Like you."

"I have no plans to relocate to Avalon."

"You know what I mean."

Falcyn looked a bit uneasy. "What? That I'd follow you any-where?"

"Would you?"

Falcyn's gaze scorched her and warmed the darkest coldness inside her. "You know I would."

He placed a kiss on her cheek, then turned toward Shadow. "Can I beg a favor?"

"Depends on the favor, especially given what happened to me the last time I did you one."

"Can you get me back into Camelot? Near Morgen?"

Shadow made a truly spectacular sound of scoffing disbelief. "And what level of special stupidity have you achieved,
dragon? I know you took a significant hit to the head, but didn't
realize it'd given you brain damage. Should we get you a CAT
scan? Dog scan?"

"Ha ha. And I'm serious."

"Yeah . . . so am I. I actually like having my bullocks attached to my body. While I don't get to use them as much as I'd
like, I still prefer the comfy feeling of having them there over
the alternative of seeing them in a jar on my desk."

"Then you'll help me or I know what to attack."

A tic started in Shadow's jaw. "Really hate you, dragon. . . .
Fine. But if you're caught, I don't know you. Never saw you and
I have no idea how you got there. And I'm sending Lombrey to
rescue or kill you, whichever. His choice."

"How have you managed to live so long without anyone
killing you, again?"

"Told you, I'm fast on my feet." Shadow sighed. "So when
do you want to partake of your suicide?"

Falcyn glanced around his crowded home. "Now would be
a good time. It'll keep me from freaking out over my OCD."

Xyn scowled. "OCD?"

"Overpopulated communal den." He pointed to the group.
"Get rid of *that* while I'm gone."

She rolled her eyes at her brother. "Ugh, you big baby. You
never did learn to share!"

"Oh, that's not true. I learned to share pain and misery,
early on."

"No, no. You learned to deliver pain and misery. *Big* difference. Being a carrier and deliverer isn't the same as sharing, *m'gios*. Do not confuse those terms."

"You're determined to annoy me, aren't you?"

Xyn smiled. "Always. Aren't you glad now that you woke me?"

"Thinking I should have overlooked *your* statue." Falcyn growled in the back of his throat. "Blaise! Why did we wake Xyn again?"

"You missed her!" he called out across the room.

"I lied!"

Xyn pushed him toward Shadow. "Go on and take him before he has a nervous breakdown. Or I kill him."

Medea laughed. "C'mon, dragonfly."

He paused at her actions. "What are you doing?"

"I know what that look in your eyes means. You're going back for Maddor. I plan to go with you."

"No. You're not. You're going to stay here."

Cocking her head, she gave him an oh-no-you-didn't stare.

Falcyn cleared his throat. "No?"

"I'm going with you," she repeated firmly.

Shadow laughed. "I wouldn't argue with that, dragon. She looks kind of pissed off, and while I'm no expert in women, that is the kind of expression that in the past hasn't boded well for my body parts being happy at a later time and date whenever a female pointed them at me."

He gave Shadow a droll stare. "Do you not have an off switch or filter?"

"Not really."

With a deep growl, Falcyn shook his head. "Fine. I can't argue with both of you. Let's get this over with. See if I can work some miracle."

"What kind of miracle are you thinking?"

"No idea. Hoping for inspiration." Falcyn took a deep breath. "All right, Shadow. Lead us in."

"Lead us in, he says. Like that's easy. Like all I have to do is snap my fingers and poof." Shadow snapped his fingers and they were in Camelot.

Falcyn arched his brow at Shadow's continued bitching.

"Well, that part *was* easy." His voice broke off as they realized they were surrounded by Adoni warriors. "But this is what I was talking about. Lousy, pointy-eared bastards tend to notice when we come and go. Worse? The little bitches attack like locusts."

He'd barely finished that sentence before they proved him right and pounced.

20

Falcyn cursed Shadow and the Adoni as Medea manifested a sword to fight them. "Really? You had to dump us in the middle of a fairy hoedown?"

"Well gee, Bubba, you didn't specify where exactly you wanted ole Miss Scarlett to put ya! It seemed as good a place as any."

"Oh shut up!" Falcyn lobbed a fireball at the Adoni nearest him.

Meanwhile, Shadow took up arms against

those nearest him. "I've got to find a better class of friends. I swear."

"Enough! Stop this!"

They all froze at the sound of Morgen's voice.

Confused, Falcyn moved to cover Medea. Just in case, as he had no idea what Morgen intended or why she wasn't ordering their deaths, when that was her normal command.

Shadow also stepped back as the fey queen materialized in front of them.

Morgen cut an evil glare to each of them in turn, but it was Falcyn she singled out for her malice. "I told Narishka you'd come."

"Pardon?"

"Beg all you want. But I knew you would return for Maddor. She thought me crazy and sentimental. However, you *are* predictable."

Falcyn ground his teeth. "Your point?"

"Simple. You want your son . . . I want your rock. One for the other. Now give it."

Yeah, right. He knew better than that.

Falcyn hesitated at giving in over her lie. "How do I know I can trust you when I know exactly how untrustworthy you are?"

"You would dare talk to me about trust after you killed my mother?"

Medea choked. "Um . . . you do get that Maddor is your brother? Right? Surely that hasn't escaped your notice in all this?"

She passed a cold stare toward Medea. "Half. And he wasn't my only one. I learned not to get attached."

Ouch.

Falcyn's reaction was a lot more violent. He lunged for her. Shadow caught him before he could reach her and cause them to be attacked.

"Temper, brother," Shadow warned. "Don't let her get under your skin. Think it through."

Shadow was right. His anger would cause him to make a mistake, and that was what she was counting on.

Slow and steady won the race.

Still, he wanted to mount her head on the wall. Forcing his temper down, he took a deep breath and reviewed his options. He could turn into a dragon. Take a number of them out.

But they were Adoni. Wizards all. More than that, they were used to battling his kind and knew how to bring a dragon down. In a group of real dragons with the powers of his brothers, he might stand a chance against them.

Alone, even with Shadow and Medea backing him, they could do damage, but would ultimately fall to the fey bastards.

And Maddor would continue to be held by Morgen and would be punished for it. Medea would be dead, and it would all be his fault.

He could never allow that.

So he made the only decision he could. He used his powers to summon his stone and held it in his palm. "Give me my son."

Morgen snapped her fingers for a grayling. "Fetch Maddor."

She practically salivated for his dragonstone.

And that caused something to confuse him as he reflected on her words and eagerness.

"Question, Morgen . . . why *is* Mordred so special to you? Above all others? As you said about Maddor not being your only brother, he's not your only child. In fact, Mordred isn't even your only son."

Her eyes flared red. "That's no concern of yours, is it?"

No, but her reaction told him much. There was something special about Mordred. Something more than her other children. Just what it was remained the question.

And that sent a chill down his spine, as whatever differentiated Mordred from his siblings could not possibly bode well for the rest of them.

Ever.

Damn . . .

But that thought scattered as soon as he saw Maddor.

If he lived another thousand years, he'd never forget the expression on his son's face. The disbelief that melted into relief and settled into stoicism so fast that it almost made him laugh. He'd be offended if he didn't understand the fact that in this company it didn't pay to show weakness.

Still, he'd seen it. No matter how brief.

His son was grateful to him that he'd come here to rescue him.

And so was he. More than anyone would ever know.

Waiting until Maddor reached his side, he used his powers to guide the stone across the room, in thin air, to Morgen.

A wicked smile curved her lips as she seized the stone and wrapped her greedy hands around it.

Then, she looked up and pinned him with a sinister glare. "Aren't you forgetting something?"

"What?"

"A dragonstone without a dragon is worthless. How stupid do you think I am?"

Honestly? Falcyn was hoping she wouldn't remember that small detail. In fact, he'd been counting on it.

Crap . . .

Reacting, he pulled away from Medea, to draw their fire in the opposite direction from her presence. "Shadow? Get Maddor and Medea out of here!" He pushed them toward him, intending to cover their retreat.

But the moment his gaze met Medea's, he realized that she had other plans.

True to her stubborn Apollite nature, she planned to stay with him.

"I won't lose another man I love, and I won't see you lose your son." She brushed her lips against his an instant before she shoved him through the portal Shadow had opened, then used her powers to seal it shut.

Falcyn was through it and back in Sanctuary before he could even protest.

He landed on the third-floor section, right beside Maddor and Shadow.

Colt cocked his brow at their group. "What the hell is this? You're back again?"

Disoriented, Falcyn scowled. "Why *are* we here? Shouldn't we be back in Kalosis?"

Hissing, Shadow rubbed at his shoulder. "Can't get in there without Medea. Apollymi would have a shit-fit. Might feed my raunchy ass to a Charonte. Not worth the chance."

Panicked, Falcyn turned around slowly as he realized he had no way to reach Medea while she was in Camelot. He felt the blood draining from his face as the full impact of what she'd done hit him.

She'd sacrificed her life for his.

What the fuck was that?

Fury scorched every part of him at the very thought of her facing Morgen on his behalf. How dare she put herself in harm's way! And for what?

For him?

I'm not worth it.

Tears choked him.

"Falcyn?"

He didn't know who spoke. He couldn't hear past his rushing heartbeat. Not until he felt a hand on his arm.

"Father?"

It wasn't until then that he realized it'd been Maddor who spoke.

Blinking, he met his son's gaze.

"We'll get her back."

"How?" Even he heard the crack in his voice.

Maddor gave him a cocky grin. "I might be a bastard, but I wasn't without some friends in Camelot."

Shadow nodded. "Ditto. Morgen wants a war? Let's give her one."

Morgen tsked at Medea. "I can't believe you did something so foolish, little girl."

"Oh, stick around, hon. My stupidity has just begun." Medea used her powers to snatch the dragonstone from Morgen's grasp.

That expression of shock would be comical in a less dire situation. As it was, Medea ran for the nearest door with no idea where it would lead. It just seemed like the best course of action would be to put as much distance between them as possible.

She hit the hallway at full speed.

Oh yeah, this was dumb. Dark and dismal, it was lit with an unholy glowing light. Sinister shadows danced around her like living creatures.

With no idea of where to seek shelter, Medea rushed toward wherever. She had absolutely no destination in mind. Just any place else but here.

Which turned out to be straight into Narishka.

Beautimous.

Medea cursed under her breath as the fey bitch tsked at her. "Be a good girl. Hand it over."

"Not a good girl. I'm a villain, too. You want it? Gotta fight me for it. Come get some, bitch." She tucked it in her bra and manifested a set of bagh nakas. For this, she wanted to feel some blood on her hands.

And fangs.

Narishka sent an invisible blast toward her.

Medea countered and sent one of her own. "C'mon. That all you got?"

They attacked en masse and quickly learned why she was the leader of her father's army, as Medea unleashed eleven thousand years of pent-up Daimon fury on them. One thing about the Spathi, they didn't hold back.

And they didn't flinch. Forget the Spartans. The Spathi Daimons were the warriors who could make King Leonidas wet his pteruges.

But that wasn't the only reason she fought. In the back of her mind was the past, when they'd come for Praxis and Evander.

That night, she hadn't fought at all. Untrained and passive, she'd been helpless before the humans as they slaughtered her husband and son. Back then, she'd told herself that it was more noble to do as the gods decreed and accept her fate, whatever it was.

To be dutiful. To submit docilely, like a good citizen.

The nail that stood out was hammered down.

Evander had believed it, too. So they had followed the rules and done what they were supposed to. They'd never made noise. Never bothered anyone.

Never harmed another living soul.

It hadn't mattered. Her loyalty had been returned to her with treachery, betrayal, and blood.

Her kindness shoved down her throat. Those she counted as friends had been the first to turn against her and cast her to the wolves. Not a one had spoken up in her defense.

Not a single act of charity remembered. No. They hadn't returned to her the respect she'd shown them. Or the regard. Rather, everyone she'd ever helped had abandoned her as if she'd never done anything for them.

Cold-hearted, selfish fucking bastards!

For that bitterest lesson, she'd hated them all.

And that night she'd learned her most vital piece. To thine own self be true. Not just with honesty, but with charity first. For no one else would ever stand up for her when it mattered most.

In the end, you come into this world alone.

Alone you will leave it.

Feet first.

She'd entered this world fighting, with someone else's blood on her fists, and that was exactly how she intended to go out.

Grinding her teeth, she caught the largest Adoni warrior a punch to the jaw that sent the giant bastard reeling.

Then, turning, she flipped the next one from his feet and delivered a punch to his throat. Her ears buzzed from the rush of blood. Fury coursed through every part of her as it demanded more and more of their life force.

The beast in her was awake and it was starving.

They surrounded her. Outnumbered her. There was no way she'd survive them all. She knew that beyond a doubt.

She didn't care.

War wasn't always about survival for yourself. It was about protecting what you loved. Preserving those you held sacred so that they could carry on after you. Making sure *they* had a future. And if that meant sacrificing your own for theirs, so be it.

One life for the many.

Medea felt a piercing pain in her side.

And still fought. Even though the pain threatened to send her to her knees, she refused to give them the satisfaction of seeing her fall. Her mother had raised her better than that.

Suddenly, someone grabbed her from behind.

With a vicious hiss, she moved to clobber her attacker, then froze as she caught sight of the most insanely gorgeous man in any world.

"Falcyn." His name was a prayer on her lips.

"You had to know I wouldn't leave you behind." He cradled her to his chest and ducked so that Shadow and Blaise could cover their retreat.

Tears filled her eyes as she wrapped her arms around his neck.

Morgen let out a fierce shriek.

Falcyn turned on her and fire-blasted her. Then he took Medea back to his cavern, where Maddor quickly joined them. He laid her down on his bed so that he could inspect the wound in her side. "I can't leave you alone for five seconds, can I?"

"It was more than five seconds, dragonfly. Do I need to buy you a watch?" She hissed and slapped at his hand as he touched a tender place.

"Oh! Hey!"

"That hurt!"

"Yeah, I know." He shook his hand.

Scowling at him, she fished his dragonstone from her bra and returned it to him. "Don't even start with me."

His jaw went slack. "How did you manage to get it back?"

"Ain't no bitch going to handle my man's rocks while I'm around. Really?"

Maddor's eyes bugged at her words. "I'm going to wait outside."

Falcyn laughed, then kissed her.

Medea sighed as she felt the heat of his kiss flow all the way through her body. More than that, she felt the warmth of his stone knitting her wound closed and healing her.

Completely.

And when he pulled back, she cupped his face and realized that Brogan had been right. She did have a future with him after all.

"So tell me, dragonfly. Where do a dragon and a Daimon make their home?"

"Simple, Lady Spathi. Wherever it is that they want. Whatever it is they want."

EPILOGUE

Medea had been dreading this moment for days. But it was something that had to be done and something that she didn't want Urian to discover on his own. Better the news come from someone he loved than to be dumped on him by accident.

And how she'd allowed Falcyn to talk her into doing this in Acheron's palace on Katateros, she had no idea.

She definitely loved the beast. Only that could account for this level of insanity.

But in the end, he was right. It was better that Urian be comfortable and surrounded by family when he learned the truth than to be blindsided and surrounded by strangers. That wouldn't bode well for anyone.

Still . . .

This was nerve-wracking. The huge marble palace was awe inspiring, as one would expect the home of ancient gods to be. It was built to impress, and she was definitely not immune to its austerity.

Acheron's throne was set off to her right on a massive dais where several small little dragon-like creatures were currently curled around and napping with Acheron's two toddler sons. The way the creatures were entwined, she wasn't even sure how many of them there were.

Simi and her Charonte sister were on the floor to her left, watching some shopping network channel on a massively huge monitor that was mounted to the wall. Completely content, they were eating barbecue-drenched popcorn out of a bowl they shared that was perched between them while Acheron's steward, Alexion, and his wife, Danger, kept it filled to capacity.

Acheron's twin brother, Styxx, met her and Falcyn in the doorway. At almost seven feet in height, he was an impressively handsome beast. Dressed in a casual blue button-down shirt and jeans, he was a far cry from Ash's preferred Goth style. "Yeah, we know. But it keeps them out of trouble and stops them from putting horns on the babies' heads."

Medea laughed as she saw that Styxx's wife, Bethany, was holding their youngest son in her arms and cooing to the toddler. "So this is the little Aricles I keep hearing about from big brother Urian."

With her black spiral curls pulled away from her face in a ponytail, Bethany rubbed her son's back. Her caramel skin was flawless over sharply chiseled features. "Would you like to hold him?"

"I might keep him if I do."

Ari smiled as he looked up at her. "Mimi?"

Completely sunk, Medea took him and was lost the moment he wrapped his arms around her neck and hugged her with a giddy squeal and bounce. It'd been so long since she last held a baby that she'd forgotten just how wonderful it felt to have such unbounded affection.

That was the hardest part about being around Daimons— they couldn't have children. Only Apollites could.

Falcyn brushed his hand through her hair. "You okay?"

She nodded. "You're screwed, though. Word of warning. I want a bunch of these again."

He wrinkled his nose as Aricles squeezed Falcyn's finger and bit it. "I don't know. He's kind of smelly and leaking out both ends."

Bethany laughed. "It doesn't bother you when it's yours who smells that way."

"If you say so." He met Styxx's gaze doubtfully.

Styxx cleared his throat. "I'm agreeing with Beth. All the way."

"That's because my brother is not a fool." Acheron came in and clapped his hands on Styxx's shoulders.

Medea froze at the sight of them together. While she knew they were identical, except for their eye color and hair color—and that only because Acheron artificially colored his black and red—it was still shocking to see them side by side like this.

If the two of them put their minds to it, there would really be no way to tell them apart.

Spooky.

"Dear gods, who's dead?"

They all froze as Urian came into the room to catch them gathered together.

"Please tell me it's Stryker." There was no missing the hopeful note in Urian's voice.

"Not funny." She handed Aricles back to Bethany as she braced herself for the last thing she wanted to do.

How in the world was she going to tell Urian about Phoebe. . . .

Now she wished she'd taken Davyn up on his offer to be here for this confrontation. But then she wasn't a coward, and Urian was her brother.

I can do this.

Falcyn put his hand on her shoulder to let her know that he was with her. She took comfort in his presence.

And with a deep breath, she braced herself for what was going to be a bad reaction.

Real bad.

"There's something I need to tell you, Urian. Something you're not going to believe."

"I've won the mega-million lottery?"

She rolled her eyes at his misplaced and extremely irritating humor. "No. It's about Phoebe."

That sobered him completely. The color faded from his cheeks. When he spoke, his tone was brittle. "What about her?"

There was no easy way to do this. So she settled on just ripping the Band-Aid off as quickly and mercifully as possible. "Stryker didn't kill her that night. She's still alive."

Gah, that sounded harsh even to her own ears. She could kick her own ass.

Delicate, thy name is not *Medea.*

He staggered back into his father's arms and would have fallen had Styxx not been there. "What?"

"Breathe," Styxx whispered in his ear. "I've got you."

Urian shook his head. "It's not possible."

I feel that, brother.

But she had to be strong for him. And she had no choice now except to see this through. "Both Davyn and I saw her. She's alive, Urian. Just not the same."

Tears filled his eyes as he met Acheron's gaze. "Did you know?"

"I swear on my mother's life, I had no idea. She's not human so I can't see her fate. It's beyond my powers. If I'd known, I'd have told you."

Urian blinked and blinked again as he slowly digested her news and came to terms with it. "Stryker knew?"

Medea nodded weakly.

His breathing ragged, Urian glared at her. "Why didn't he tell me?"

"He didn't want you to feel guilty for what she's become. For what she did."

He scowled at her. "What she did?"

"She attacked the commune where you had her housed. He said that she became corrupted by the souls she was consuming to live."

A tear ran down his cheek as he stared into space. Raw, tormented anguish radiated from him. It was obvious that he was blaming himself, just like her father had predicted. "Ash . . . is there any way to get her back?"

"Not that I know. But I'm a god of fate. Not one of souls." He looked at Bethany.

She shook her head. "Wrath, warfare, misery, and the hunt. You need someone hunted down and killed with extreme prejudice, I'm your girl. But I was never in charge of souls, either. Sorry."

Falcyn sighed. "And I'm a war god, too. What a worthless lot we are."

"Although . . ."

They turned to stare at Acheron.

Ash bit his lip as he considered something. "This is a long shot. I mean it's a Hail Mary pass of all time."

"What?" Urian stepped away from his father.

"I might know somebody who can help with this. . . . Xander."

Medea scowled. "Who's Xander?"

"A Dark-Hunter currently stationed in New Orleans. He was a sorcerer. One of the darkest powers. So much so, Artie only got a part of his soul. He deals with transmutations and is the only non-demon I know who can bargain with Jaden and Thorn. If anyone can help you, he'll be your best bet."

"You think he'll do it?"

Ash let out a nervous laugh. "I don't know. He's a tricky son of a bitch. But he does have a weakness."

"And that is?"

"Brynna Addams and Kit Baughy. They can talk him into most things. Maybe, just maybe, they can talk him into this."

Apollo froze as he saw Morgen approaching his throne. Her hair was singed, her dress torn and filthy. "You look a little worse for the wear, love."

She actually shot a blast at him. "You bastard!"

He arched a brow at her. "Temper, temper. Be careful with that, lest I take offense."

"Take all you want! What happened to the dragonstone you promised me?"

"Patience. The game isn't over. Just a slight reset on the board."

She frowned. "What do you mean?"

He let out a long, weary sigh. "I forget that you're not a god. Playing with people's lives isn't something you've much experience with. Sometimes you have to let things run their course."

"Meaning?" she repeated.

"Meaning the good guys had all the dragons . . . now they don't. And Urian holds the blood of Apollymi, Bet, Set, *and* Acheron. . . ."

Morgen sucked her breath in as she finally understood. "He's the key to bringing them all down."

"Isn't he, though. And you know what we've just discovered?"

A slow smile curved her lips. "The source of his undoing."

Apollo nodded slowly. With Phoebe under his control, he didn't need to find out Acheron's father, after all. He had something even better at his disposal.

Acheron's comeuppance.

Because that was the beauty of being a god of prophecy. He knew the future.

The final fate of the world—of all humanity—wasn't really in the hands of Acheron, or even Apollymi.

It was actually in the bloodline of *Styxx's* family.